THE BELL FORGING CYCLE, BOOK I

The Stars Were Right

K. M. Alexander

The Stars Were Right

Print Edition ISBN:978-0-9896022-1-1
eBook ISBN: 978-0-9896022-0-4

Published by K. M.Alexander
Seattle, WA

First Edition: October 2013

This is a work of fiction. Names, characters, places and incidents either are products of the author's imagination or are used fictitiously. Any resemblance to actual persons, living or dead, business establishments, events, or locales is entirely coincidental.

K. M. Alexander asserts the moral right to be identified as the author of this work.
Copyright © 2013 by K. M. Alexander, All Rights Reserved

No part of this publication may be reproduced, stored in a retrieval system, or transmitted, in any form or by any means without prior written permission of the publisher, nor be otherwise circulated in any form of binding or cover other than that with which it is published and without a similar condition being imposed on the subsequent purchaser.

Cover Design by: K. M. Alexander
Cover Lettering by: Jon Contino at http://joncontino.com/

Did you enjoy this book? I love to hear from my readers. Please email me at: hello@kmalexander.com.

WWW.THESTARSWERERIGHT.COM

WWW.KMALEXANDER.COM

For Kari-Lise

When the stars were right, They could plunge from world to world through the sky; but when the stars were wrong, They could not live.

—H.P. Lovecraft, *The Call of Cthulhu*

THE STARS WERE RIGHT

PROLOGUE

The doorbell sang out its soft tinkle as the shopkeep shuffled to place his new product on the shelves behind him. He slipped old worn boxes and small leather clutches with frayed edges into the various cubbies that covered the wall behind the shop's small counter. Bifocals here, trifocals there, red boxes, blue boxes, brown pouches, and cases that were the faded gray of granite. He hummed tunelessly along with the shop's crackly radio as he worked.

The spectacle shop was old, long, and narrow, with a glass front and a small thin door that opened onto a somewhat busy avenue in the antiques district on the South side of Lovat. It was a quiet enough area, away from the rougher warrens, but not particularly elevated. Across the cramped street hawkers sold vases, while up the road outside a rug merchant's shop a man sold antique suits. There was also Dubois' new storefront to the East; he dealt in religious artifacts and trinkets. The shopkeep hadn't liked when he had moved in; it had somehow changed the feel of the warren. Odd folks had started showing up shortly after Saint Olmstead Religious Antiques opened: black-clad priests, Hasturians in yellow robes, and a few Deeper cultists dressed in their gray sackcloth rags. It had set the entire warren on edge.

The optics shop had been a hand-me-down from the shopkeep's father. By rights it should have belonged to one of his older brothers, but his father had chosen to skip tradition and had given the shop to him. Why he, a middle son of the brood, had come to inherit the old optical shop he would never fully understand.

"You have a good head on your shoulders. Not like those worthless ingrates you call your brothers," his father had declared. It hadn't been much of an answer, yet he had been grateful for the responsibility. He had many children of his own and the shop brought in a modest income with little effort on his part. He and his expansive family were quite comfortable—not rich, but comfortable.

It had always amused the shopkeep that he dealt in spectacles. He had never been particularly interested by the human fabrications. His own kind had keen eyes that didn't fade with age. It was almost comical: an anur dealing spectacles. His father had loved the little contraptions of glass and metal. He treated each like a precious gem, even if the old fellow couldn't wear a pair himself. He would go on and on about the styles, explain how glass could be ground into various concave shapes to readjust a human's vision, and he was also known to speak at length about proper fitting.

The shopkeep chuckled to himself. Even now, when visiting

his father in the convalescent home, the old anur would spend more time inquiring into the shop's latest procurements than asking about his numerous grandchildren.

"I'll be right with you. Just putting away some product," the shopkeep said to the newly-arrived customer. He could hear the footsteps slow behind him. He slid a boxed pair of single focus lenses onto a shelf with some others, listening to the muffled footsteps of his latest customer cross from the wood floor near the door to the soft carpet that covered most of the shop's floor. The radio continued its crackly cadence adding a little bit of noise to what would otherwise be an eerily silent shop.

The selection from the caravan master had been varied. Lots of unique prescriptions, a few odd styles, and a pair of browlines that were in near perfect condition. Browlines had fallen out of style decades earlier, but the shopkeep had a particular client who preferred them. This pair would fetch nearly triple what he had paid.

He had always felt that his shop was a necessity for the races of Lovat. While his own kind didn't suffer fading eyesight the city was full of humans, dimanians, dauger, and maero who all had the need for spectacles. The multileveled city was crawling with the dim-eyed, and unless you were flush with coin and lived in the elevated levels, finding an eye doctor—let alone a manufacturer of spectacles—was nearly impossible. That's where Russel & Sons Optics, Maynard Avenue, Fourth Level, South Lovat stepped in.

"Sorry for the delay," apologized the shopkeep, shifting around to look at his customer. "Now, what can I do for you?"

He blinked his bulbous eyes and distractedly scratched behind one, a nervous tick he had developed over years of haggling. Waldo had always called it his "tell."

"I can always tell when you're going to try to screw me," the caravan master would say with a laugh. "You scratch behind your left eye. Then you lowball me."

"I do not," he would declare.

"You do so, and that skin of yours darkens a deep gray-green. Like an anur blush."

Waldo was right, of course. The shopkeep knew it, but his tick was all for naught. His shop was empty.

Bizarre. He could have sworn he heard someone enter even as Wal had left. The bell had rang out, hadn't it?

The shopkeep looked around the small space, turning his gaze left and right, his wide frown deepening. It was midday and the shop was shadowed and dark, the small lamps on the ceiling providing little light among the dark wood shelves that lined the walls floor to ceiling. Hundreds of precious pairs of eyeglasses filled cubbies all around him, each labeled in the shopkeep's meticulous hand, but there was no one to be seen.

Outside gray streaks of rain cascaded down in sheets from the streets above, their colors shifting as they passed in front of the sodium and neon lights that lit Maynard Avenue. Pedestrians moved past the glass front, collars turned up, hats pulled low, papers tucked under their arms. Steam rose from the streets below. It looked downright miserable and cold. But this deep in Lovat it was always cold.

The crackle of the radio faded as another song came on; a

wail from ages past sung by what sounded like a maero voice. The voice rasped through the speaker, filling the shop. Low and rumbly, a tune about a summer long since past, before the stars had been right, before the earth had changed.

The shopkeep shrugged at his empty shop and settled his thick body on a stool behind the counter. He read his newspaper and sipped at his chicory with wet slurps. It was dull, but it passed the time.

He was halfway into an article about new construction approved for Holgate Hill when he felt the eerie sensation of being watched. He looked up from his paper.

A shadow stood across from him. It was both opaque and transparent at the same time, seemingly there and not, vaguely human in form, and female. He could recognize the curve of hips and the swell of breasts in the shadow, but it was hardly discernible.

He half fell, half slipped off his stool in surprise, crumpling to the floor before shakily rising, his back pressed to the cubbyholes as he held his paper out before him like a shield. The shadow turned its head slowly, studying him. Eyes that glowed like coals stared at him from within black pits.

The shopkeep had only seen a few umbras in his life. Their kind usually hung out in the warrens to the North or could be seen in rougher cities like Destiny in the South. They were a rare sight in Lovat. Those he had seen usually wrapped themselves in multiple layers of clothing to make their forms as discernible as possible. It was considered more polite. Openly flaunting their forms like this one was threatening behavior.

The shopkeep's hands shook; the loose curtains of skin that hung from his chin quavered. He yelped in surprise. One moment the umbra was on the other side of the counter and the next she was atop it. If she had moved the shopkeep didn't see it. She was just there: a black mist standing above him. Coal red eyes stared down at him as tendrils of black drifted away from her shoulders, elbows, ankles, and toes. No wonder he hadn't seen her; she had probably blended herself into the shadows of the shop.

"C-can I help y-you?" he squeaked. His mouth had gone dry. He licked his lips nervously with a thick, amphibian tongue.

No response. The shadow stood there. Menacing. Silent. That odd tilt to the head as she looked down at him at once both innocent and eerie.

"We have a wide selection of frames and lenses. I am sure I can find something for you."

Did umbras even need glasses? He hadn't recalled seeing one in his shop before. The shopkeep pressed backward into the cubbies behind him and felt the old wood pressing lines in his flesh. The umbra stepped down before him in a fluid, supple motion. She was at least half a head taller than he and significantly more lithe.

He smiled a wide smile and then let out a nervous chuckle that died as he saw what she held in her hand. A large straight razor hung loosely in the shadow's left hand, the naked blade reflecting unintelligible, twisted shapes.

The shopkeep dropped his newspaper and raised his hands defensively.

"Look, I don't want any trouble," he began.

The straight razor flashed out. It was perfect, smooth, and deadly sharp.

He tried to react, but the umbra was faster and he was graceless. She caught his neck: the blade of the razor cut into his throat sack, split arteries, and shattered both his windpipes. A surge of blood gushed from his throat and seemed to pass through the umbra as if she wasn't there. The shopkeep gurgled and clutched at his throat, his thick, black blood covering his hands and soaking into his white linen shirt and gray trousers. He slid down to his knees and then collapsed, his back against the wall. He could feel his body convulsing as his hearts pumped blood out of the open wound.

He didn't understand.

The shadow bent over him. Looked at him again with that strange tilt of the head. He wanted to cry out; wet tears rolled down his cheeks and by the smell he knew he had pissed himself. Slowly, methodically the umbra drew the straight razor across his face, cutting above his lips, below his nose. He felt the blade continue its cut, tracing an oval around his upper and lower lips, across his chin. The shopkeep gurgled through hot flashes of pain.

The umbra drew back, peeling his lips away from his face like a sticker. She looked at him and then at his lips, holding them in the black of her palm almost inquisitively. Blood dripped from the flesh, seemed to pass through her hand and spattered on the floor.

The shopkeep stared in horror. Seeing his mouth sitting in the hands of this umbra woman was too much to bear. He was panicking, but his arms refused to move. He wanted to kick out, but his feet felt anchored to the ground. He felt his three hearts slowing, and somehow he knew he wouldn't be going home. He would miss the family meal. He would not see his brood. He would miss his wives. He would never see his aging father again. The radio droned on, the maero's voice a rumbly lullaby.

The umbra stepped away, taking the shopkeep's lips with her. Drifting across the room towards the front of the narrow shop, she disappeared out the front door. The doorbell tinkled softly.

ONE

I blew into town like the murmur of a warm sigh. The air was muggy and hot—high summer in Lovat. Clouds churned above the city like cake batter, promising rain. The island caravansara buzzed with activity as I led my party through its gates and into the open courtyard. The smells of grilled meat, dust, sweat, and animal dung competed for the attention of my nose. I could hear someone playing music, the rumble of discussions, and raised voices arguing.

I was home.

Other road-weary travelers swarmed around us, moving in and out of the caravansara, slipping past the ponderous cargowain. I looked over my shoulder at the ridiculous thing. It was enormous, slow, bogged down by the massive crate that dwarfed its frame. The oxen pulled slowly and the large wheels creaked along. The crate was made of fresh pine the color of whiskey and a brand for Wilem, Black & Bright, the crate's owners, blazed on the side.

This had been my charge. Normally a trip across the Big Ninety would have taken us a week, but with the laden cargowain behind me the trip had lengthened three times over. I was exhausted, covered in road dust, and hungry. Pierogi sounded good right now.

"By the Firsts, we made it. Another trip complete; more money in our pockets," mumbled Wensem dal Ibble, my partner in Bell Caravans. I looked up at the lanky maero. He smiled a wrinkled, crooked smile, his small dark eyes shining.

"That we did," I said, reaching up and clapping him on the shoulder. "What do you say we sign off on the delivery and go get our money?"

"Sounds good to me," agreed Wensem.

The driver of the massive cargowain dropped down from his seat and walked across the hard-packed earth to where my partner and I stood. He was a scrappy fellow with a rough tangle of white hair that stuck straight up. He pulled the goggles off his face and squinted up at me.

"Well, we're here," he said, swatting a fly away from his bulbous nose.

I grinned. "We are, and I'll need to have your signature confirming delivery."

He shook his head. "My signature won't mean a damn thing to the bosses. You'll need to get the cargo master's sign off. Wilem, Black & Bright have an office on the second story, right over there. See them."

He pointed.

I nodded, trying to hide my annoyance at being sent scrambling to get a simple signature. A few of the travelers who had accompanied my caravan approached me, shaking my hand, dropping extra lira in my palm to thank me for my guidance and protection.

Don't tell anyone but, truth be told, the Big Ninety isn't that dangerous. It begins somewhere East of the territories, cutting West like a lazy river between the mountains. For me, the open road begins and ends at Syringa, the trade town to the East. From there, I guide caravans west across the open plains and through the lofty western mountains before descending towards Lovat itself. There's something open and free about that big road that gets into my blood. Makes a roader crave its expanses. If you have the itch, it's easy work. The Lovat Municipalities and the Syringa Nation do a decent job at keeping companies moving between the two cities: armed militias mean raiders and thieves aren't generally a problem. The route's fairly straightforward as well. Sure, there's some knowledge needed in crossing the Grovedare Span, and there can be some confusion when you get to the mountain passes, but it's not like crossing the continent or trying to get behind the walls of Victory. Still, I graciously accepted their thanks, took their payment, and shook their hands, playing the part of a dutiful caravan master.

That duty finished, Wensem and I crossed the courtyard of the caravansara melting into the crowd as we made our way to the second story office of Wilem, Black & Bright, Import and Export.

The office was small and cluttered with papers and crates bearing the brand and documents explaining where the various objects were due to be shipped. It was located in an external corner of the building. I tried to see the fabled Lovat skyline, but the layers of dirt that clung to the office's windows like moss prevented me from even seeing the time of day. I guessed they hadn't been cleaned in a hundred years.

"I can't pay you," explained the cargomaster, a surly kresh. His fleshy, V-shaped mouth chewed on a musty cigar. "We don't keep cash at this office. Not allowed. We're strictly for receiving and shipping. I'll sign a proof of delivery and services rendered, but you'll need to go to the main office to receive payment."

Wensem frowned and rolled his eyes. He was as eager as I to get paid and get into the city. I was just excited to be back in civilization, but Wensem had a more noble purpose: to see his newborn son.

"I was really hoping I wouldn't be required to run all over the city just to get paid for services rendered," I explained, trying to sound professional. I probably failed.

The kresh looked at me unabashed through clouds of pungent blue smoke. "Welcome to Wilem, Black & Bright. We like our protocol."

"Clearly."

He gave a bitter smile and scratched out a proof of delivery on official-looking stationery with a boney claw. "You'll find the main office in Pergola Square. Know the Hotel Arcadia?"

"I do," I mumbled. It was partially true. The hotel was too elevated for my kind: seventh level, extending up through the eighth and ninth until its upper floors touched the sun itself.

"They like their protocol as well. Roaders aren't allowed in, but show this to the doorman and he'll let you in. He won't like it, and he'll sneer down his nose at you, but he'll let you in."

"Thanks," I said, taking the slip of paper and tucking it into a chest pocket.

"Might want a shower first," the kresh added as we left, letting the old door swing shut behind me. We said brief goodbyes to the rest of our party. I settled accounts with the men and women of our company: Hannah Clay, my go-to scout whom I would undoubtedly see again on our next caravan; Eli Pascal, one of our occasional caravan guards; and a few others, doling out three weeks' wages from my billfold to each of them.

The trip had to have been excruciatingly boring for them, spending most of their days languishing along the road as the caravan fought against the slow pace of the cargowain. I gave each a healthy bonus which cleaned me out of most of my money. I told some to keep in touch because I was planning on leading another caravan out of the city in a month's time. A good crew can be hard to come by.

"Let's get paid," I said to Wensem, feeling a slight wave of déjà vu that rolled over into annoyance. "I'm nearly broke. Remind me to have a stern talking with August. I appreciate the numbers behind this job but all this running around is a bit ridiculous."

Wensem nodded in agreement, repeating the kresh's line about Wilem, Black & Bright liking their protocol. I gave him a sarcastic smile.

The caravansara sat on an island close to the mainland. In ages past it undoubtedly had been a place of residence and business, but as the waters had risen after the Aligning most of those were swallowed up by the sea. In this era it was significantly smaller, serving only as a port of call. Twin floating bridges lead away from the island, through a tunnel, and into the mighty city of Lovat beyond.

We began to cross one of the massive floating bridges. Bits of old buildings half-submerged and rotted stuck up from around the edges, eventually fading into the murk as we passed over deeper water.

We moved among the thinning crowd heading into the city. Motor-coaches and fourgons passed us, belching the black smoke that followed the rich around like a noxious perfume as they made their way to more elevated levels. Fuel was hard to come by, and as a result, expensive; only the ultra-elevated burned it over trivial matters like personal transportation.

The silhouettes of Lovat now dominated the skyline. Nine levels stretching skyward. Five hundred meters high at its apex. Each level housing buildings of various sizes sagged on the backs of buildings below. Thousands of sodium lamps twinkled in their recesses.

Lovat was the oldest and largest city on the coast, and it showed its age by the haphazard mess it had become. Roads rose and dipped, elevators and staircases criss-crossed, and floors would end and then begin across the city leaving large empty spaces between levels.

The lower levels of Lovat were darker, shadowed by the more elevated levels. As residents were fond of saying, "Sunlight doesn't shine in the depths." Smoke from fires and cooking stoves hung around the city like a permanent fog. You could see the sunlight from the seventh, eighth, and ninth levels, but rarely did it penetrate the murk. Down here, life was lived beneath sodium and neon."

The bridge deposited Wensem and me on the eastern side of the Fourth Level warren known as Frink Park. Frink Park sat one level above the only dry land in central Lovat: an island known as Broadway, named after the central street that ran its length.

The streets of the warren were lined with modest apartment blocks, small restaurants, commercial vegetable gardens, bars, a gym, and a few pool halls. The residents had taken to draping colorful lines of flags from the roofs, which gave the neighborhood a festive feel. It was a quaint, quiet warren, safe enough but not totally free from the street gangs or pitchfork dealers operating out of broken telephone booths.

"Have you decided on a name?" I asked Wensem as we made our way along Cherry Street toward Pergola Square. We passed by a group of teenage maero playing squares on the corner and took care not to disturb them.

"Considered my father's name," said the maero in his soft tone, stepping around one of the teens. Wensem was big and strong, but his voice had a surprisingly soft quality—almost delicate. It always took people by surprise.

We were moving away from the residential buildings and into the more commercial area of Broadway Island. I looked up and couldn't see a single hole into the upper levels. No sunlight penetrated this deep. Just the soot-blackened cement of the buildings above and the slowly spinning fans of air circulators.

"Ibble dal Ibble?" I asked as Cherry Street came to an end and James Street began.

Around us the streets were lit with the yellow glow of sodium lamps, occasionally broken by the vulgar bloom of neon. The bright colors hawked all manner of goods and services: food, tailoring, liquor, weapons, loans, entertainment, barbering, and cheap sex.

The air was heavy with exhaust, grease, and sweat; odors came and went as quick as a breath. Hawkers filled the streets with their carts shouting at passersby in crude calls like angry crows. Nearby street musicians strummed on out-of-tune guitars and shabby beggars pleaded for a spare lira, dirty hands extended to hurrying pedestrians.

Wensem chuckled and shook his head at my mistake. "Ibble dal Wensem. In maero culture our father's name becomes our follow name—er—last name as you humans put it. Dal means 'son of.'"

I sighed and I wondered if I was blushing. "Ah, yeah sorry," I mumbled.

My embarrassment was forgotten as the smell of spiced meat filled my nose. Food. Real food.

"Hold up," I said, and stepped up to the cart. A handsome dimanian with two red horns growing from his cheeks smiled at me.

"What will it be?" he asked, waving his hands over the grill before him.

"Chicken skewer," I said, handing him half a lira.

He nodded and removed one of the hot skewers of meat from the grill, wrapping the lower portion with a wax-coated paper before handing it to me. In the yellow lights it glazed, sticky with some mystery sauce. My stomach rumbled.

Knowing dimanian cooking the meat would be on the spicier side. Possibly paprika and chilies, often a thickened curry. The scent wafting from the meat made my mouth water.

I generally try to hire a decent chuck but the fellow we parted with back at the caravansara had been terrible. The food he prepared was bland and overcooked. Ingredients on the Big Ninety are sparse even with a dedicated chuckwain; no matter how well we stock, half our trip always ends up consisting of dry hardtack.

I bit into the chicken, letting the juice run down my chin. It was utter delight. The meat was fresh and perfectly grilled. The heat from the spices (chili, I was right) burned my mouth. I regretted not buying a second skewer.

"It's a wonder you're not enormous," said Wensem as we continued to walk.

"What makes you say that?" I asked through a mouthful of chicken.

"You're eating. All the time. I'm shocked you didn't buy a bowl of noodles at the caravansara. I saw you eyeing those vendors."

"I hardly eat on the trail. Besides, I didn't want noodles; I really want pierogi," I said. It was true. Eat too much and it makes you slow, and it's never good to be slowed down out on the Big Ninety.

"That," he pointed to my half-devoured skewer, "isn't pierogi."

I ignored him. "Anyway, the vendors at the caravansara aren't very good. You buy there, you risk a sour stomach. You know that."

Wensem chuckled in agreement as he walked beside me.

We continued to make our way toward the Arcadia Hotel. The city grew taller around us, the ceiling above us rose, and we could see a few spaces through which the upper levels were illuminated.

Pedestrian traffic increased as we moved closer toward the center of the city. A used-suit salesman stood on a small crate near one corner and shouted at passersby in a rough, thickly accented language I couldn't understand. Just down the street another hawked broken radios from a folding table.

Lovat buzzed with life, and I was glad to be home.

A gruff-looking doorman in a sharp black suit stood next to the gilded doors of the Arcadia Hotel. The first floor of the Arcadia rested at Level Seven and rose upwards beyond Level Nine. It was one of the tallest buildings in the city: sixty stories and elevated well above the lowest levels of Lovat.

"We have business here," I said, hastily wiping my greasy hands on my trousers. It wasn't my finest moment.

The doorman wrinkled his nose and, without a word, took a step back from us.

"Look," I said, pulling the proof of services rendered from my pocket and handing it to the doorman, "We have business with Wilem, Black & Bright. We'll go on up, conduct our affairs, and then bugger off."

The doorman studied the note for a long moment before handing it back and stiffly opening the door. Wensem and I walked inside.

The interior of the Arcadia Hotel was overwhelming. Chandeliers of crystal and glass hung from a baroque ceiling of cream and burgundy. The walls were papered with hand-painted linen. Ornate tables squatted around the room holding up enormous bouquets of fresh flowers. Waist-coated bellmen moved trollies of luggage around the main floor through doors and into elevators.

The luxury washed over me, caught me in its tide. For a moment I felt adrift.

My father was a wheelwright, and I had grown up a wheelwright's son in the small town of Merritt on the outskirts of Lovat. We didn't have much: a small bedroom I shared with my brother, a narrow single bed. Our house smelled of my mother's plum bread and my father's favorite tobacco. His workshop had been equally small and was filled with the scent of wood being cut and soaked before it was bent into wheels. A decent life.

I met all types in my father's shop: Reunified Road Priests, beggars, traveling salesmen, wanderers, mercenaries, and of course roaders and caravaneers. Living along the Big Ninety is what led me to caravaneering. Now I couldn't imagine not sleeping under the stars or being without that bustle.

The dense bustle of Lovat. The smells of its market, the flavors of King Station, the sounds of a couple fighting in an apartment above. Food carts and dim sum, antique dealers and used clothing. The Arcadia Hotel, with its eight-course dinners, cloth napkins, diamonds, and custom-tailored anything, was not my Lovat.

We approached the front desk. The clerk behind was a young girl with golden hair and a face caked with makeup. She smiled at me, her eyes betraying the greeting. I felt out of place. Under her gaze I could feel the road dust plastered to my shirt, the mud that stained the cuffs of my pants, the brambles that lodged themselves in my hair.

"Can I help you?" she asked with a strange pressed tone.

"Wilem, Black & Bright?" I requested.

"Ah," she began, the smile wavering. Her hands played over a brass autodex with faded yellowing cards. "Wilem, Black & Bright, yes. They're on the fifty-first floor. West side of the building. I'll ring them and ah...tell them you're both on your way."

"I'd appreciate that," I said with my own, fixed smile. Damn this protocol.

"The elevators are around the corner," she explained. "Here is a token."

"Token?" I asked, taking the odd-shaped plastic disk.

"Yes, you'll need it to operate the elevator. Keeps the homeless from wandering the halls."

I nodded and we left, making our way to the elevators, eager to find Wilem, Black & Bright.

The ancient lift's doors clattered open at the fifty-first floor. We were far above Level Nine's streets. Bright sunlight flooded through windows at either end of the hallway. I could see other towers that stretched away from the jumbled mess below reaching for the sky. Squinting after the low light of the sublevels, I shielded my eyes as we walked toward the west side of the hotel.

"I don't like this place," said Wensem coolly.

"Me neither. Let's find the offices and get out of here."

We found the offices easily enough. Near the end of the hall, an elegant frosted frosted glass door with hand-painted letters led to a smartly decorated waiting room. Square leather furniture ran along a wood-paneled wall and detailed etchings depicting scenes from some distant past hung in extravagant frames. A receptionist sat behind an antique desk, the value of which could probably feed a brood of anur for their entire lifespan.

"Can I help you gentlemen?" asked the dauger from behind the desk. Her mask was reflective, with a sheen of cobalt that matched the eyes that moved behind the slits. It was impressive, elevated, and had the intriguing effect she desired.

"Yeah. I'm here to get paid for a delivery."

"Ah, the caravan master. I got the telegraph an hour ago. Bell Caravans, was it?"

I nodded.

"Mister Black will be quite pleased."

She tilted her head to one side, a motion I took as a smile despite not being able to see her mouth. I returned the expression.

"Just doing our job. Sorry it took longer than we had expected, that crate was heavy and with the summer thaw at the pass, things were slow going."

"Well, the estimate was a month," she said. "And you beat it by a whole week. Better than we could have hoped for and better than your competitors' bids."

"Well, I suppose I did say a month, didn't I?"

She ignored me. "Here, let me fetch the coinbox."

The dauger disappeared behind a door, leaving Wensem and me standing awkwardly in the middle of the reception area. A man in a dark red jacket walked in and took a position behind us, forming a short line.

I had the dull realization that I had probably tracked dusty footprints across the lush carpet, but decided it was better if I didn't look down and check.

The dauger receptionist returned in the flustered breeze of the perpetually busy, a gray metal box in her hands. She glanced at the newcomer and said she'd be with him in a few moments. He took a seat in one of the waiting chairs.

"Ah, here we are. Three thousand, correct? Are Lovat liras acceptable?"

"Three thousand is correct and, yes, ma'am, liras are fine," I said, smiling politely. I watched as she laid out the bills, counting them twice.

A window occupied the wall behind her desk. As she counted, I watched the rich of Lovat play on their Level Nine terraces, the midsummer sun baking down on them. Laughter, wine, and cuts of meat sizzling on outdoor grills.

In the distance massive cargo ships and ferries pulled in and out from terminals, heading out into the world towards the distant island city of Empress and parts unknown. Cargo cranes littered the skies like pigeons, raising more towers and cramming as much life as possible into this small corner of the world. It was a lovely view, an expensive view.

The receptionist spoke, snapping me away from my skyline reverie, saying: "Mister Black has authorized a five hundred lira bonus. He wants to thank you for your hard work and prompt delivery. He's sorry he cannot thank you personally, but he's a very busy man."

"Well, that's very kind of him, ma'am. Tell him thank you," I said. I had expected the bonus. I had also expected the trip to only take three weeks. Telling the client it would be four had set me up in a position to bonus. It was an underhanded trick but I had a feeling Wilem, Black & Bright could spare the extra five hundred lira.

"Receipt?" she asked.

"We'll be okay," I said, thanking the receptionist and shaking her hand.

"It's about time I go see my son," stated Wensem. He was getting fidgety. I couldn't blame him, when we had been told we'd have to come all the way to Pergola Square he had deflated. I forked over his portion of the payment, plus a little extra from the bonus. It left me with a little over fifteen hundred lira in my pocket. A decent wage and it would easily hold me over for the month I planned to stay in the city.

"You take care of yourself, Wensem, and that little man of yours."

"Little maero," Wensem corrected with a grin that followed

the crooked line of his jaw. We started walking north. I was heading south, but figured I'd walk with my partner a little longer.

"You settled on a name?"

"Honestly? I was thinking Waldo, after you. Waldo dal Wensem," said Wensem.

I sucked in a gasp, then beamed. "Are you sure?"

"I spoke about the naming with Kitasha before we left. She felt it was an honor. You and I, we built Bell Caravans, and you're as much a member of my clan as any of my brothers. It would be an honor to give my son your name."

"Well," I said, taken aback. "I'd be honored, my friend."

"It's a good name: rare, noble," said Wensem as we walked down a caged stairwell from the ninth to the eighth level of the city. "The kind of name that a maero should feel pride in wearing."

"Don't know how noble it is."

"You make it noble," stated Wensem.

We got in an elevator and dropped to the city's fifth level, passing out of the light and re-entering the murk of the sublevels.

When we stepped out of the lift and in between two small buildings on the fifth level Wensem extended his big hand. I took it and we shook, his small black eyes flashing.

"See you in a month," I said.

Wensem nodded.

"Telegraph me if you get bored," I chuckled.

"Hardly. I'll probably be unreachable for most of the time. I intend on spending as much time as possible with him and

Kitasha before I drag my ass back out onto the Big Ninety. We have a family ritual to perform, a bonding between father and son. It's long overdue already."

"At least invite me over for dinner before we head out again. Let Waldo dal Wensem meet his namesake."

Wensem grinned. "I'll see what I can do."

I laughed and slapped his shoulder. "Get out of here."

Wensem departed, moving in his long stride, arms swinging at his side as he disappeared down an alley and headed north.

The smell of the street vendors was alluring. My stomach rumbled again. I needed a snack.

TWO

Hunger had set in. Before dinner, I had a few errands to run. The first of these, of course, was an evening snack. Priorities, right?

I found a noodle cart on the fourth level of the King Station district. It was a comical little thing, boxy and rusted with a faded canvas umbrella of red and yellow. At one time it probably was mobile, but time had turned it into something a little more stationary. A line of stools and a small bar sat opposite the grill. It was currently devoid of customers.

A pot-bellied man stood behind the cart, wearing a sweat-stained undershirt, gray trousers, and just the brim from a wide-brimmed hat. He probably hadn't shaved in days and it was impossible to tell the last time he had bathed.

He whistled the first bars from Mother Holiday's "Gloomy Sunday" as he seared a small mountain of noodles. At opportune times he would squirt various oils and sauces from a line of plastic bottles that stood in formation on the top of his cart.

Settling on one of the stools, I ordered a bowl of the house noodles and a small glass of ruou de. The vendor nodded and worked at my order. Steam rose in wisps disturbed only by the passing pedestrians and the occasional bicyclist.

"Rain's coming," said the cart owner, his voice thick with alcohol and an accent I couldn't place. He smiled a toothless grin and poured a small glass of foggy ruou de for me. I nodded along and took a sip of the rice liquor.

"There was sun earlier," I said. The liquor was good. The right amount of burn. It helped me forget about my blisters, and I found that with a bit of a buzz the mugginess of the sublevels was easier to bear.

"How'd you go about seeing if there was sun earlier?" asked the vendor as he looked around the dimly lit street. King Station was southeast of Pergola Square and had no real view of the outside. It could've been months since he'd seen the sun—maybe years.

"Just came into the city this morning," I explained.

"Ah. I see. What do you do?" he asked as he handed me my bowl of noodles and a pair of pull-apart bamboo chopsticks.

I dove into the noodles. "Caravan master."

"Ah. A caravaneer. What do the elevated call you, roaders? Something like that. Could never do that work. Personally I don't like the open sky so much—feels too, I dunno. Open."

"Not for everyone," I said with a nod.

The cart owner nodded and turned the conversation back to the weather. "Mark my words. It'll be rain before too long. I can feel it." He tapped his elbow meaningfully.

Rain. I didn't like that idea. It was hot, high summer in Lovat and rain only meant one thing: more mugginess. It brings out the worst in people, drives them mad.

I shoveled noodles into my mouth and continued to make small talk with the cart owner. He did his best to follow along in his half-drunken state. Nodding at the right time. Asking a few questions about caravanning. I didn't mind, the ruou de had me buzzing and the noodles were good, spicy with a zing of citrus. We spoke of sports, politics, and the recent violence to the south in Destiny. It was the same routine I'd be having with cart owners all over the city for the next month. I was relishing it.

I lingered at the cart longer than I really should have. My feet hurt, and sitting down and drinking a few glasses of the rice liquor went a long way toward making my blisters feel better. The cart owner matched me drink for drink, and though thoroughly drunk, was still able to resume his whistling of "Gloomy Sunday" as I walked down the street toward my next appointment.

You meet a lot of interesting folks on the trail. Scavengers, traders, and caravaneers like myself make up the bulk of the traffic, but you'll still come across lawmen, barristers, Road Priests, wandering judges-for-hire, and the occasional pilgrim. The roads of the territories are a great source of stories and an even better source for goods to trade. A week's supply of hardtack can mean life or death to a professional wanderer, so they're willing to let goods that would sell for a lot more in a city go for a pittance. This often works in my favor.

Russel & Sons Optics was a few blocks from the noodle cart on Maynard Avenue. It was a small hole in the wall shop tucked between a seamstress and a small distillery that brews some of the worst gin I have ever tasted. I had known the proprietor for a few years now: an anur who claimed to have fourteen sons and eleven daughters from his first wife and six boys and eight girls from his second. Thaddeus Russel had inherited the shop from his father a few years earlier, and had made a decent little living selling spectacles to the poorer inhabitants of Lovat.

You can get custom spectacles elsewhere, but it'll cost you dearly. So the rest of us make do with hand-me-downs, older pairs, and guys like Thaddeus to sell them to us. He has quite a collection and claims some of his stock is over a thousand years old. It's one of those tales you never question and it's what makes Thad's place unique among the eyeglass vendors.

The cart man was right: a soft rain began to fall as I walked toward the spectacle shop. Rain in the sublevels is different. It doesn't fall in showers; instead, it collects in pools in more elevated levels that eventually overflow. Then the water streams down in sheets, finding random paths, continuing down and down. Even light rains become torrents, running down the edges of buildings or between cracks in the road, creating waterfalls that pour from level to level until they reach the Sunk.

Russel's shop sat behind one of these sheets and I had to charge through, soaking my hair and the shoulders of my shirt. It wasn't the smartest move, but it sure felt good. I looked forward to a proper bath later.

The doorbell tinkled as I entered and the fat Anurian looked up at me from behind his paper. The anur are an interesting race, large tapered heads with bulbous eyes that stick out to the sides, thick throats, and wide mouths. If you imagined a human-frog hybrid, you wouldn't be far off. They live short lives; I've known Thaddeus for five years, and he probably only has another five in him. His own father is eleven, which is almost unheard of, but the old cuss doesn't show a sign of ill health. They make up for their short life span by breeding enormous families they refer to as "broods."

"Wal!" Thaddeus declared, as he rose and waddled over to me. I could see the folds of skin shifting beneath his shirt, and he enveloped me in a musty embrace.

"Hey, Thad," I said jovially. "How's the business?"

Thaddeus smirked and shook his head, the motion sending his throat jiggling. "Slow, only sold a few pairs last week. I don't know where this sudden souring has come from. If I had half a mind I'd say it was due to that new shop up the avenue."

"New shop?" I questioned, following Thaddeus to the counter at the far end of the shop. The walls of Russel & Sons Optics were lined with shelves and crammed full of boxes of spectacles sorted first by prescription and then style. They smelled of glass cleaner.

"Aye. Some religious trinket dealer named Hagen Dubois. It has brought all manner of riffraff into the neighborhood. This used to be a quiet place. Didn't see any weirdos down here like you see up north. I mean, we'd get the occasional vagrant and the random street mystic, a few mindless pitch addicts, but nothing like those weirdos. Nope."

"What do you mean weirdos?" I asked, laughing.

Thaddeus leaned forward conspiratorially. "You know. Religious types. Monks and such. I can deal with the Reunifieds, but these fellas are fringe types. Fellas wearing robes and shaving their heads clean. I've seen Hasturians and even a few Deepers seeking their tentacled idols. Those tattooed types as well. All sorts. Scaring away my customers."

"Hey!" I said, grinning and holding out my tattooed arms. "Do I scare away your customers?"

"Don't be silly—you know what I mean. These are those fellas with head and face tattoos. Those cultist types. They wear those jumpsuits."

"Sorry, drawing a blank on those types."

Thad frowned.

"Just yesterday a pack of them walked by and returned with an armload of cheap statuary. If you wait here I'm sure we'll see more of them. I see a few almost every day. Ever since that shop opened up they swarm like hornets."

Thaddeus blinked at me and scratched behind his eye.

"So, you interested in some new stock, or is business too slow?" I asked. This was a typical conversation with Thaddeus. Business was always slow and there was always something chasing off his customers. Last time it was the weather, before that he claimed people were scared to go out because the serial murderer the papers dubbed the "Lovat Strangler" had been apprehended. When I had brought up that "apprehended" meant he was caught, Thaddeus had said he believed people of Lovat feared a copycat. Either way, business was always slow and Thaddeus used that as a ploy to try to barter even cheaper prices for my goods.

Thaddeus frowned and grumbled, "Let's see what you have."

I brought out four pairs and laid them on a cloth pad that rested on the counter. A few wire-framed spectacles I purchased off a scavenger from the territories to the south, and a rimless pair I'd found on the side of the road that was unfortunately missing one of the nose pads. My prize this round, however, was a pair of mint condition Browlines spectacles I had bought off a trader heading to Syringa. I knew Thaddeus had a special place for Browlines and would love those in particular.

For his part, Thaddeus didn't break his stride. He slid the cloth closer to him and puzzled over the four pairs, lifting them to one of his bulbous black eyes, inspecting their prescriptions, noting scratches, and mumbling to himself. Often he would stop and make notes on a ratty old notepad he kept near his register.

"Well?" I asked after ten minutes of his perlustration. "Can we make a deal or what?"

"Patience has never been your strong suit, Waldo, my boy."

I gave a good-natured frown.

"You smell awful by the way. You been swimming around in the Sunk?"

"I haven't bathed yet. Came here right after collecting my pay for my last caravan."

"Well aren't I lucky," Thaddeus chuckled. He pushed the four pairs back toward me, having satisfied himself with their inspection. "You're missing a nose pad on that rimless pair, but I might have a match; the others are in decent enough shape."

"How much?" I asked.

Thaddeus scratched behind his left eye. "I'll give you fifty for the lot."

"Fifty? Those browlines are worth twice that by themselves. I'd need at least a hundred and fifty," I declared. "And don't pull the 'how much do you really know about spectacles' line with me. I've learned quite a bit over the last few years."

"One hundred," said Thaddeus, completely deadpan.

"One twenty-five and you throw in a bottle of that brandy you keep in that desk of yours."

"One fifteen and the bottle," he said. "Final offer."

He extended his hand and pulled out the bottle of brandy.

I shook it and took the brandy. We avoided a paper trail. Made both of us more profit without the city's tax collectors dipping their hands into our pockets.

"You know, every time you try to haggle with me, you scratch behind your eye."

Thaddeus frowned. "I do not."

"You do so. Don't ever play cards, Thad. You'd be terrible at it."

He handed me a wad of bills, which I slipped into my pocket.

"It's going to be humid tonight," he said, looking outside the windows of his storefront at the curtain of water. "Rain's really coming down. Maybe you should just forego the bath and go stand under that."

I grinned at him. "I might. Want to get dinner later this week?"

Thaddeus turned his amphibian-esque face to me and nodded. "Sounds good. How about this weekend? I usually close up around six—come by then?"

"Sounds good to me," I said.

We shook hands again as a farewell and I walked out of the narrow shop and onto the street. The bell at the door sang out as I passed through.

Maynard Avenue was quiet. A few folks milled about. I passed a group of dimanian teenagers—their horns just sprouting—and I bought a newspaper from a friendly guy on the corner. His eyes crinkled as he smiled, taking the small bit of change in wrinkled, leathery hands. I tucked the soft newsprint under my arm and cast a look toward the end of the street where Thaddeus had indicated the religious artifact dealer had set up shop. None of his "weirdos" seemed to be around. I considered checking it out, but I didn't need an idol or prayer book or some charm for a necklace. And at this moment, hunger took precedence.

The rain hadn't let up but I was careful now to avoid the spouts of water that had cropped up. I walked west, toward a lift that would take me down to Level Two. There was a place in King Station that sat just above the Sunk. It was always where I ate my first real meal upon returning home.

That was my plan. Grab dinner. Find a room to hole up in for a month. Spend the rest of the evening drinking brandy and letting all the dirt soak out of my pores in a bath somewhere. Glorious.

I really wished things had worked out that way.

THREE

The waiter set down a warm beer the color of piss. I looked out the dirty window of the small shop and absently ran the tips of my fingers over the butcher paper. Spills from previous diners stained the top in greasy splotches. Outside the rain continued to drip and wash down from the upper levels. I could see some of the lower races walking past: anur and their broods, cephels moving in that awkward gait on their powerful leg-arms. An occasional pitchfork addict stumbled past, scratching at scabs while hunting down his next fix.

I don't normally seek out restaurants this close to the Sunk, but I didn't come to Shuai Tan for the atmosphere.

The best places to eat in this city aren't the elevated, celebrity chef-run restaurants with a cover charge just to see the inside. I'm sure they are fine in their own right, with interiors richly filled with gilded columns and hanging tapestries, with ingredients sourced from the finest merchants, fishermen, and ranchers. In places like those, the cost of dining alone could pay a small family's rent for months.

Not my style.

It's places like Shuai Tan where the true culinary treasures can be found. It's in the grubby down-in-subs, hole-in-the-wall dives; that's where one finds the best Lovatine cuisine. In a city of ninety-three million souls with generations of families going back to the Aligning, some recipes have been perfected. Dishes that are prepared following traditions, hundreds even thousands of years old. Food made from the heart.

Shuai Tan only had two customers at the moment: me, and a fat old kresh with long face whiskers that passed as his beard. He spooned mouthfuls of fried rice into his face. His bulging, heart-shaped eyes were cloudy with cataracts; a walking stick leaned against his table. He breathed heavily when he wasn't smacking his lips. He was taciturn, eating and watching a monochrome that blazed gray and white light across the back wall of the small restaurant.

A lone waiter flittered between the two of us. Human. Probably a member of the family that ran Shuai Tan, a grandson in a long line of grandsons. Most of his muttering was drowned out over the hum of an ancient air cycler that clattered above us, small paper streamers fluttered from its grate.

Shuai Tan was small, thrust into a space built in another time and for some other purpose. Four small tables with room for nine customers occupied the dining area of the restaurant. An extra table sat outside, though the chairs that went along with it had been stolen years earlier, never to be replaced.

The exterior and interior brick walls had been painted a dingy aqua blue; the paint so thick it was impossible to see the pattern of the cinderblocks. A dirty awning lit by flickering sodium lights kept the rainwater off the necks of hungry customers.

A hand painted sign advertised "good food" for "cheap prices," and above me, the ancient tube monochrome broadcasted, whipping through the day's news in a language unknown to me. I had sat near the window intentionally. I preferred to keep my eyes off that image-filled box and focused on the more interesting stories that play out in the streets. The hustle and bustle of life itself.

Noises echoed from the kitchen, and I leaned back in my chair to drink it all in. This was my ritual, my first meal upon returning to Lovat. Before bed or even a shower, I had to first come to Shuai Tan and eat a mountain of bao yu.

"Can I take your order now, sir?" asked the waiter, fluttering next to my table and wringing his hands impatiently.

"I'll have some of that fried rice the fella over there has, and the bao yu in the sweet pepper sauce, with the ah...." I checked the menu. "...Ah, yes, the asparagus?"

"Ah," winced the waiter, his Strutten only slightly accented, "We're out of the asparagus, we could substitute..." he thought about it." ...mushrooms? Would mushrooms be all right, sir? Anything else?"

"That'll be fine," I said, taking an ill-advised sip of my warm beer. I fought back a shudder. "Can I get a vermouth?"

"Yes, sir."

"With ice if you have any."

"Ice. Yes, sir."

The waiter nodded and fluttered off and left me alone near the window, watching the street. Bao yu. "Abalone" in Strutten, the common language of the territories, Bao yu in a language so ancient and dead no one could remember the name. My mouth watered. I couldn't imagine living farther inland. In cities even as close as Syringa, seafood was scarce. The trip across the Big Ninety took too long and seafood spoiled easily. Lovat was lucky. The archipelago brought in sea life by the droves. Shrimp. Seals. Mussels. Clams. Otter. The occasional whale. The bounty of the ocean crashed against her gates, and the city was hungry.

According to some censuses, Lovat is also home to one of the largest populations of gathered cephels on the planet. Not sure how much I believe it—they tend to keep to themselves, spending most of their time in their underwater colonies in the Sunk.

Cephels' octopodian heritage make them excellent fishermen and shellfish collectors. They tend to run massive shellfish farms somewhere below, and even larger spreads farther out into the sea. Huge swaths of seafloor growing acres and acres of some of the best shellfish you could bite into, and Lovat got first choice.

That meant the hole-in-the-wall, down-in-the-subs restaurants rarely visited by elevated citizens had some of the freshest seafood this side of the Eastern Mountains, and were handled by people who knew how to prepare it.

I turned my gaze from the window back into the narrow restaurant. The waiter had paused by the rear counter to stare at whatever was playing out on the monochrome above me. Probably another random shooting in Destiny or a Purity movement march. The waiter's face was painted with the lights of the screen: grays and whites of varying luminosity. Like the mirrored reflection of a stormy sky in the sea.

I settled myself, trying to ignore the horrible aftertaste of my beer, and waited for my vermouth. I caught the half-blind kresh glance at me and then back to the monochrome, awkwardly shoveling another spoonful of rice into his mouth. Ignoring him, I continued my vigil at Shuai Tan's storefront.

In the distance I could hear sirens.

You know that odd voice in the back of your head that knows something is off, but the rest of you is too stupid to comprehend what's going on? Yeah. That part of me was screaming, and the rest of me? Well, the rest of me just wanted some vermouth and to be left alone.

I heard voices near the back of the restaurant and glanced over, seeing the waiter talking in hushed tones into the telephone. He glanced over his shoulder at me, once, twice, three times, and then back at the monochrome. The rest of me caught up. I could feel the eyes of the other patron as well. He had stopped eating and was staring with those cloudy, heart-shaped eyes. Something wasn't right. It felt off.

I rose.

"Cancel my order," I announced. "I think I need some air."

The waiter turned and backed into the counter. The sirens wailed outside loudly and a few large fourgons rolled up. Flashing red and blue lights reflected against the painted aqua walls, and the old kresh cowered behind his table, the cane falling to the floor in a clatter.

Lovat police burst inside before I could do anything.

"That's him, officer," I heard the waiter stammer. "That's him! The man from the mono!"

The grey and blue clad cops all turned toward me, as if guided by some powerful hand.

I reacted.

I would not be pinned down, I would not be trapped. They would not take me. Something snapped. Escape.

I shoved my way past the officers, knocking over two deputies before barreling into a third just entering the door.

The waiter kept yammering behind me, his voice rising as I moved farther away until he was screaming, "That's him! That's him! The murderer! That's the man from the monochrome!"

I somehow made it out the narrow door, falling face first onto the level two street and bloodying my nose. The scent of piss, sewage, and spoiled raw meat hit my nostrils like a battering ram. I struggled to my feet, confused and wanting only to escape.

I was tackled from the right. The officer who hit me was a burly maero, his shoulders as hard as iron. I collapsed onto the street feeling a shooting pain on the left side of my chest. My head bounced off the pavement right near the edge of a large, exposed portion of the Sunk.

Under the water I could see the barnacle-covered ghosts of a society long since drowned. A lamppost. A vehicle of some sort. A warehouse. All had succumbed to nature and drowned as the seas had risen. Now they served as homes for fish and crabs. A few cephel had stopped and gazed up at me through the water, their bulbous hourglass irises fixated upon my arrest.

Pushing with my hands I tried to rise, but felt the weight of the maero's knee press against my spine.

"Don't think about it," came a growl. Low, throaty, dripping with unspoken threats.

I turned as best I could and saw another Lovat Central patrol arrive. A small scooter with a detachable light. Unmarked.

A dimanian in a sweeping tan coat stepped off his ride. A cigarette dangled dangerously from his dry lips. He was overweight, with a moon face and two sweeping black horns that followed the curve of his bald pate before rising upward into points. Two black beady eyes stared knives at me under a menacing brow. He scratched a greying goatee.

"Waldo Bell? Waldo Emerson Bell?" he asked, almost casually, but his voice had a sharp edge to it. The kind of voice that could tell a dirty joke and berate an uncooperative witness in the same breath. A cop's voice.

"Yes," I said, feeling the pavement press hard against my cheek.

He thrust a silver-plated badge in my face, snatching it away before my eyes could focus on it.

"I'm Detective Carl Bouchard. I'm placing you under arrest for the murder of Thaddeus Gil Russel."

FOUR

Y ou stink."

I sat in a room the color of rotten mint. The pale green that had once covered the walls was stained by centuries of cigarette smoke, sweat, blood, and humidity. On my left was a metal door painted the same color as the walls; a small window showed the buzz of the hallway beyond it. Too high to see anything, but visible enough for prisoners to know that a free world existed just beyond its frame. The tops of heads drifted past.

Before me sat my captor; behind him, an obsidian-dark glass wall, which reflected a shadowy version of myself back at me, as if I was trapped in oily tar. I looked worn, beaten, and tired. My caramel-colored skin was darkened by the sun and my dusty brown hair was longer than I typically preferred. My brow was caked with weeks of road dirt broken by rivulets of sweat, and a drying stain of blood trailed from my nose to my lips. A month's beard obscured my square jaw. Below my heavy brow, my dust-colored eyes peered back at me, darker than in reality, yet somehow reflecting how I felt. I wasn't handsome. I wasn't ugly. Just dirty—dirty and exhausted.

I ignored the detective sitting across from me and continued staring at the black mirror. I've seen enough cop serials on hotel monochromes to know that a group of police officers and maybe a department chief or two stood behind that glass watching me. I visualized them smoking and imagined a few drinking whiskey from mugs.

I gave them the finger.

It just felt right. Probably something else I picked up from the monochrome. The surly suspect. It was probably a stupid idea, but it made me feel better. My way of broadcasting that I knew they were watching me.

You can't pull a fast one over ol' Waldo Emerson Bell, I thought.

Yet there I sat. Arrested. In questioning.

So much for feeling better.

"When's the last time you showered?"

My eyes flicked from my reflection in the glass wall toward the cop sitting across the metal table. Nothing moved but the steam wafting out of his ceramic coffee mug. Bright letters skipped across the mug, proclaiming the detective as the "World's Best Dad!" He looked like a mess. Probably an alcoholic. His right hand was missing the traditional wedding tattoo, but I saw some scarring. Divorced?

He settled slightly, his eyes fixed on me. The detective was fat, in that thick bouncer sort of way: wide neck, thick hands, and a broad chest. His suit was too tight, and his arms were enormous. He probably lifted weights in years past. The muscles remained but they were now buried under mounds of fast food, day old doughnuts, and booze. It takes a long time for strength to fade, and I would bet he could snap me like a twig if he desired, though I'd wager I could probably outrun him.

He grinned. A big grin, with straight white teeth like pillars propping up his fleshy lips. He was dimanian, with large swooping horns that were faded to a dull gray and clung to his bald head, lifting and tapering upward at their apex. A single horn sprouted from his chin, which I had earlier mistaken for a goatee. Dark beady eyes matching the mirrored glass behind him watched me from beneath heavy lids. He looked like some ancient drawing of a chubby devil. His grin faded into a smirk.

Detective Carl Bouchard.

My captor.

"Three weeks? Maybe four now." I sighed, shrugging. They were the first words I'd spoken in an hour, and my voice was raspy and dry. When was the last time I bathed? Syringa? That little inn I stayed in outside the city? I honestly couldn't remember. I don't bathe often on the trail, and I'm aware how grubby I can look. The road clings to a roader, placing its mark upon him like the Lord's upon Cain, as the ancient tales go.

I usually bathe my first night in the city—that would have been tonight. Instead, rather than relaxing in a steaming tub in my rented room, I was chained to the floor of the LPD building in downtown Lovat, watching a fat cop drink himself to death. Lovely.

"That's disgusting," said Bouchard, matter-of-factly. He

sniffed, as if to double check his statement.

I watched him lean back in his chair and slip a flask from his jacket, pouring a few ounces of whiskey into his "World's Best Dad" mug, careful to block his actions from the eyes behind the glass. My eyes turned from his mug toward the wall. Bouchard glanced over his shoulder before leaning forward, only inches from my face. I smelled the potpourri of cheap aftershave, tobacco, whiskey, and coffee drift over me.

I wasn't the only one who stank.

"Medicine," he whispered conspiratorially, as if my watching him catch a nip was enough to make us chummy. "Bum knee."

I shrugged, hoping my face remained placid. This rough cop act—if it was an act—did little for me. He was doing his job like everyone else. Holding me, waiting for me to snap and reveal everything. It was lazy. He was as much a slave to the serials as I was; he might have wanted to wrap this up in a neat hour, but I had all the time in the world. He'd have a long wait.

I continued to sit in silence, still wondering why I was here. The arrest was still swimming in my head—the reading of my rights, the accusations—it was a blur and more confusing than anything else.

Murder? Had he accused me of murder?

Bouchard watched me, the tick of the clock the only noise besides his occasional slurp from the coffee mug.

"You want something?" he asked, finally willing to break our silence. "Coffee? You thirsty? Water? Hungry?"

"Hungry," I said, my voice sounding like a wheeze. My stomach growled, and it felt like a week since I ate my small bowl of noodles from the cart outside Thad's. I never got my bao yu and I was both disappointed and frustrated by this.

Bouchard still said nothing. He leaned back, his enormous gut rising like the moon over the horizon of the metal table. His tree-trunk arms crossed his boulder chest. He looked disheveled, unprofessional. A three-day patch of stubble dotted his jaw. His tie was frayed, ancient, second-hand, worn out of requirement rather than any desire to appear stylish. His coat was too small, and the cuffs ended almost mid-forearm, exposing a tangle of dark hair that sprouted like barnacles in the Sunk. He distract-edly licked a space between two of his pillar teeth with a sharp red tongue as he sized me up.

"Muffie, get the kid a sandwich," he eventually said. He tossed a lira to the only other person in the interrogation room: an emaciated human in a baggy tan suit leaning on the wall near the door. Detective Muffie caught it after a second of fumbling. I turned to look at him. The silent partner. There was no good cop, bad cop routine between these two. Just the personality and the spook. Bouchard and Muffie. Partners? Seemed like a stretch. Bouchard was the brains and the brawn. Muffie? He was just along for the ride. He didn't look more than a few days out of the academy. His suit looked like he borrowed it from someone two sizes bigger, and he twitched and scratched like a pitchfork junkie. Probably was one.

He disappeared through the metal door, giving me a glimpse of the outside hallway and a pretty female officer walking past.

Bouchard yelled after him, "And a cup of coffee!" before turning back to me. "You like coffee, don't you, kid?"

I nodded.

"The coffee here is shit...," he said amiably, like we were buddies.

Of course it is. Maybe the serials are more accurate than we all believe.

He continued. "But it serves its purpose. Wakes a fella up. Puts hair on your chest."

He smirked as he opened the manila folder on the metal table between us. It was a shoddy thing, and it matched Bouchard's tie. Frayed edges, worn well beyond its years. The little tab at the top had white labels layered on top of each other for generations, creating a gummy mess of gray stickers stained with ink. My name was scrawled atop the pile in blocky handwriting.

Waldo Emerson Bell.

I tried to fold my hands and lay them on top of the table, but I realized that the chains holding me to the floor prevented that. I considered pulling them again, but the smarter portion of my brain won out and I rested my hands in my lap. I briefly wondered how I'd eat that sandwich, and in response my stomach growled.

Silence fell between us, a silence too heavy to be outmatched by the small air conditioner humming in the window, or the buzz from the sodium lights. We stared at one another like old jai alai masters sizing up opponents. Bouchard continued to lick at the space between his teeth; it was vaguely lizard-like, though I didn't point that out. I tried to reveal nothing in my stare—just my boredom.

"Waldo Emerson Bell. Six feet tall. Brown hair. Hazel Eyes.

Tattoos of cargowain wheels on your left and right forearms. You were raised in the Merritt township. A wheelwright's son, father is Talbert Olsen Bell, correct?"

I nodded. Placid.

"Named after your great-grandfather on your mother's side. Waldo Emerson Scot. You're a caravan master and part owner of Bell Caravans alongside your partner, Wensem dal Ibble. How am I doing so far?" He grinned.

I nodded again.

"You're 32. Moderately successful. You make monthly runs between Lovat and Syringa and occasionally make a run to Hellgate and operate your caravan company in one of the caravansaras outside the city. Beyond the scrape and the span." He looked up. "One of the islands?"

I nodded a third time, hoping my face didn't betray my annoyance.

"How's your father?" he asked. Easy questions first.

"He's well," I responded coolly.

"Enjoying retirement?"

"He's not retired."

I watched him make some notes.

"Rough life in Merritt?"

"No. It's a small town. Lots to do for a young boy. Haystack mountain, the forest, the river."

"Who taught you caravanning?"

"You pick it up."

"Did you know a Thaddeus Gil Russel?"

I looked up, my dust-colored eyes meeting his inky black

ones. Bouchard smiled a sterile smile and scratched next to the small horn jutting from his chin. Clearly he meant the question to take me by surprise.

It did.

"Yeah, I know Thad. He's a business partner of mine. Traders don't often come into the city, and those that do don't like to talk with anur. So while on the trail, I acquire spectacles for him from merchants and scavengers. When I return to Lovat, I sell them to him, and in turn he sells them at a tidy profit. Good money in eyeglasses."

"Is there now?" questioned Detective Bouchard.

It was a leading question, but I obliged. "They're lightweight. Relativity cheap—it's hard to find a single pair that works. You need to shop for eyeglasses in bulk, you see? New caravaneers tend to go for the items that are extremely valuable. Iron. Steel. Aluminum. Problem is those are bulky and heavy, so you don't have room for more delicate items. Necessary items that people will pay good money for, items that are hard to acquire."

"Spectacles."

I nodded. "Unless you're in such an elevated position that you can hire an artisan to make you a custom pair."

"How long you known Mister Russel?"

"Few years." I thought about it before answering. "Maybe three?"

"Three?" Bouchard questioned.

"Maybe four." I shrugged. I honestly couldn't remember. I felt sick to my stomach. Murder. That was why I was here. I was arrested and charged with murdering Thad. It rolled over me like a dust storm.

Thad was dead.

Dead. Gone. Carter's cross, his brood! His kids. His wives.

My head drooped. He was such a nice guy, had a heart for people. All people. Anur don't need eyeglasses. They don't live long enough for their eyes to degenerate, but he wanted to help other races. Those whose eyes grew old, whose sight dimmed. It's a rarity to find such a generous person. I felt horrible for his wives and children. This would break his father's heart.

I watched the detective make notes in the margins of some document with a badly gnawed pencil. Finally, he nodded and looked up, satisfied after a moment of scratching.

"Are you a member of the Purity movement?"

"I beg your pardon?" I said, my voice betraying my irritation.

"Are you a member of the Purity movement?" he repeated.

The Purity movement is a pro-human speciest organization operating out of West Lovat. Their leader was a fellow named Conrad O'Conner, a charismatic blowhard that preached a return to a pre-Aligning world where humans were the dominant species.

They were particularly hard on non-humanoid races: cephels, anur, and kresh. O'Conner's xenophobic preaching had tied the Purity movement to several murders of non-humanoid races over the years, though there had never been any convictions. They were a black spot on humanity, and I detested the association. I had been called a great many things over the years, but never a speciest. Hate mongers like O'Conner disgusted me.

"I'm no bigot," I said. My voice was laced with anger. "Carter's cross, my best friend and business partner is a maero. O'Conner would hate me just as much as he hates non-humans. He preaches guilt by association; you should know that as well as I do."

Bouchard's eyebrows raised and he nodded. His small eyes blinked slowly as he continued to scratch notes.

"So, if you're not a Purist, please tell me, Mister Bell: What led you to kill Mister Thaddeus Gil Russel of Russel & Sons Optics? Jealousy? Anger? He cheat you?"

"Thad wasn't a cheat, bit of a tightwad but not a cheat, and I didn't kill him," I said, my voice going cold. I felt my hands knot into fists. I jerked at the chains holding my arms to the floor, hearing them rattle. Bouchard smirked and I continued, "Thad might have liked to think of himself as a cheat, but he was about as honest as they come."

"He's dead. Murdered. His lips cut away. I'd show you pictures, but you were at his shop earlier, weren't you? You already know all of this. Why would you want to see pictures?"

My mouth dropped open and I felt cold.

His lips? His lips cut away? The thought horrified me.

"He was a friend. A business associate," I explained, my voice cracking with emotion. "I sold him several pairs of spectacles before heading down to Level Two for some dinner. A couple wireframes and a particular pair of Browlines – he loved Browlines."

"You have receipts for these spectacles?" asked Bouchard, a faint smile playing over his lips.

Damn it.

I stared silently at him. He knew I didn't have receipts.

It was a trap, and I had blindly walked into it.

He grinned, his white pillar teeth flashing. "Receipts would lend a lot of credence to your story, Mister Bell."

I wanted to lunge at him from across the table.

I seethed as the rotten mint door swung open and Muffie returned. The emaciated detective carried a wrapped sandwich and a steaming paper cup of coffee. I could smell the bitter beverage from my seat. The sight of the sandwich made my stomach growl. I wondered if it was audible in the small room.

The skinny detective set both sandwich and beverage before me, just out of my reach.

My stomach growled louder. Bouchard and Muffie glanced at each other. Was that a smirk I caught passing between them?

"We have you at the scene, Mister Bell. We have your fingerprints all over the counter, all over the door. We have a witness who saw you come out of the storefront a few minutes before one of the Missus Russels found her husband dead, his throat slashed, his lips cut off. The guy you bought the paper from, remember him?" He slapped my paper down on the table next to my untouched sandwich and coffee, making the dark beverage ripple. Bouchard wrinkled a thick round nose that matched his moon face perfectly before adding, "He places you there. Perfect description."

I ignored him and repeated, "I didn't kill him."

Bouchard leaned forward, grabbing the sandwich with a thick hand. The plastic wrap reflected the lights above us. I could see the dirt under his fingernails. He unwrapped the plastic and gave the sandwich a perfunctory examination before frowning deeply and then glaring at Muffie.

"What is this shit? Did you get me a damn curry chicken sandwich, Muffie? You did, didn't you?" He glared at the detective leaning next to the door. Muffie shrugged distractedly. Bouchard's eyes were fixated on me the whole time.

"I bet you added mayo, didn't you, you treacherous bastard."

I pulled at my handcuffs, hearing the chain rattle below my chair.

"Nervous?" asked Bouchard.

"Annoyed."

Bouchard chuckled.

I continued, "That's why I'm here. You're hoping I'll crack. Break under this pressure from your act and Muffie's silent routine. The facts are: I didn't kill him, you got nothing, there's no murder weapon, there's no motive. If you did even a little police work you'd know I was friends with him."

"Victims are usually murdered by people they know. Friends often kill friends."

"You just want to fill your quota for the month and I'm the easy target. I'm the lazy target. Do you always hang your investigations off conjecture?"

"We got you at the scene."

"So? What does that mean? You'll work extra hard trying to pin me to the Purity movement and mark me as part of O'Conner's flock? Meanwhile, as you bumble about, the real killer is out on the streets.

"It's all circumstantial; you can't pin this on me. You have no weapon. No motive. You have nothing."

I leaned back as much as my chair allowed. Bouchard grunted

in response and took a massive bite of my sandwich. He chewed thoughtfully, and rose to face the one-way glass, watching me in the mirrored surface.

"It is circumstantial," he admitted, swallowing his mouthful of food. He grinned at me from the mirror, his white pillar teeth reflecting in the ebon surface like a line of stars. It reminded me of the stories my father used to tell me of the girl and the magic cat with its haunting smile. A smile always more visible than the cat itself. "Fingerprints and a witness saying you were there. There were probably hundreds of people on Maynard Avenue today."

That was the one moment where I felt smug. Felt like I won. Then Bouchard dropped a bombshell.

"It's also circumstantial you're connected to Fran Nickel, I suppose. The flute player."

"What does Fran have to do with any of this?" I demanded. My heart thudded in my chest. Fran was the cousin of my broker, a fellow named August Nickel. She was a musician, a flutist in the Lovat orchestra. My one and only connection to elevated society. We had been introduced years earlier by August and hit it off. Went on a few dates but it wasn't meant to be, yet we decided to remain friends. Our relationship was once close but always platonic. As much as I enjoyed her company, I never saw myself with a woman in a mask. I hadn't seen her in years. What did she have to do with this case?

I felt sick at the thought, my hunger pangs were devoured by worry, and I realized I didn't want to know.

Bouchard spun, his lackadaisical expression replaced by a fiery one. His eyes were wide, his brow knitted. He bellowed at me, "Like you don't know, you sick son of a bitch? You starting some collection? Some sick trophy case? Is that it? You come into my city, and already I have two murders, both of which are connected to you."

"Fran's d-dead?" I managed to stammer. The shock was overwhelming.

Bouchard ignored my ramblings. "Why the trophies? Her ears, Russel's lips! This some sick perversion? You get off on this stuff, or did they piss you off? Jealousy? Talent? What did they do to make you snap?"

He leaned across the table, continuing to swear and shout at me. I hardly heard him. It all crashed in on me at once. The realization of what had happened. Fran. Thad. Gone forever. I had been angry with Bouchard up until this point, annoyed at the whole fabrication, unjustly accused of murder; that anger had masked the reality. I had wrapped myself in it, and in one fell swoop Bouchard had torn it away.

I hadn't seen Fran in years, but I still cared about her. First Thad and now Fran? Fran with her gleaming mask of silvery-white metal, and the lively blue eyes that shone from behind it.

Few dauger played music, especially wind instruments, but Fran had modified her flute and made it work, and she was good. She had risen quickly, achieving the rank of first chair in a matter of months. I remember sitting in the audience, her flute carrying me to far away places. A melody that was now forever silenced. Gone. I felt sick. I was shaking. Hot tears cut through the dirt on my face, and I realized I was crying.

My stomach ached with the loss.

My friends. My friends were gone.

I convulsed, my arms pulling at the chains fastened to the floor. Bouchard moved closer, continuing to shout. He slapped down an image of Fran's body, the mask smashed in, her ears cut away. Her stomach ripped open.

I gagged, feeling bile rise in my throat. Bouchard ignored it.

"You knew her. You knew him." He slapped down a picture of Thad. "They thought you were their friend!"

I heaved, puking up the noodles from earlier. The vomit spilled all over my clothes, the desk, the photos. It knocked over the coffee. I gagged, coughed, and wept. Bouchard's rant came to an abrupt end, and he backed away quickly. His face was an expression of repulsion. I tried to wipe my mouth, but my hands remained chained to the floor.

"Muffie! Get him out of here! Throw him in a drunk tank for the time being. I'll see if I can't get the chief to sign him into a proper holding cell."

He turned to me. I could barely register what he was saying.

"I'll nail you with this, you piece of shit. By the bloody Firsts, I will nail you to the wall."

Bouchard's cold eyes followed me as Muffie half-dragged me out of the interrogation room and into the drunk tank.

FIVE

The world was a blur and looking back, it was hard to remember the hours that passed between the interrogation room and the drunk tank. I moved through the motions automatically. Shuffling down the hall, Detective Muffie behind me, club in hand, saying nothing. He'd prod me when I moved too slowly for him. Eventually we got to our destination.

The cage was located on the main level of the station, near processing and just down the hall from the front desk. Made it easy, I suppose, to move the drunks and small-time criminals from processing and into holding.

I moved into the cage, not really taking in my surroundings and ignoring my fellow prisoners. I followed orders, placing my hands through the bars. Letting the officer unlock the cuffs. Feeling the metal slip away from my wrists. Rubbing them absently and sitting when I was told to sit.

Sit and wait.

I took a seat next to a sleeping cephel. He smelled like seawater, kelp, and gin. His skin was a faded gray, dry from his time in the cage. The huge bulbous eyes on the side of his body were closed, and the sack that served as both head and torso seemed to expand and contract with his breaths. His leg limbs curled up below the bench where he rested.

Across the cage were a few exposed metal toilets. A lanky maero sat atop the stainless steel, his pants down around his ankles and his head drooping. He was about as awake as the cephel next to me.

Another Saturday night in the drunk tank.

Hooray.

I sat in silence for what felt like days but was probably only a few hours. A whole parade of stereotypes were ushered in and out of the cage. Pitch junkies, thugs, prostitutes, drunks, outfit enforcers, cultists, vagrants, and even a Purist came and went in the night. Some released after sobering up. Others bailed out by husbands, wives, or friends. Admitted and discharged and in a few cases readmitted.

Yet I remained.

A few characters attempted small talk but I made it obvious that I was uninterested. I needed to think. I needed to mourn.

Fran's mask and Thad's missing smile filled my memories. I hoped August was okay; he was close with his cousin and a death in the family is never a pleasant affair. Thad was only middle-aged. He would have lived another five years easily. This must have hit his brood hard. I wondered who'd provide for them. A lot of hungry mouths, and none old enough to take over his duties at the spectacle shop.

I got angry. I wondered who would want to kill Thad, who would want to murder Fran. It seemed so bizarre. So wrong, and somehow I was stuck in the middle of it. Why was it all pinned to me?

What had Bouchard said? Two deaths since I'd arrived in town, two deaths, and both were connected to me on some personal level. It felt arrogant to assume I was the reason both of my friends were dead, but what other connection was there? Thaddeus didn't know Fran, and Fran didn't associate with anur. As an elevated member of society, it would be bad for her career. I puzzled over the connection for a while, coming up dry.

The cephel next to me woke up. He clucked at me for a while. Humans don't have the beaks to speak Cephan, but if taught it's fairly easy to understand; likewise cephels can understand Strutten, although it's not perfect and often things need to be repeated. We passed some time making a bit of small talk, the weather, some local politics, the jai alai rankings. When he was ushered out of the cage I remained on my bench alone, pondering my position and starting to itch with that feeling of being trapped.

I had to prove my innocence. Though it would take real, solid proof. Bouchard's inquisition played through my head over and over, like a skipping record. Endless. Repeating. It was clear to me that his mind was already made up. He wanted me for the murders. Me and no one else. He was probably finding a judge to sign off on my conviction. It'd be the easiest route, and if the monochrome serials are right, corrupt judges are as common as pitch dealers.

Leaning back against the bars, I ran my hands over my tattoos.

Twin cargowain wheels printed in fading black stained both my forearms. They meant a lot to me. I shuddered involuntarily, feeling like the cage was pressing in on me.

I couldn't stay here. My skin grew itchier. Moving away from the bars, I began to pace the cell.

I don't mind the crowded streets of the city. I don't mind layers of buildings built atop one another; there in those crowds, among those levels of the city, I can move where I want to move. If I choose to take a caravan across the Big Ninety, I can. If I choose to find myself in a kreshian restaurant on Level Two, I can. If I choose to spend days holed up in some cheap motel watching serials, I can.

There, in the holding cell, I was like a caged animal at the Wilcox Exchange. I was trapped, my world shrinking from vast and unreachable to a twenty by twenty cement floor, and if I was convicted it'd get even smaller.

I need to be free; it's burned into me.

"Wensem," I said out loud.

My answer.

A homeless man who had just drifted off to sleep near where I stood grunted with displeasure at the outburst. He rolled to one side, exposing the soiled ass of his jeans. I shifted away, taking up a standing position near the corner next to the cell door.

Wensem was my answer. He was with me all morning, until I went to Thad's shop. He could prove my innocence, at least in Fran's death, and if I wasn't guilty of Fran's murder, why pin Thad on me? There was no motive. It made Bouchard's case that much more difficult. How could I have collected my payment with Wensem if I was off murdering Fran?

My telephone call. I never got my telephone call. Hoping that was not just another serial misconception, I turned to face the bars. The walls opposite the cage were the same rotten mint color as the interrogation room. Must have been a common theme throughout the building. I could hear the ringing of telephones and the babble of raised voices. A few cops passed by, either off or just freshly on duty—I couldn't tell.

"I want my call!" I yelled, making my demand to anyone who could hear it. I pushed my face between two bars as my hands gripped them. I shouted again. No response. My racket added to the noise, but didn't draw any attention from outside the drunk tank. Inside the cage was a different story. My companions were much more free with their jeers and insults. They shouted at me, waving arms and hurling profanities.

Ignoring them, I shouted again. "Bouchard! I demand my telephone call! You hear me, detective? You hear me?"

"Shut up," I heard a deep voice growl from behind me.

I shouted again.

"Keep it down, tiger!" sneered a cross-dressed prostitute with purple hair and olive skin. "Some of us are nursing hangovers the size of a First's nutsack."

I ignored my cellmates.

"I want my telephone call!" I shouted. "I haven't got my telephone call! Detective Bouchard, you own me a damn telephone call!"

Nothing. No response from the other side of the bars.

I waited.

Bouchard didn't appear. Surprisingly, it was the emaciated Muffie who showed up. Sunken cheeks and hollow eyes. Even his hair hung limply. Fat, wormy lips drew back in a sneer and he stared at me cockeyed. He held a small club, and menacingly slapped it against an open palm.

"Keep it down," he drawled. I couldn't place his accent, but it was slow. Sloppy. Like he was talking through a mouthful of cotton balls and tripping over his own tongue.

"I get a telephone call."

"When you're officially charged, yes, you get a call," Muffie said; his smile wasn't a perfect row of white teeth like Bouchard's. It was broken, full of wide gaps, and his teeth jutted off in awkward angles. His breath rolled out like a cloud, reeking of fish.

"I was arrested."

"Aye," said Muffie. "You were arrested."

"You have to charge me to arrest me."

Muffie disagreed. He slapped the club against the bars. I stepped back in surprise, blinking. It only encouraged him. He leaned close.

"That's a good boy," he slurred. "You stay back and don't crowd the bars. It's unruly. Know your place, don't you be quoting Lovatine law like you understand how it works. You were arrested under suspicion, not formally charged. When you're arrested under suspicion we can hold you for five days, and then you'll get your telephone call. If we don't formally charge you, you'll eventually be released..." Muffie grinned his undertaker's grin before finishing, "...at the detectives discretion, but we both know there's not a chance in hell of that happening, don't we, killer?"

He sneered and I glared; we stared at one another like this for some time, but it was Muffie who rolled his eyes and lost our silent competition. "Don't try that tough guy routine with me, killer. It doesn't phase me. I've faced off with harder men than you. Now, you just settle down and wait for Bouchard and me like a good little killer, see? You behave and we'll see you get some breakfast in you." He wrinkled his nose. "Maybe see that you get a shower and a fresh jumper as well." His sallow eyes looked me up and down. "I think prisoner red will suit you just fine."

I slammed my hands against the bars and shouted a few obscenities as Muffie disappeared into the station, leaving me to pace a nearly empty drunk tank. I was getting restless. Feeling frayed at the edges. I needed a meal, needed sleep. I was exhausted. No windows were visible from the drunk tank, but the station did feel lighter. Had I been there all night?

I sat on an empty bench and tried to nap, but sleep didn't find me despite how my body ached for it. My insomnia only frayed me further. I stood, paced the small cell, and then sat again. Wondering what my next plan would be.

I couldn't stay there.

If they formally charged me I might have got my telephone call, but would I really be able to contact Wensem? He said he would be unreachable. Besides, he didn't even own a telephone. Who else? Who else could vouch for me?

Wilem, Black & Bright.

My payment.

I was with Wensem, but they paid me. I regretted not getting the receipt when the receptionist had offered it, but remembered her scratching the payment into a ledger book.

Bell Caravans. Waldo Bell. Wensen dal Ibble.

They'd have records of me collecting my caravan master fee and my bonus. It'd be hard for Bouchard to refute that evidence. I wondered if they'd take my call, if the receptionist would even listen to me.

Probably not.

I paced some more. Exhausted, I decided it would be better to visit them in person. You can't hang up on someone standing in front of your desk. Maybe August could get me in to see one of the partners? Wilem? Black maybe? August had contacts. He had said as much before I took the Wilem, Black & Bright job.

I moved near the door of the cage.

A plan began forming in my mind. I would have to act quickly. Escape seemed insane, but what other option did I have? It was either fight my way outside and try to clear my name, or risk prison for two murders I didn't commit.

"Back away from the door," said a voice, snapping me out of my daydream.

A pair of uniformed officers stood just outside the cage door. A drunk beggar was hanging between them. One scowled at me when I didn't jump at his command.

"The door. Away. Now," he commanded, drawing a club with his free hand. I stepped back cautiously. This was my moment. I needed to time it right.

"Move it, drunk. Come on, I don't have all day."

The man that hung between him hiccuped and rolled his head back, a long moan belching from his throat and a stream of drool dripping from his lips.

"I think he's going to puke," said the other officer nervously.

"You hear that, buddy? This fella is going to puke. Now step back so he's not puking on me."

I stepped back again. Enough to appease the officer. He grumbled thanks and pulled a set of keys from his belt and unlocked the door. It swung open with a long metal-on-metal creak.

The two cops, drunk slung between them, stepped one foot inside the cage, cocking their shoulders. It was clear they were going to throw the poor bastard forward and slam the door behind him.

I pushed against the drunk right as they started to release him. He reeled and fell backwards into the officers, the contents of his stomach an arching rainbow. The three went down in a tangle of limbs and a spatter of vomit. The drunk's loud moans were broken by a hiccup.

I leapt the tangle and landed on my heels, feeling a hand try to grab my ankle. I kicked backward, connecting with the jaw of one of the officers. His club clattered from his hands and I scooped it up, pushing forward on the balls of my feet and taking off down the hallway in a sprint.

I could hear cops shouting from behind me.

"Escape! We have an escape! Drunk tank! Escape! Bar the doors!"

Another officer appeared before me, a look of shock on his

face. I pushed him through an open door, sending him sprawling.

"Get down!" came a command.

Muffie came into view, club in hand, a panicked look flashing across his face.

"I knew it was you, you son of a bit–" I hit him with my stolen club, catching him across the nose and jaw and sending him spinning. I dropped and shoved my shoulder up until it connected with his gut, lifting him slightly and sending him falling backward. He yowled in pain. I could feel the air gush out of him as he went down, and heard the smack as the back of his head slapped on the tile.

"Stop or we'll shoot!" came a command from behind me. "Stop!"

Right.

I didn't stop.

I plunged through an open door and into the lobby of Lovat Central Police Headquarters. A mass of stunned cops greeted me with blank stares. Looks of shock and bewilderment crossed their faces. What idiot brazenly attempts to escape from the drunk tank—the drunk tank of all places—surrounded by police?

I seized the moment, slipping over a nearby counter and landing on my feet. I heard boots pounding on the tile behind me.

"Stop him!"

"Get down!"

"Stop that man!"

Arms and hands reached out to stop me, quick instincts

working through confusion. I jerked away, roughly pulling free.

I passed through another open door and was sprinting toward the lobby entrance as the sound of gunfire opened up behind me.

Pop. Pop. Pa-pop!

I tried to duck, wondering if it really made me a smaller target or just a slower one. Hard to know when my education on police evasion came from the police procedural serials.

Slugs zipped past my ears and I could smell gunpowder. My heart pounded as glass shattered and burst around me. I considered dropping to the ground, but knew if I did that I'd never get out.

Almost to the door.

Red hot pain exploded through my left arm.

I was hit.

In slow motion, I watched a shower of my own blood spatter across the floor. I slowed and stumbled as the pain hit my brain. My arm felt on fire.

Escape! My brain shouted. I stumbled, correcting myself before I fell through the glass doors that lead to the streets outside. I could feel blood run down my arm, and I slapped my right hand over the wound. I didn't need to leave a blood trail. I needed to escape.

More gunfire shattered the air behind me. I started with every shot, expecting another slug to bring me down.

None did.

Civilians stared at me awkwardly. I was filthy, I stank, and I was stumbling down the street with a bloody arm and a crazy look in my eyes. I'd stare at me too. I probably looked like some fever-mad pitch addict.

I ignored the crowds; the more distance I put between myself and the police, the better. I sprinted away.

Pushing past stunned civilians and a few equally stunned cops.

Pushing through and out into open streets.

Pushing toward freedom.

SIX

Taking the stairs two, sometimes three at a time, I sprinted away from Lovat Central PD. The bullet hole screamed at me with every step. I could feel the warmth of my blood as it gurgled from the wound and down my arm.

I ignored the pain as best I could (which wasn't very well) as I flew down the caged stairwell descending from the fifth level down into the fourth. The stairwell had been close to the station, but I gambled that the officers in pursuit of me would expect me to take a public lift rather than the stairs.

I had won the hand.

The sub-floors of Lovat Central Police Department hung like a stalactite from the ceiling of Level Four. The mirrored glass windows hid any prying eyes, but I swore I could feel the presence of lookouts watching my hasty descent, reporting my location, directing the hunters.

Level Four's street rose to meet me, but I ignored it, slipping past a homeless man and continuing my descent. Downward.

Ever downward. My mind raced, thinking back to lessons I had learned on the trail.

Keep a distance between yourself and other travelers.

Never stop moving.

Trust no one but your company.

Rest only for short periods of time.

Never rest in the same place.

They were solid rules. For this occasion I added one more: *the police can't catch what they can't find.*

I needed to get lost. Really lost. The police wouldn't stop looking for me, I knew that: my face would be all over the monochrome news by morning. Person of interest. Top suspect. I would probably get a nickname. I could see the headlines and they left a bitter taste in my mouth.

I continued to descend.

Body parts stolen? Both victims tied to me somehow? Why? There was more to these murders, a reason why I was connected. It was a spiderweb, and I couldn't make sense of the strands. Thad was a close friend, Fran was once close. Now, both were gone.

Gone.

Hollowness rang out inside my chest, clanging like an old church bell. I felt sick to my stomach. I wanted to just slump against a wall and mourn properly. Say my goodbyes. None of this made sense. Bouchard's fleshy face sneered at me from the shadows of my imagination, that smug Detective Muffie standing over his shoulder.

I slumped into a stairwell wall, smearing a streak of blood

along the graffiti and causing my arm to scream in protest. Almost there.

Level Three.

I slipped out from the stairwell. My momentum sent me stumbling to the sidewalk, scaring an old woman and a group of teen maero who rushed away on their long, spindly legs. I let go of my arm to catch my fall. Blood fanned out before me, and I clamped my hand back over the bullet wound, squeezing tightly and gritting my teeth against the lightning bolts of pain that buzzed in my skull like static.

The police can't catch what they can't find.

Get lost.

My motions were feral, desperate as I spun, trying to get a sense of my bearings. I was only two levels below Lovat Central. A five, maybe ten minute lift ride. Perhaps fifteen if traffic was heavy.

Still too close to the station.

Pedestrians moved across the street to avoid me. I couldn't blame them. I probably looked awful. Dirty, covered in puke and blood, gripping my left bicep, and gritting my teeth. All these people would remember me, remember me and report to the police when my face showed up on the news.

I needed to get away. Away from the stairwell, away from the public.

I began to wander.

It was clear how different Level Three was compared with the more elevated levels. It was older. Shabbier. Remnants of ancient towers poked through the street like nasty weeds; crowns of the old city. The back of the forgotten metropolis upon which Lovat had risen.

That is the way of it: cities built upon the bones of cities that came before them. Adding, mixing, destroying, and rebuilding. The penthouse suites of one generation become the vomit-soaked dens of addicts in another. The city grows, ever upward, ever changing.

It gave Level Three an unusual otherworldly quality. Oddly shaped buildings of diametric angles, bulbous domes, and broken half circles dominated the area. Slabs of rusted steel and mildew-darkened glass hunkered over the streets like broken old men. Large, sprawling open squares were lined with heavy machinery that had once circulated air in the floors of the tower below them. Skeletons of cranes that had once lowered window washers now became the supporting structure for an apartment building or the makeshift roof of a block of stores. A few old twin-wheel cycles rumbled past, belching black smoke that hung in the stagnant air, their occupants glowering from the seats as they clung to the handlebars.

I headed west along Cherry Street, hoping it'd be the opposite direction the Lovat Police Department would expect. East was the caravansara encampments.

The open road.

The Big Ninety.

Freedom.

East was where one would be expected to run. Cross the bridges. Hit the mainland. West was the sea. A dead end. No fool in his right mind would head in that direction.

The police can't catch what they can't find.

I hoped it would be enough. I stumbled along, blind to the street signs, pausing for a moment to rip my right sleeve free from my shirt and try to tie a makeshift tourniquet around the bullet hole. It was painful. I'm no doctor, but I needed anything to staunch the flow of blood from my arm. I needed medical attention desperately, but I needed to hide even more.

I passed a huddle of kresh grouped near a street corner wearing dirty rags and the small round hats of monks. They hissed as I rushed past, their beady, heart-shaped black eyes following me. Marking me. More witnesses. The wild man of Level Three, he'll be on the news later, I'll need to remember where I saw him.

I ignored them.

Walk the hundreds of miles between Lovat and Syringa twelve plus times a year, and you end up with a skill in trail work. I pride myself on being fairly quick on my feet, but I was exhausted, hungry, and despite my tourniquet feeling light-headed from blood loss.

I was leaving a trail. The roader in me knew it would take very little to track. I was resigned to the matter; even if I could get some distance with my current strategy, they'd eventually find me.

My new rule repeated in my head. *The police can't catch what they can't find.*

My trail needed to end here.

I slumped to the sidewalk and allowed myself a few minutes to catch my breath. I felt cold. Shivers ran along my spine and a cloying numbness began to seep into my bones. My brain was fuzzy but somewhere inside I knew I was in shock—no sense ignoring it.

Lovat hospitals were expensive and exclusive; most folks simply couldn't afford to move through the automatic doors to reach the caring hands of their highly trained physicians. The lira in my pocket could have bought me medical care, but professional physicians would turn me back into police custody as soon as they had sewn me up.

I needed someone less reputable.

I needed a Bonesaw.

I don't know how long I sat on the street corner. A few more people milled about, giving me a wide berth. One even tossed me a lira like I was some beggar. A street mystic stumbled past, smelling strongly of gin and urine. I considered taking one of the monorails that crisscrossed Lovat but thought better of it. Too public.

A cephel dragged a rattling rickshaw down the road toward me. The ancient construct squeaked and clattered as the eight-limbed octopod pulled it. I flagged the cephel down and climbed into the seat behind it. My motions were slow and cumbersome.

It clucked at me. Suspiciously eyeing the blood on my clothes, it nodded its head in a motion akin to a man pointing with his chin.

"No questions," I said. "I need to get to Collins Street."

It considered this. Staring at me, softly clucking as it thought. It clearly wasn't pleased with my demand, and didn't like the look of me, but the fare would be large enough to allow it to eat for the week. I avoided mentioning that my stack of lira was in some lockbox deep inside Lovat Central.

A moment of decision passed between us until the cephel clucked again, this time louder and sharper, and nodded its huge head towards the rickshaw's seat. It would take me.

The rickshaw was wood, worn smooth by countless numbers of passengers over what could have been centuries. I slumped in the seat, exhaustion and numbness creeping into my limbs. I laid back and let the cephel's thick leg tentacles push us down Second Avenue, carrying me away from my blood trail and toward my freedom.

The police can't catch what they can't find.

I got lost.

My trip down Second Avenue was a blur. A broken series of mental photographs. A few odd storefronts. The flashing, verdant green of commercial and community vegetable gardens. The taunting scents from food carts that jolted me and my stomach awake. I drifted in and out, eventually waking with the looming presence of the rickshaw driver above me, its massive oblong head blocking the headache-inducing glare from the cement gray sky.

Sky.

No roof.

No upper level. I was far from the central area of the city.

Giant eyes stared at me with concern. I jolted upright. Thanked the driver. He nodded, and tsked over the smear of blood I left on the old wood of the rickshaw seat, my legs shaking below me.

Now it would get awkward.

I shrugged when the creature extended a hand for the fare. Its eyes went cold and it clucked louder. I shrugged again, feeling genuinely bad. I explained what had happened. Told him I'd owe him double. Told him to visit the caravansara in a month's time and ask for me. He seemed suspicious. Who wouldn't have been?

I promised a second and then a third time.

Finally, he waved me away, making the cephel motion for one month. I nodded. One month.

I stumbled away. Leaving my savior behind, and starting a fresh trail of blood.

Lovat rises and tapers like the waves of the ocean. Around its central point it reaches its apex: the ninth level. Stretching to the heavens like some improvised minaret, yet as you move away from its apex it drops away. Level Nine quickly ceases, then Eight; Seven continues for a while, and Six for even further. Level Five covers most of the central archipelago but even it eventually ends, and then Level Four and finally—miles away from Lovat Central—Level Three is exposed.

I stood on a corner and drank in the sky. Thick dark gray clouds buffeted above me. The humidity caused me to sweat instantaneously. To the north the central city was nearly obscured by fog and haze. A light rain spattered my face and my hair; rivulets formed and ran down my skin, dripping off me. It wasn't a proper shower, but it was the first I'd had in many, many days.

It felt clean, it felt good. It cleared my head.

Time had lost all meaning in the rickshaw. I inspected my makeshift bandage and saw that it had finally staunched the flow, if only slightly. My arm was red and sticky.

My head swam. I had lost a lot of blood. I needed to be patched up, and quick.

I found a Bonesaw in a haze down an alley on Level Two, below and west from where the cephel had dropped me off. A hand-painted A-frame sign offered "simple medical advice for cheap" and pointed down an alley. I followed it to another door under a small dirty awning, lit by a yellowing lamp that hung next to it.

A pitch addict leered at me from a pile of trash bags and waterlogged cardboard; the rot had begun to take his arms, and he cackled as he injected more of the vile stuff into his veins. In my current hazy state it was nearly nightmare inducing.

"Knock for entry" was painted across the door in an elegant hand that seemed comical this far down-in-the-subs. I knocked. The old door swung open, and I was greeted by a blast of crisp, cool, clear air and a pudgy dauger in a pressed white coat. Her dark hair was pulled back in a long ponytail. A few loose strands fell over the edges of her stainless steel mask. Behind the metal, bright blue eyes peered at me from the eye slits.

"D-d-do-doct—" I sputtered, stumbling forward and pointing to my arm. "Shot…"

She was quick, and stronger than she looked. I'm not a big fellow, but I am dense. Years of trail miles have knotted my muscles into strong, heavy limbs. Still, the doctor had no problem dragging me inside and locking the door behind me. She helped me to a small table in a small room that served as the waiting, examination, and operating room all at once. My mind wondered vaguely what had happened to her medical career to send her chasing the cash-on-hand work of an unlicensed Bonesaw in a Level Two alley office.

"Sir? Sir? Sir?" I heard her ask.

I lolled my head toward her.

"Sir, are you maero tolerant?" She asked. Her soft voice was muffled by the fuzziness forming in my head.

I mumbled a response.

She repeated the question, "Sir, are you maero tolerant?"

I tried to respond again, but slumped. Maero tolerant, it really meant maero blood tolerant; of all the races that occupied the earth after the Aligning, the maero were the most like traditional humans. Superficially they are a lot like us. Two arms. Two legs. Two eyes and ears. Their faces are similarly shaped, and they are often handsome and beautiful, but cosmetically it was their seven fingers on each hand and seven toes on each foot that set them apart.

Maero also tended to be taller, and lankier, but extra digits aside they differed from us in one very unique and particular way. As Wensem was fond of telling me, "Maero are hard to kill."

He's not wrong. Resilient to disease, infection, and even trauma, according to the local superstitions the only surefire way to kill a maero was incineration. They lived to be one hundred and nine, on the dot. They died on their birthday. They could expect to live healthy long lives free of the normal breakdowns and ignorant of sickness, headaches, even sore backs.

Some in the Reunified Church believed they are inhuman, sullied by the blood of fallen angels or some nonsense. Deepers believed they were post-human, the next evolution of our species, touched by the Sleeper. Hasturians refused to acknowledge their personhood, issuing documents stating that maeros are beings without souls and therefore untouchable by their Cold Shepherd. Mystics teach they are the sons and daughters of giants. To me they're just people.

Whenever I spoke with Wensem about these stories he always smiled that crooked smile, gave me a wink, and said the same thing: "I know as much about my great-great-grandfather as you do, Wal. Probably less."

Regardless of the stories, rumors, and legends, the point is: maeros are resilient, and some folk—people like me—could accept transfusions of their blood to speed up and help the healing process. It was rare to find maero blood outside an elevated hospital, and even rarer to find a Bonesaw that had stock on hand. Maero blood—as one would expect—is an expensive commodity.

Generations ago the capture and draining of maero for blood was common within the black market. It continued like this for years until a few enterprising maero formed Lifeblood Incorporated in West Lovat. With legal, willing donors, cheap maero blood flooded the market and put the black market dealers out of business. Maero tolerant individuals demanded it, and Lifeblood Inc. made millions.

The doctor quickly cleaned the wound. I felt a needle slide into my forearm, and could feel the rush as saline and blood were pumped into my veins. The pain was constant, but the knowledge I would be all right placated me.

The doctor hummed and spoke to me, words I couldn't understand.

I let myself drift off to sleep.

The Doctor gently shook me awake.

"You need to move on," she stated, not unkindly.

I blinked. My eyes sharpened around the square shape of her stainless steel mask. Blue eyes. The metal "nose" was shorter than most and a few scratches marred the polished surface. I sat up slowly, feeling my head lurch.

"How long was I out?"

"Few hours. You lost a lot of blood, so it's lucky you stumbled in here."

"I'll say," I said, rubbing my temples. "My head is pounding."

She nodded, "Side effect. You were dehydrated. You needed a huge transfusion; you drank me out of maero blood. It'll be a while before I can get more."

"I'm sorry," I said.

"That's what I have it on hand for, hon," she said with what sounded like a smile. "That persistent hangover feeling will last a few days. Get some pain meds from a pharmacy and it should cut it down some. You'll want to rotate those bandages at least once a week. I'd suggest once a day, but I doubt you'll do it."

I smiled. "That obvious, huh?"

She chuckled but didn't respond.

"I...well...er—I don't have any money on me. I have the lira to pay, just not right now."

She nodded. "You aren't the first. I run on a thirty day cycle. Just pay me before then."

"You have a name?" I asked.

"Inox," she said with that same warm tone in her voice. "Eliza Inox. You're Waldo Bell."

I swallowed the lump in my throat and worried what she would say next.

"Your face is all over the monochrome, you know that? They're not saying what for yet. Just that you're a person of interest and a dangerous escapee from Lovat Central." She whistled. "Bold. Escaping Lovat Central. They the ones who have your money?"

I nodded, remembering the bottle of brandy Thad had given me. "Among other things."

"If spotted, I'm supposed to alert the authorities immediately and avoid any and all contact."

"Too late for that," I said with a sheepish grin.

"Am I going to regret patching you up?" she asked, crossing her arms over her ample chest.

"If you take Lovat PD at their word you might. I can assure you none of what you'll hear is true."

"They the ones who shot you up?"

I nodded.

"By the Firsts, you are trouble!" she said, humor lacing her words.

"I know. It's dangerous lingering, so I'll get out of your hair."

"First, here's twenty lira. It'll get you some food, rent you a bed and such. I'll add it to your bill. Second, you need a new shirt. I have an old box of lost and found that previous patients have left behind. Maybe you'll find something in there. Finally, I do expect to be paid. I'll do what I can to help you out, but I'd like to avoid the Collectors if I can, a messy bunch. You play fair with me, I'll play fair with you. And I'm not into that compounding interest bullshit."

"I appreciate the help."

"If you need a place to stay, there's a hostel a few blocks over. It's not especially clean or especially nice, and it's usually full of pitch addicts, but it's off the beaten path and folks there know how to keep quiet. Good place to lay low. Tell them Inox sent you and first night's on me."

Charity isn't something you ignore in Lovat. "Thanks. Seriously."

"Don't mention it, and I mean what I said about the bandages. You don't want an infection."

I nodded and extended my hand.

Doctor Eliza Inox shook it and smiled. "The box is in the corner. Get what you need and get out of here."

The coat was too small and smelled of sweat, but it covered me up enough. I kept the collar flipped up and my head down as I walked slowly away from the alley office. I could still hear the pitch addict behind me moaning in ecstasy from his throne of trash.

I was exhausted.

Arm bandaged. Head pounding. I found myself excited to fall into a bunk, any bunk, and get some sleep for the first time in what felt like weeks.

SEVEN

The telegraph office was empty. I sat on an uncomfortable wooden bench and waited for a response. Wensem had said that he didn't want to be disturbed, but this was an emergency. I'd also had a troubling dream and I hadn't been able to shake it. Feeling like I needed to warn Wensem, I sent the telegraph. I looked up as the operator received an incoming message. He shook his head at me silently. No one home. On some level I expected that.

I considered trying my luck a second time: sending the messenger out to knock on Wensem's door again, but I wasn't sure it would do any good. If he was home, Wensem would have answered. Maero are straightforward folk in that regard.

Putting my failed telegraph behind me, I made my way to a small consignment store down the street. The waters that flooded the Sunk lapped against the edge of the pavement. Higher up, you'd find guardrails keeping citizens from tumbling over the edges of levels, but the police, politicians, and the more elevated class preferred to ignore Level Two's existence altogether.

Through the murk of the water an occasional shadowed form rushed past. The Sunk was the flooded remains of Level One; the citizens who lived beneath the waters lived a life similar to (but separate from) the dry races. Strictly the realm of the water-breathing, it was a city in itself. They had lights down there, illuminating corners in the flooded streets of the old city. Underwater traffic would flash past like a shadow in your peripheral vision. Cephels, anur, some kresh, and the occasional bok dwelled in the watery depths of the Sunk, loving, living, and dying. There are tales of vast structures even deeper below the Sunk in the flood tunnels of Humes and Moran. Rumors were they had their own police force, government, and laws. Thad always said those rumors were a load of bullshit.

I watched a heavy, naked anur pull himself out of the brine and shake himself dry. The flaps of skin that hung around him like a heavy robe jiggled in the lights hanging from Level Two's roof. I pulled the borrowed rusty-crimson jacket Doctor Inox had loaned me closer to my chest. It was uncomfortable and bizarrely cut, with little to no collar and was a size and a half too small. On the right sleeve was a faded circular patch embroidered with eight narrow rectangles arranged smallest to largest. Down in the murk of Level Two it would be largely ignored, but if I wanted to move about freely on the more elevated levels of Lovat I needed something less...conspicuous. As grateful as I was for the Bonesaw's help, I needed some better clothes if I was to stay hidden.

The consignment shop was empty when I arrived. The clerk

was an indifferent cephel who hardly glanced at me as I purchased a new shirt, a ball cap, and a black hooded jacket. Mundane items. Boring. Easy to melt into the crowds and not stand out: urban camouflage.

After the consignment shop I stopped at a corner market for some much needed personal supplies. Then I made my way back to the hostel, dodging prostitutes, pitch addicts, and a few thugs. The hostel was quiet and I was checked in until noon, and Carter's cross, I needed a shower. I checked the clock behind the front desk: three hours, plenty of time.

Inox had been right about the hostel; it was full of the downtrodden. Most of the bunks were still occupied by patrons sleeping off the previous evening's binge. A few winced as I pushed my way through the door from outside and passed into the dark interior. They groaned, mumbled curses, and rolled over in their sweat-stained bunks as the light penetrated the gloom; a few gave me the finger.

The common room smelled of alcohol, latex, hot metal, piss, sweat, and vomit—a wholly revolting little medley. It wasn't the worst place I had stayed, but it was definitely in the running. After last night, however, I wasn't in the mood to be picky; it was safe, hidden, and it had a bed. I had cleared things with the proprietor, a surly dimanian with an underbite and horns that splayed out nearly horizontal, before making my way to a bunk. I was the walking dead, intent on sleep, not even bothering to remove my boots as I collapsed into blissful unconsciousness.

I woke hours later and ignored the mumbled insults as I passed as quietly as I could to one of the shared bathrooms. Locking myself in, I started the shower and withdrew the toiletries I had bought at the corner market. The naked bulb above the sink was the only light in the room, and it flickered and hummed as I shaved. I had grown a beard during my last run, so it felt good to go down to bare skin. Cleaning myself up and exposing my jaw made me feel one step closer to being alive. There was also the added benefit that the recent photos the police were running featured me in my trail regalia: bearded and shaggy haired, in a road-stained shirt, looking more like a wild hermit than any respectable Lovatine.

I let the water run as I took a pair of cheap clippers and murdered my hair. I did the best I could, taking it down as close to the scalp as the shears would let me. Slathering my skull with cream, I attacked it with the straight razor, shaving it bald. The battle was hard fought but over quickly, and I was pleased with the result. Having lost so much blood the day before, escaping a self-administered shave nick-free was a relief.

Taking a moment I examined myself in the mirror. Nearly hairless, I looked like some sickly, penitent monk. My face was still filthy despite the odd clear spots where I had shaved. My skin was paler than its normal russet color. My cheeks were sallow and sunken from blood loss, and I had dark circles under my dust-colored eyes. Frankly, I looked like I had been run over by a cargowain.

Satisfied, I turned my attention to the shower.

In a perfect world, that first shower in almost a month would have been glorious. That's what you normally see on the monochrome serials, isn't it? The trail-hardened cowboy soaks in a boiling hot bath, drinking a whiskey and smoking a cigar. Letting the hardships of the trail wash off him as he's tended to by busty tavern wenches. There were times when I would and could have said I experienced as much. There's nothing quite like a hot shower or bath after a month on the road, and a whiskey would have sat quite nicely, an ice-cold vermouth doubly so.

But the shower at the hostel was a pitiful thing. The water at its highest setting was barely tepid. It sprayed brown and smelled of old pipes and seawater. Even as the dirt, sweat, and blood from three weeks on the trail and two harrowing days running through Lovat's streets washed away, I couldn't help but worry that I'd end up catching some disease.

I cleaned myself with the help of some strong lye soap that stung my skin and a shampoo that claimed to smell of warm honey but seemed more akin to axle grease. After a few minutes I conquered the road dirt and exited the shower feeling cleaner than I had entered. Small victories, I suppose.

Showers are a good place to think, and as I changed my bandages per doctor's orders and dressed in my new clothes, making sure to pull the ball cap down tightly over my brow, I had come up with a rudimentary plan.

First, I would seek out my broker, August Nickel. He ran his business out of a storefront somewhere north of me on Level Three between the city center and here. He had a good head on his shoulders and could probably help me out.

Second, I would see if I could get him to put me in touch with Wilem, Black & Bright. I would have contacted them outright if it hadn't been for their location. The Hotel Arcadia was heavily fortified, the doorman being only the first trial a caravaneer would have to endure to make his way to the elevators. As much as I wished I could, I doubted that even my new look would allow me to walk into the Arcadia unmolested.

Third, I would—with the help of Wilem, Black & Bright—prove my innocence. Their books recorded when I was on the trail and should be solid enough evidence to clear me of any wrong doings in Fran Nickel's murder. I hoped that seed of doubt would help to clear me in the murder of Thad as well; if Bouchard believed the two murders were linked, then I would have had to be present to commit both, right?

Nickel's office occupied the second story of a two-story building in South Dome, sitting just below the section of the city where Level Four ended and Level Three stretched south under the open sky. As I stood outside the offices I looked up, seeing the round faces of a gathering of children staring down at me from Level Four. I waved awkwardly and they waved back. The edge of one world and the beginning of another.

Two signs hung above the street level door. "Sardini Market" was painted in a graceful brush script; above it the name of Nickel's business blared in neon block letters: "Comings & Goings, Ltd." Elaborate signs aside, whitewashed and two stories tall, the building looked more like a flophouse than an office for one of the most powerful commodities brokers in the city. I had said as much to Nickel, and delighted in giving him a hard time over the state of his office. It had become something of a pastime of mine.

"Return on investment!" Nickel would say in his always too-loud voice. "Cost per square foot! That's where it really matters, see? All the big firms spend thousands on their spaces, and for what? To impress clients concerned with the bottom line? Clients don't want to see their money being spent on fancy chairs, antique desks, tits, and short skirts. They want results and I deliver results, my boy. I deliver! I thrive in the cramped and don't waste their money on unnecessary resources. They can spend ten thousand lira a month for that elevated corner office overlooking Level Eight. I'll funnel that money into my next venture!"

Nickel had an ambitious streak.

The stairs that led to his offices were only accessible through the deli market on the first floor. It was small but clean and neat, offering a wide variety of groceries. A few aisles of wine, an aisle of canned goods, and a cold case stocked full of cheeses, milk, beer, cured meats, and other assorted and unique ingredients. The whole place smelled of rich foods and hearty wines. It made me hungry.

Along the south wall was a glass counter stocked with all manner of fresh, handmade pastas, salads, and sandwiches. Near the western wall by the stairwell that led to the second floor was a small bar with three stools for customers.

I gave a wave to Elizabeth Sardini, proprietor of the deli. Mrs. Sardini was human, and had to be at least a hundred. She was beautiful once, but time—as it always does—had worked away at her beauty like rain on a trail. She now stood stooped, wrinkled, smiling a smile that was absent a few teeth. Her eyes, however, were sharp, and they glittered with recognition as she saw me.

"Waldo!" she said, her tone friendly even as her voice cracked. "It's so good to see you. So good. It's been far too long. Look at you!" She gestured at me with both her hands. "You're all skin and bones. Skin and bones! You lack color."

"Hello, Mrs. Sardini," I said, smiling and looking around, grateful I was the only patron in her small market. She meant well, but having my name shouted out loud in public wasn't something I was really keen on at the present time. She must have not seen the news reports.

"I saw you on the monochrome last night," she said, sadly. Guess she had.

"I can't believe the police would be so wrong. There's no way you could be involved in any of that funny stuff. No way, no how!" She clapped her hands together and shuffled out from behind her counter and gave me a big hug. "It's good to see you. So good to see you."

"Thanks," I said, returning the hug. "It's good to see you as well. Is August in?"

"He is, he is. I think he has a client upstairs right now, but I am sure he'll send them away if you pop in."

"Thanks," I said, moving toward the stairs.

"Ah, ah ah! Not so fast. You need to eat. Look at you!" she declared, her eyes twinkling. "I have a delicious bolognese tossed with some of my handmade ravioli. Stuffed with cheese and sausage."

My stomach rumbled. I hadn't settled enough to eat properly since my ill-fated attempt at Shuai Tan. Since yesterday the only thing I had to eat was a handful of roast walnuts from a street vendor that morning.

"I suppose I can spare some time for your cooking." I smiled.

Mrs. Sardini laughed delightfully. "You go up and see August. It's nearing his lunch time as well, and I'll just make an extra batch and you can eat with him."

She shooed me up the stairs and shuffled behind her counter to prepare my lunch.

Years earlier, Nickel had struck a deal with Mrs. Sardini: she would make his lunch, and he would cover half her rent. For Nickel it wasn't about the money—he had plenty, and even though he could eat cheaper pretty much anywhere else, there were other benefits of having what amounted to a live-in cook. Wining and dining clients being chief among them.

As I stepped onto the second floor, a stout gentleman heading down the stairs brushed past me.

"Excuse me," he said, politely. I nodded, and was struck with a sense of déjà vu. I turned and caught a glimpse of him disappearing around the corner. His coat. He was wearing a garish, close-fitting red coat with no collar, similar to the hand-me-down I had procured from Inox. A large tattoo dominated the right side of his neck. It was circular and familiar, and for a moment I thought it was a wagon wheel like mine before I realized it was the same design as the patch on my borrowed jacket: enclosed in a circle, eight narrow bars were arranged smallest to largest, hanging from a shared plane.

I stood at the top of the stairs and watched the guy leave.

Twice in one day? It was an odd coincidence.

"Waldo? Is that you, Wal?" a loud voice jolted me from my hazy stare, emanating from behind the frosted door labeled Comings & Goings, Ltd. Main Office.

"Come in! Come in! Carter's cross, Waldo, get your skinny ass in here!"

I slipped past the door and entered August Nickel's office.

The room was cramped. Boxes of documents were piled six feet high against every wall. Only the windows remained unobscured. August sat behind his massive second-hand desk, leaning back in a worn leather chair that seemed ready to break under his weight at any moment.

August Nickel was a dauger. His mask, as his namesake, was heavy nickel, though it was dwarfed against his massive fleshy head. His eye holes were bigger than other masks, the mouth an open slot instead of the grate preferred by most dauger. Behind the mask his eyes were a rich brown, the same color as his desk, and the mouth opening always showed a row of bright white teeth like those windup mechanical dentures from the monochrome comedies. As with most dauger I knew, I always wondered what he looked like without his mask, but knew it would be rude to ask. Only dauger saw other dauger without their metal masks, and even then masks were only removed among close relations.

"Ha!" said August, slapping his desk. "The escapee comes home to roost."

I grinned and shook his outstretched hand. "Hello, my friend."

"It's damn good to see you. You okay? I heard you were shot."

"I'm fine. I found a dauger Bonesaw named Inox, and she patched me up."

"By the Firsts," he swore, "a Bonesaw? You trusted one of those quacks?"

I shrugged. "What choice did I have? Not like the city hospitals would have taken me in anonymously. Also, I'm broke."

"You need money?"

I nodded. "I'm good for it. Most of my possessions were taken when I was arrested."

August opened a desk drawer and withdrew a stack of lira. He gave me half.

"Here's five hundred. No, don't act like you don't need that much. Pride is overrated. Take it. Pay this Bonesaw—last thing you want is a Collector on your ass. You can pay me back when this is all sorted out."

"Thanks," I said, pocketing the cash. "Really...I mean it."

August waved a hand dismissively. "It's no big deal; as you said, you're good for it. So, care to tell me what exactly happened? The details in the monochrome news reports are always spotty."

Settling in, I told my tale, sparing nothing. August, for his part, was quiet. Nodding at the right moments and asking clarifying questions the next. We took a small break when Mrs. Sardini brought our lunch. I wouldn't have been able to talk anyway. I shoveled the ravioli in my mouth, ravenously hungry. When we finished eating I wrapped up my story, finishing with the doctor and my stay in the flophouse.

Nickel leaned back in his chair and studied me from behind his mask. "Shit," he said, the word hanging between us before his mind caught up with his mouth. "Shit, Wal. That's heavy stuff."

"I'm sorry about your cousin. I had no idea."

Nickel nodded his thanks. When he finally spoke, his voice had softened considerably. His normal flamboyant bluster was gone. "Felt like a punch in the stomach when Detective Bouchard told me."

"I had nothing to do with her death. You know that, right? You know where I was."

"I know, Wal. I know. You weren't in the city," began Nickel, his voice cracking. "She was a good kid, and talented. The earth ain't been graced with a better flutist in my opinion. Hit my family hard. Carter's cross, it hit me hard. Came out of nowhere and we were left dumbstruck. Who would want to kill Frannie?

"My Ma was beside herself for days. She practically raised Fran. She was her sister's kid, see? When my aunt died, Ma stepped in. Kinda an ol' dauger custom, but Ma went all the way. Really stepped in and filled the role vacated by Frannie's own Ma. In a lot of ways Frannie was more like a kid sister to me than a cousin."

He stared out the window for a moment before looking back at me.

"We buried her in the family plot up near John Noble. Quiet spot. A nice warren."

"I would have been there had I—"

Nickel waved a hand, stopping me. "You were halfway back

from Syringa. I know you would have been there, don't apologize."

We sat in silence for a moment, our thoughts on Fran.

"Carter's cross, I need a damn drink," he said, breaking the silence. He pulled a blackened bottle from a desk drawers. "I know you're partial to that vile vermouth, but you ever had hundred-year-old scotch?"

"No," I admitted.

"Me neither, so let's crack this open and toast Frannie."

We did, and the scotch was excellent. I rolled it around my tongue and let its warmth replace the numbness I was feeling. I tried not to dwell on my lost friends, but failed. When I had drained the glass, Nickel offered me a refill. I graciously accepted.

After our third glass I had a healthy buzz. Nickel looked across his desk at me. "So you came to me. I'm glad you did, but what help do you think I can give you? I don't have any pull with Lovat PD; even if I knew someone on the inside, what would you expect them to do for you?"

Swirling the scotch around in my glass, I thought about what I wanted.

"Nothing. I need to know who to contact at Wilem, Black & Bright."

"Ha! There's really only one fella you can contact there. Both Wilem and Bright died before you were born. Peter Black is the only remaining partner."

"Peter Black?"

"Aye. Dimanian bloke. Older fellow. Shrewd businessman. He's good people, but keeps to himself. Been working the Lovat trade since before the day I hung my shingle. Does a lot of work in the archeology business and pre-Aligning salvage. I guess that sorta goes hand-in-hand these days with professors uncovering huge caches in cities buried during the Aligning."

My mind went immediately to the massive crate I helped guide across the Big Ninety. "Know anything about his latest delivery?"

Nickel pursed his lips and was oddly silent. His eyes seemed to focus on the wall behind me before he snapped back to reality. "That crate you were guarding? Not much. Know it was bound for some lab in Brookside. My guess is it's old tech; I know a few of the professors at the college are trying to backwards-engineer a bunch of old shit. See if they can't get it working again."

"He acquire it in Syringa?"

Nickel shrugged. "Don't rightly know."

I waved my hand, my curiosity subsiding. "It's neither here nor there. How can I get in touch with Black? I'd go to the offices, but..."

"...but there's no way you wouldn't get caught again."

I spread my hands in defeat.

"What you need is to contact his gate."

"I beg pardon?"

Nickel fished around in one of the desk drawers and brought out a small card.

"His gate."

When I still didn't get it, he spelled it out for me. "His assistant. Secondary channel. His gate. It's an old outfit term from back in the bygone. Zilla's her name. You want to talk to

Black and avoid the traditional channels, you go through her. She's his eyes and ears, if you can call her that. Ol' Peter Black doesn't get out of the Arcadia much these days. Tends to run things from his suite and let his operation take care of the dailies."

"She trustworthy?"

Nickel snorted a laugh, his heavy shoulder rocking. "With me, sure. Does that mean she won't sell you upriver for a bounty? I can't rightly say. If you want I'll telephone her and put in a good word. Don't know how much it'll count for you."

"How do I reach her?"

"Telephone. It's the only way. She won't answer a telegraph. Number's on the back of the card." I flipped it over and saw Nickel's scrawl.

"I appreciate it," I said, slipping the card into a pocket and checking the clock over his shoulder. I had been at the office nearly four hours. It was time to move on. Lingering didn't help my chances of avoiding capture. "I should get going. I've been here too long already."

"You need a place to stay? You can crash in my spare back room."

I shook my head. "I've put you and Mrs. Sardini in enough trouble as it is. I'd hate to see Bouchard drag you off for aiding and abetting."

"I'll call Zilla immediately," Nickel said. "How can I reach you?"

"I'll telephone later. I think I'll have to play it safe until I can get my life back to normal."

"You sure you don't want to stay here?"

"I'm sure. Thanks for your help, my friend," I said, rising from my chair and draining the last of my hundred-year-old scotch. I needed to keep my wits about me... but you don't let scotch like that go to waste.

He stood and came around the desk, his heavy stomach quaking back and forth with each step. He grabbed me in a big bear hug, and I swear it looked like he had teared up. It meant a lot.

"I'm glad as hell to see you safe, Wal. You take care of yourself. If you need anything, you just let me know. I'll pull any strings I can."

"Thanks, August."

"Don't mention it, kid."

EIGHT

Hi, my name is, um, Waldo Bell and I'm one of the, er...
partners of um, Bell Caravans, and I had some recent business with your employer, Mister Black. So...uh, the problem is, I
am being accused of some crimes and er...when they were com-
mitted, I was on the trail from Syringa with a crate of yours.
Inbound to Lovat. So uh, if you get this and could let your boss
know I'd like to talk to him, I'd, um, appreciate it. Er...hello? I'll
try calling later. This is Waldo Bell."

I hung up the pay telephone with an angry clang. Fifth time
I've tried making a call and gotten only a message machine. All
I could do was hope Zilla would get in contact with her boss.

Before returning to my bunk for the night, I telephoned
Nickel's office. He answered and I explained where I would be
crashing.

"I'll ring you in the morning," I said. "Just to check in."

"Be careful," he said, a worried tinge in his voice. "Level Two
is rough territory, and a pitch den is rougher still. Where is it

again? Corner of Third and what?"

I told him, and then said, "I can handle myself with junkies. It's late enough, and most of them will be well into their next trip before they realize I'm sleeping in their midst. It's a good place for me to lay low."

"If you say so."

"I'll call you in the morning."

"Do that. Stay safe, Wal," he said, hanging up.

My visit with Nickel had raised my spirits, and it was nice knowing there were folks out there pulling for me. Having a friend in my corner made me feel good. I wanted to keep going. I wanted to get this over with and set things right.

Stopping outside the telephone booth, I considered calling one of Wensem's neighbors. Wensem didn't have a telephone but one of them might. Maybe I could reach him that way.

Something about this whole ordeal didn't sit right with me. Wensem was my partner, he was with me when we arrived back in town. My connection to these killings felt personal. All the people connected to this weird little mystery were related to me: old friends, business partners. Maybe he was involved as well? Maybe he had his own problems?

His voiced echoed in my mind: "I'll probably be unreachable for most of the time. I haven't seen my son, and I intend on spending as much time as possible with him and Kitasha."

He lived way up north, past downtown and the swarming cops of Lovat Central, in a neighborhood called Reservoir. It would be half a day's travel at least to get up there and I had already spent too much time out on the street. With posters of my face showing up on street corners and lamp posts it would only be a matter of time before I was made. I had lingered on Level Three for far too long. I needed to keep moving and disappear, and the easiest place for that was right above the Sunk. Level Two beckoned and I was intent on hiding myself in the twisted makeshift hovels of its narrow streets.

Still, I had to contact Wensem. I had to warn him. The pictures of Fran and Thad's bodies still haunted my mind. So I put in a call to his neighborhood's main switchboard. The operator was cool, and I did my best to dictate a message for delivery, warning Wensem and telling him that I'd try and contact him first thing in the morning.

Hoping for a chance to feel normal, I bought a copy of the *Lovat Ledger*, the city's big paper. I prayed I didn't make the front page. When I saw I hadn't, a wave of relief washed over me. Last thing I needed was my mug on the front of every bloke's paper.

I did, however, make the eighth page. "Killer on the Loose," the headline read, and it included a small image of me taken at the time of my apprehension. The quality of the paper's printer and the graininess of the police photograph made my features difficult to make out. I looked like any of the homeless Lovatines wandering the streets of the city: bearded, with long dirty hair and a dirty face.

Feeling a bit more relieved, I tucked the paper under my arm and returned to my bed for the evening.

Level Two is rough. It is the junction between the Sunk and the upper city, and it draws a host of illicit activities. The presence of the underworld outfits is apparent in the graffiti that lines the walls of the buildings. The police avoid it. The streets are wild and makeshift. Trash piles up everywhere, usually washed down from the more elevated levels by the rains. Lovatines forced to live down on Level Two build shelters out of crates and boxes. It's difficult to navigate these shanty towns; the streets become an incomprehensible maze for an outsider like myself.

I'm no stranger to Level Two, though. I have my haunts, but those are usually near a lift or a stairwell. I rarely navigate away from those lifelines to the upper city. The innermost parts of Level Two—those were as foreign to me as the city states to the south or the fabled sprawl of the eastern territories.

I needed the safety of the unfamiliar. I needed its labyrinth of streets.

Stepping off the stairwell, head down, I quickly disappeared into parts unknown.

I wandered for what felt like hours before I located the pitch den I had discovered earlier.

Pitchfork, or "pitch," is a harsh blend of common chemicals. Codeine, iodine, phosphorus, a bit of gasoline, some lighter fluid for flavor, and a dab of industrial cleaning oil, and you have yourself the chemical makeup of pitch. I don't know the damn measurements, so don't ask. It's dangerous stuff. Caustic, numbing, and apparently so euphoric that addicts ignore the dangerous side effects.

There's no mistaking an addict. Their arms nearly skeletal. Covered in open, festering sores. With prolonged use the injection areas rot away, exposing muscle and bone; in some cases gangrene sets in, causing whole limbs to decay. Still, the pitch addicts inject away, eyes rolling up into their skulls and thin streams of drool dribbling from their open mouths.

Addicts are rare in nicer warrens and on more elevated levels, usually shooed away by police or shopkeepers. Like most of the downtrodden they go where they won't be bothered, tending to set up small communes down on Level Two that the papers liked to refer to as "dens."

This is where I found myself. Down in the subs in a pitch den on Level Two. A pocket full of lira, a *Lovat Ledger*, an arm with a hole in it, a few bruised ribs from my arrest, a belly full of Mrs. Sardini's ravioli and bolognese, and coming off a buzz from Nickel's hundred-year-old scotch.

I suppose there are worse places.

I settled down between two passed out addicts. On my left was a cephel, missing two tentacles and a third showing advanced degrees of rot. To my right was a young man, human by the look of him, with a shaggy beard and long brown hair. He looked similar enough to my mug shot in the *Ledger* that he could have passed for me. An empty needle hung from his arm. Sediment from the home brew concoction settled near the plunger. I pushed my way softly between them, pulling my cap low and my jacket's hood up over my head. I unfurled my paper and set to reading.

I fell asleep this way. Tucked between two junkies, paper in hand, and feeling relaxed for the first time since my arrival.

Screams woke me.

The flailing of arms. The occasional slap of a tentacle.

I jolted awake, leaving the paper I was still clutching and scrambled to my feet.

"RAID!" came the scream from somewhere deeper in the den. "RAID!"

Were they after me? Were the cops here to flush me out? How could this have happened? I wondered briefly if Nickel had betrayed me, wiping the thought from my mind as soon as it had come.

Ridiculous. I must have been spotted.

Flashes of red and blue illuminated the dingy windows on the wall opposite me. More screams issued from deeper in the den. A burly human burst through a cheap cardboard wall next to me, dragging the body of a junkie by one hand, a bloody knife in the other. He grinned a yellow smile and let out a roar as he turned and rushed toward the entrance and the flashing lights.

I backed away quickly, hoping to make an exit out the rear of the building before Lovat's finest burst in and had me in cuffs for a second time.

My heart hammered as I pushed past a few dazed junkies staring blankly at the mad confusion that churned around them.

A weight hit me from behind.

Damnit.

I was slammed forward and down to the floor. My face was buried in a filthy mattress older than I was. A metal spring pushed against my cheek as a massive hand pressed my head down into the dirty fabric.

Mumbles from behind me I couldn't make out.

I rolled, twisting in the grip, expecting to see the yellow smile of the burly human. Instead I was looking into the face of an angry maero. It was clear in an instant that neither of us were pitch addicts. Both our eyes were too clear, our gazes too leveled, our movements too smooth.

I fought back, hand on his chin, pushing him away from me. He punched at my stomach with a free hand. I grunted, feeling the wind blast out of me as I brought my knee up.

My knee struck his crotch. Say what you will about the maero toughness, but no male can withstand someone messing with their tackle. He rolled off me with a high-pitched yowl. The blue and red lights decorated the movement in a strobe-like stutter.

I scrambled backwards, watching the maero turn his head toward me, a wicked grin splitting his ugly face. Back to the wall, I steeled myself.

The maero launched himself toward me and I kicked out, landing a solid kick to his chest. It hurt him, but with his momentum he still crashed into me.

Shouts from the entrance of "Stop!" and "Police!" boomed through my head like thunder.

I pushed upward, my wounded bicep screaming at me and my ribs adding to the racket. The force pushed the maero off me and he fell aside. I felt a tear in my arm and hoped I hadn't ripped my stitches. I didn't imagine Doctor Inox would be keen on seeing me again. *If* she saw me again.

I scrambled to my feet, planting a kick squarely across the attacking maero's jaw as he struggled to his own. Teeth scattered across the pile of mattresses absurdly reminding me of candy tossed from a parade float. The maero whipped its head back around toward me, mouth bloody, hate in his small dark eyes.

He wasn't a junkie.

He wasn't a cop.

I took a step back. Confused. Who was this person? I wondered ever-so-briefly if he was an outfit enforcer. One of the organized crime thugs who preyed on the weak and shook down shopkeeps. It was possible, but why me? Was there a bounty on my head?

He leapt with a roar, and I reached out, grabbing for anything. Feeling my fingers tighten around the collar of his jacket, I pulled and swung with all my strength, carrying him past me. He smacked against the cinderblock wall with a thud. The collar of his coat ripped away and remained in my hand. He didn't stir.

A cop rushed past me, tackling a junkie who had been staring awkwardly at my tussle with the maero. One of the vanguard with more behind him, batons raised, angry looks on their faces.

I ran. In danger of capture yet again, I ran, sprinting away from the police, away from the maero, and toward the rear of the den. I could see the reflections from the cops' flashlights shine against the brown walls; shouts of "Stop!" and "Get back here!" broke against my heels.

I burst out a rear door and into some Level Two alley. The torn collar still in my grip.

I disappeared.

NINE

Eyelids growing heavy, I lay among the trash, listening to the rain. My body surrounded by stinking plastic bags, rotting half-eaten meals, and the buzz of flies. I had no idea where I was. Probably for the best. I breathed lungfuls of the reeking air and tried to calm down, my heart punching at my ribs from within.

I ignored the humidity and listened to the settling sound of the summer rain; it was soothing. In the distance I could hear the wail of the sirens drawing away. Somewhere a man screamed, elsewhere a baby cried, nearby a motor-coach rumbled. Its pistons fired like a great mechanical heart.

The continuous rush of a downspout or a broken pipe added a layer of white noise to the sounds of Level Two. I was exhausted and the constant woosh lulled me into a sense of ease, and for a while I felt all right. I felt at home. Among the trash bags I was safe. I was well-hidden. I had disappeared.

Relaxing, I stretched out, hearing the plastic bags groan in protest. A smile crept sleepily across my face. I chuckled even as

I began to drift off. How was it that now, here in the trash, I felt more at home than I had since returning to Lovat?

Here—behind a random dumpster, in a random alley, off a random street, my mattress a pile of trash bags—I passed out from exhaustion.

It's funny. That feeling of home. It's so temporary, like bathwater: the warmth eventually grows cold.

Hours later, the buzzing of a yellow sodium light roused me. It flickered, casting spastic shadows in my trash-filled alley. Rubbing sleep from my eyes, I woke stiffly. I was wet. I was cold. I felt miserable. My whole body complained, not just the gunshot wound in my arm or my sore chest. I felt bruised everywhere.

Not knowing how long I was out, I took in my surroundings. I felt disoriented. Waking up violently in a pitch den and passing out later in a pile of trash bags will do that to a fellow.

My alley was tucked off a narrow street. It was early yet. Not quite breakfast and the streets of Level Two were quiet. I could hear water from the Sunk lapping somewhere nearby and a clucking argument in Cephan from one of the open windows above me.

In my mad rush to hide myself, I had apparently placed myself behind an overflowing dumpster that was covered with a phosphorescent moss. Rolling my neck to loosen it a bit, I watched a forearm-sized rat tear into a wet paper bag full of some half-rotted food.

Lovely.

Standing groggily, I stuck my hands in my pocket. To my surprise I felt the collar I had torn from my assailant. The previous evening's excitement came back to me in such a rush, I had to take a few deep breaths to calm myself.

Pulling the collar out, I examined it for the first time in the daylight brightness of the lamps.

The collar wasn't very wide, maybe three inches. I had only gotten half of it; the rest remained on the maero's jacket somewhere in a dark pitch den.

The material was a deep red fabric, a color that reminded me of a rich claret. I turned the piece of cloth in my hand, revealing a small patch on the opposite side sewn tightly against the fabric.

It was familiar. My heart skipped a beat.

Eight narrow bars arranged vertically smallest to largest. It was a mark I had seen before. First, larger, on a similar patch on the coat I borrowed from Inox. Second, darker, black on light skin as a tattoo on the neck of the man I saw leaving Nickel's office.

Chills played the nerves of my spine like a guitar.

My eyes widened. This was all too eerie. Too many random events were connected by this symbol. My evidence was thin—the more rational part of me said—this could just be happenstance, perhaps this was only the logo of a local jai alai team, or a popular restaurant.

What did I know?

I played through the scenarios in my head: the doctor in the alley just so happened to have a deep red jacket with this circle and bars symbol sewn on the sleeve. Innocent enough, I suppose.

It was in her Lost-and-Found box after all.

What else?

That man at Nickel's office. The same mark tattooed on his neck. Coincidence? Maybe it was the logo of a band? Somehow I knew that was incorrect.

Finally, the third time, my attacker attired in a jacket similar to the one I had found, embroidered with the same circle and bars on the collar. How did he find me in the maze of Level Two? Inox? Nickel? The tattooed man?

My location. My telephone call. Me, telling Nickel where I had bedded down for the evening, even giving him the street address.

I could feel the hairs on the back of my neck rise.

Nickel.

August Nickel was the connection.

It all swirled around my friend. He was tied to this. He was a part of this game.

I could remember hate in that maero's eyes. He was ready to kill, but why me? There was a warrant out for my arrest—probably a bounty. The maero could have held me down and handed me over to the police, but he hadn't paid them no mind. Focusing only on me.

Did this symbol belong to Thad's killer? Was this some sort of gang? Were these the people who killed Fran? Is that why they were after me? Was I next?

My head spun. The rat in the wet paper bag shrieked as I moved past. It scrabbled backwards, tearing the bag from the side, and then disappeared under the dumpster in a brown blur.

The group behind this symbol had found me. Attacked me in the middle of a police raid. Hunted me down. Me.

Nickel. The name blared through my mind.

Seething, I turned the piece of fabric over and over in my hand. My mood grew darker. I've never been good at keeping my temper in check.

I stood by the alley entrance, leaning against the gray-stained brickwork of an old building, fighting to bite back what was welling up inside me. I punched at the bricks, my fists lashing out. Waves of pain lurched up my right arm, a harsh reminder that I had been shot not twenty-four hours earlier.

My arm and knuckles protesting, I slumped down against the gray-stained building.

I *did* ring him. I *did* tell him where I would be.

My *friend*. My *trusted* friend.

I screamed a guttural scream. Rage. Red rage filled my head.

I kicked out, grinding my heels across the pavement, my boots leaving streaks across the dirty sidewalk. Pedestrians jumped out of the way to avoid the human kicking at phantoms.

That had to be it.

Nickel.

Nickel betrayed me. That had to be it. I seethed, then stopped. Like a break in the clouds I was hit with a wave of calm. I had known him for years. Why would he give me over? If this circle and bars group was really after me, why would he help them?

Had they killed Fran? She was like a sister to him. He wouldn't blindly associate with killers.

Maybe they weren't connected.

This could all be a misunderstanding. Coincidence, nothing more.

Doubt crept back in. It seemed ridiculous thinking about it. It felt so wrong, so ludicrous. I rubbed my eyes with a thumb and forefinger, feeling a headache crawl back into my skull.

"Go with your gut," echoed my father's voice. "Folks spend too much time in their head. A man shouldn't second-guess himself; if his gut says something is a sham then it's a sham. Experience means a lot. Ain't no lengthy blathering of retrospect going to change a man's mind about what he knows."

I smiled, hearing my old man's words play through my head.

I stared at the torn collar, the passing of time lost to me. Citizens who lived in Level Two or who came up from the Sunk to do business continued to ignore me, passing me by. To them I was just another pitch addict. Just another junkie.

I didn't care. It didn't matter. I was lost in thought. My gut told me to second-guess myself. I was out of my element. August was suspect, true, but I needed to be sure. Needed to know. Everything was questions.

I looked at the torn collar, wondering if I could find someone to identify the symbol. Under normal circumstances I would have just gone to the police and reported the assault. These weren't normal circumstances and that was out of the question.

I considered the old glass library on Level Three; that would be my next best option, but I had little idea as to where to begin. I had only been in the place once, maybe twice, and the police presence there made me nervous.

Nine times out of ten an officer won't notice a wanted suspect.

They're people, too. They get the same warnings as the public, and just like the public they look at the faces, file them away, and move on. It's the nature of existence in a city like Lovat. There're too many junkies, transients, thugs, grifters, thieves, con men, ramblers, and beggars in this city to remember one face out of millions, even if that face has been all over the monochromes.

Still.

I'd rather not take even a ten percent chance.

I studied the marking. The border was filigreed with bright gold and rich brown threads forming the shape of sapling branches. I ran a thumb over the pattern. It was intricate. A relief in string. Expensive, with an odd religious bent to it.

Religious.

My mind hummed along.

Religious.

Memories were excavated from the recesses of my mind. What had Thaddeus mentioned? Religious...something.

I snapped my fingers.

He had complained about the religious types. Cultist, monks, the occasional Reunification priest—weirdos as he called them—heading down Maynard Avenue to visit the newest shop in his warren: a trinket dealer specializing in religious artifacts.

Religious artifacts.

I looked at the patch intently.

Maybe he could be of help.

I struggled to remember his name. Debil? Dubin? It was something like that.

I rose.

Level Two's slummy charm had finally worn out on me. I stopped at a pay telephone to try to ring Wilem, Black & Bright during normal business hours. I was holding out hope that someone would pick up and I'd have this whole business with the Lovat PD settled before lunch.

"Wilem, Black & Bright," I said to the operator.

"One moment."

A click, then a hum.

"Connecting," said the operator. Her line went silent. The telephone rang. And rang. And rang. And rang. Finally, after the fifth ring, a singsongy and slightly annoyed voice radiated from the earpiece.

"Wilem, Black & Bright!" the voice sang. "How can I help you?"

"Hi, my name is Waldo Bell," I began.

"Good morning, Mister Bell."

"Ah, good morning."

A pause.

"Hello?" asked the voice.

"Er...yes, sorry, I was hired by Mister Black a few weeks ago. Bell Caravans. Me and my partner came in to get our check a few days ago. Completed a run from Syringa. Maybe you remember me?"

"I'm sorry, I don't. Did we hire you?"

I tried to explain, "Yeah, actually. My partner and I, er...we came to the office. I'm human, he's a maero. Caravan master. Bell Caravans."

"We employ a lot of caravan masters."

"Yeah, I'm sure you do. We helped guide a big crate back from Syringa, anyway, I was hoping—"

A sigh.

"We get over three hundred ingoing and outgoing shipments a day, Mister Bell, if you can be more specific..." she drifted off and paused, the earpiece going silent, waiting for me to answer.

I stammered incoherently.

"Do you remember the shipment confirmation number?" she asked.

I tried to remember but drew a blank. I had a sickening feeling that Wensem would have been far better at this than I.

"Er, I can't remember. Sorry," I apologized.

"It's on the receipt."

"I didn't take a receipt."

"Well, I can't help you then," said the receptionist, her voice dropping an octave.

"Surely you'd be able to—"

"You get me the shipment confirmation number. I'll check our records," she said, pausing before finishing coolly, "Have a nice day, Mister Bell."

Click.

Great.

The religious artifact dealer. That was my next stop.

I had considered calling Nickel but decided against it. Confrontation wasn't in the cards. Not now anyway, and not over a telephone. I had no idea what I would say to him and all it would do is fill me with rage. Both Lovat PD and this dangerous circle-and-bars gang were still after me. Keeping my wits about me needed to be my primary focus.

A brief pit stop on Level Three waylaid me from the religious artifact dealer.

The old public market still existed in the belly of the city, and it was there I knew I could find what I needed. It would be crowded, and there's no better place to hide than in a crowd.

Also, I was hungry.

I stopped at a doughnut cart and bought a small bag of greasy doughnuts for breakfast. The scent of cinnamon and sugar had made my stomach rumble. I stuck my nose into the grease-stained paper bag and inhaled. It was far more pleasant than the scents I had faced on Level Two.

The crowd moved about me, ignoring the guy with the ball cap and the dirty jacket. I wasn't anyone special. Just one of the throng. It felt safe.

My purchases made, I headed south back to King Station.

Thad's old neighborhood.

I'd be walking by his place. I realized I'd never again step foot through his narrow door and see his wide, fleshy mouth break into a smile. I felt sick.

The massive cage moved slowly, rising from one level and into another. I leaned against a corner in the back, head down, the brim of my cap covering my face. I was starting to feel like I was getting good at this inconspicuous thing.

"Level Four. King Station," called out the elevator's conductor.

Level Four was as I had left it. I walked down Second Avenue, took a left on Main Street passing bars, sushi shops, nightclubs, a few nail salons, and a crematorium. When Main arched left and became Maynard, I followed it the rest of the way down to Thad's old neighborhood.

Water dripped down from unseen holes in the street above. The white brick that made up the majority of the buildings here was stained with soot and a gray moss.

A gaggle of old women moved in a herd down the sidewalk, clucking to each other like cephels and nodding to themselves.

I saw the same noodle cart from the other day with the same pot bellied vendor. He was still slinging his noodles while whistling old jazz numbers. I considered stopping; the doughnuts weren't enough for breakfast and I was hungry, but being recognized was too risky. Odds were Bouchard had already got to the vendor when they examined the murder scene. Surely the guy would recognize me a second time and report me. As much as my stomach complained, spending today running wasn't appealing.

Thad's place creeped up on me. I almost didn't recognize it. Police tape blocked the entrance to Russel & Sons Optics. Yellow and black. A stark contrast to the soot-stained white blocks that made up the storefront. The tape looked garish in the midday sodium lights. Harsh in the greyscale of Maynard Avenue. I stepped to the front stoop and laid a bunch of flowers down that I had bought from the public market. The scent of marigolds was heavy around the stoop. I hadn't been alone; many others had also laid flowers and mementos over the last few days. A few candles poked up from the jungle of color. A photograph or two of Thad's smiling face.

A memorial. A memorial to a great anur.

I felt guilty. Weighed down by my connection to Thad.

Move on, I told myself. *For Thad's sake. For your own.*

I said my goodbyes as I stood in front of the shop. I shed a few tears, then I left.

Was this whole idea of seeking out the artifact dealer really worth my time? It was a long shot but I needed answers. I looked down at the patch still attached to the torn collar. I flipped it around in my fingers and walked the rest of the way to the end of the block.

The bell above the door to Saint Olmstead Religious Antiques tinkled as I passed through the door. My boots thumped on the wood floor as I closed the door behind me. Shelves. Everywhere, shelves, covered with all manner of things.

An unseen shopkeeper grunted out a greeting as if he couldn't be bothered with customers as I moved through the shop. It wasn't large but was quite cluttered, making navigation difficult.

I had no idea where the counter was, so I resigned myself to wandering around the store until I found it. Three lines of shelves broke the shop into four aisles. I weaved between them inspecting the inventory.

Religious items from the mundane to the downright bizarre were presented in seemingly no order. Statuary occupied shelves with mosaics of brightly colored tiles. A collection of carved wood and ivory icons depicting a stern-looking cephel sat among a stack of blue robes. Antique daggers with jeweled handles were arranged carefully next to what appeared to be a phallus of hammered gold. Wooden reliquaries labeled carefully with the saintly possessions inside them were stacked beside hoods and mitres lining one whole shelf, each bearing a different mark to various gods. Jewelry was mixed in with everything, some of it simple and some extravagant. Rich browns and luminescent golds reflected the dim light of oil lanterns that hung along the shop's walls, warmly lighting the interior.

I passed by another customer browsing a collection of crucifixes. A Hasturian priest in his yellow robes. His head was shaved and his beard was braided into the eight braids dictated by his Cold Father. Hasturians don't traffic in Reunified iconography and he seemed slightly embarrassed to be caught looking. He gave me a weak smile, his expression a mix of shame and guilt.

Nodding at him, I rounded the corner and saw the counter. A dimanian sat behind it, head down, nose in an old leather-bound book that seemed to be made up of more dust than parchment. He looked up at me as I approached.

"Can I help you?" he asked. A single wild horn sprouted from his right temple. Its odd twisting angle made it clear he avoided the dimanian barbers who shaped horn growth.

"This your place?" I asked.

"Yes, I'm Hagen Dubois, and this is Saint Olmstead Religious Antiques." He waved his hand around, moving automatically into his pitch. "We specialize in pre-Aligning antiquities, though we do carry all manner of holy and consecrated objects; for the more discerning customer I have access to all manner of items I can get delivered. Now, introductions out of the way, can I help you?"

He smiled a forced smile. It was obvious I was keeping him from the dusty book he had been so engrossed in.

"Nice place," I began. "I'm hoping you can help me. Truth is, I'm kind of suspecting this is a long shot, but figured I'd check. Have you ever seen this mark before? Looked kind of religious to me."

I dropped the collar with the patch on top of the old tome. The proprietor tsked and moved it aside, shutting the book and folding it gently into purple threadbare velvet. Squat spurs extended from each of the knuckles on Hagen's narrow hands. I wished I'd had a set like those the night before, they would have been useful.

"That is a pre-Aligning manuscript: The Treatise on Iram," he said. I nodded as if I understood. It was clear he didn't believe me. "Very expensive and very fragile. Please have some respect."

I gave an apologetic shrug.

"Now to this symbol." Hagen slipped a pair of spectacles from his tangle of black hair and settled them atop his sharp nose. He squinted at the patch for a while, silent except for occasional odd grunts and pensive humming. He turned it over, examined it upside down and on its side. All the while he drummed the spurs of his left hand on the wooden counter. Eventually he dropped the collar and looked up at me.

"I honestly can't say what it is, though it does look familiar. Where'd you get this?"

"Down in Level Two."

He nodded. "Could be a gang symbol. Where in Level Two?"

I ignored the question. "That was my first thought as well," I lied. "It seemed too...I don't know...too well thought out? Too intricate? Gang symbols tend to be crude, quick things right? Something you can scrawl on a building."

"Good point," said Hagen, nodding. "You thought about checking the library?"

I nodded. "That was my next step if this fell through."

Hagen rubbed his eyes and pointed at the patch with his little finger. "The circle and bars are both common elements in religious symbolism, but I've never seen them laid out in this fashion. Are you sure it's of religious origin?"

I shrugged. "That's why I brought it here."

The shopkeeper held out his hands apologetically and scratched behind his horn. "Look, I'm pretty busy these days, and I don't know if I would be much help in tracking this down. I'd say you shoul—"

I cut him off. "Please. I'll pay you. Just give it a couple hours."

He looked up and seemed to study me for a while.

"All right," he said with a sigh. "I'll give it a couple of hours. My going rate is fifty lira. I bill at three hours minimum."

I pulled the lira out of my pocket and laid them down on the counter; my little slush fund was running out quickly and I still needed to pay Inox. Regardless, I felt this was worth it. I needed help. I needed a direction. Right now everything was gray. I needed some black and white: some absolutes.

A good friend potentially betrayed me. Another was unreachable. More were dead. Someone was after me, possibly even the people who had killed my friends. Even if I had to pay him, just having this antique dealer on my side eased me somewhat. Someone to help would be beneficial, for my sanity, if anything.

"Three hours," said Hagen. "It's all I can spare."

"Thank you, Mister Dubois. Three hours will be plenty. This means a lot."

"Just Hagen," he said cordially. "I have a few manuscripts I'll consult and some telephone calls I can make. It should give me a direction at the very least, if not the answers you seek. What's the best way for me to reach you...Mister?"

"Boddins," I said, coming up with a name off the top of my head. "Wal Boddins, and I don't have a telephone in my...er, hotel room." More lies. "I'll contact you. Is two days going to be enough?"

He nodded, pocketing the lira. "I can put aside some of my own personal work for a real client. Why not telephone tomorrow morning and check in; if I need a little more time I'll let you know then."

"Thanks," I said.

"Have a good afternoon," added Hagen, turning back to the old, dusty tome.

For the first time since returning to Lovat, as I left Saint Olmstead Religious Antiques, I felt like I had some control.

TEN

Darkness had settled over Lovat by the time I made my way back to Doctor Inox's office. The pitch addict I had seen on my last visit still sat atop his pile of trash. A vague outline in the dim twilight glow of the overhead lamps.

It was good that I had returned. I owed the doc money and I paid my debts.

Collectors are serious business. Loans happen daily, and in a city like Lovat where millions upon millions live above and below one another in an ever-changing maze it's easy for a creditor to lose track of a debtor. For years, before the Society of Collectors was formed, banks would loan money and then never see their debtor again. As you can imagine, things spiraled out of control, banks quit loaning money, and Lovat was thrown into a serious economic depression.

From the rubble of that depression, the Collectors emerged. They weren't just good at their job, they were astounding. Bounty hunters, focused solely on loan repayment. Creditors hire one of the Society to go after a delinquent and collect their outstanding balances. It's effective.

The Society of Collectors operates under a series of principles: twenty-five percent of the debt is paid to them upon completion and—this is where it gets darker—they claim organ rights on the debtor if the debtor refuses, or is unable, to pay.

The organ market in Lovat is quite lucrative. If a Society contract cannot be reclaimed the Collectors assume the debt upon themselves and take not only the debt, but an extra twenty-five percent based on the sale of organs.

It keeps people honest, I suppose. As you can imagine, debts here get paid quickly. No one wants to have a black-clad Collector showing up at their door, knife in hand, demanding some outrageous sum—or your heart. With two sets of goons after me already, a third group wasn't something I was keen on.

I stepped into the alley that led to Doctor Inox's office. Her door was wide open, and bright white light spilled out from the interior into the narrow alley. As I drew closer I noticed the pitch addict hadn't moved. It wasn't that he was passed out. He wasn't sleeping. He was dead. With a bright red slash across his throat, his glassy eyes bloodshot eyes stared up at the roof of Level Two.

I slowed.

Unprepared for what greeted me, I stepped inside.

I gasped.

Doctor Inox was tied to the gurney set up in the center of the room. Her mask hung crookedly off her face, lines of blood dripping down from the mouth grate and the eye slits. Blood pooled around the tile floor, leaking from a ragged cut in her throat. Beneath her lab coat the rolls of flesh that made up her arms, breasts, and belly stacked on top of one another giving her the appearance of a melted candle.

But where were her hands? Bile rose in my throat. Her hands were missing.

I stepped closer. Her forearms had been bound to the gurney by roll after roll of surgical tape. A bloody bonesaw lay next to the stumps where her hands had been. The front of her stainless steel mask had been dented as if someone had smashed it into the side of the gurney.

Another death.

Another murder.

Another death connected to me.

I could see Bouchard's smile. That smug, I-told-you-so expression.

I rushed to the doctor's side and used the bonesaw to cut her free of the surgical tape. She slumped backwards to the floor. She was at least twice my weight, a mountain of a woman, her skin brutally pale in the fluorescent lights of her office.

I checked for a pulse, knowing the answer before I did so. Her skin was like ice.

She was dead.

"You!" snapped a wispy female voice from behind me.

I spun.

Standing behind me in the small living area was a smoky, formless shadow of a woman. She seemed fuzzy, her edges blurred like wet watercolor paint. Slits of red-orange glowed in the murk. It was clear from her posture that I had surprised her.

"You're the Guardian," she said, sounding surprised.

I took a few steps back, putting Inox's corpse between me and her.

I had met very few umbra in my time on this earth. The shadow race tends to keep to themselves. Closed off, tight-knit communities far away from the masses. You'll see a few of them working in Lovat, but as a society they like their privacy. Folks tend to distrust them almost immediately; the fact that they are impossible to see in the dark doesn't help.

Most cities have passed ordinances requiring umbra to clothe themselves, Lovat included. Those that choose to blend in do so willingly, wearing heavy layers of clothing so they can be identified in a crowd. This female was scantily clad, however, which was considered rude, as well as threatening. It was also illegal.

The shadow figure advanced toward me, taking long, confident steps, and I instinctively took another step back, finding myself against the wall of the small Bonesaw office.

I fumbled at the nearest tray of utensils, withdrawing a spiky-looking instrument that reminded me of a thick stake with cross beams. I spun it, holding it out as if she was a vampire. The knuckles of my hand grew pale as my grip tightened.

The umbra laughed. It was a delightful sound. Like honey. It felt out of place in this gory scene.

"What are you going to do with that, Guardian?" she taunted. Why was she calling me that?

I remained silent.

At her side, Inox's fleshy hands hung in a partially translucent plastic bag. Blood had pooled near the bottom, and it sloshed lazily as the shadow figure sashayed closer.

She followed my gaze and patted the severed hands.

"Hands of a doctor," she said vaguely, as if this explained everything.

I flicked my eyes from the hands and tried to fixate on the glowing slits in the shape that was her head. A wicked-looking straight razor hung loosely in her left hand, blood staining the blade.

"She wasn't much of a fight. Not like that flutist. By the Firsts, she struggled." The figure tilted her head, watching my reaction.

"You," I growled. "You killed Fran."

That inappropriately sweet laugh again.

"Me."

She lunged, and I swear I saw the straight razor outstretched, its wicked blade swiping in my direction. I sucked in a lungful of air.

The world went dark.

Wait.

She didn't cut me. I wasn't dead. She flicked off the lights.

More laughter. This time from farther away. To my left? Right? It was hard to tell. I was disoriented.

My eyes struggled to adjust to the darkness. She had the upper hand. I tried to move as quietly as possible. Creeping along the wall, one hand on my makeshift weapon, the other flailing about looking for obstacles.

Even if I lasted long enough for my eyes to adjust, I wouldn't be able to see her. Naked, the umbra was living shadow, invisible in the dark.

I stepped carefully, my eyes useless in the inky blackness. I expected an attack at any moment. I swung the spiky instrument before me like a stubby sword, my trajectory and awkward slashes never powerful enough to do any real damage.

"Behind you," came a whisper in my ear, the heat of her breath hot on my neck. It spooked me. I spun, swinging the makeshift dagger around. Catching only air.

"It was you. You killed Thad, and Fran, and now Doctor Inox."

She chuckled, almost pityingly, and I rushed to the spot, striking out but hitting nothing. Feeling a breeze as she fled.

So close.

Umbra are as solid as you or me, they just appear formless. So my striking out was as dangerous to her as her razor would be to my throat. They can die just like the rest of us, *if* you can find them.

I waited.

I tried to remember more of my rules of the trail.

You have more than one sense. Use them all. Listen.

I kept one eye on the lit doorway leading to the alley and tried to focus on noise. If she stepped in front of the doorway I'd be able to see her, and if I could see her, I could strike. She was physical, I reminded myself, she made footsteps, she made noise.

Nothing.

I could hear my heart beating.

Ba-dum. Ba-dum. Ba-dum.

She made noise. I focused on sounds beyond my own heartbeat.

Then, the soft padding of bare feet on tile. Just to the left of Doctor Inox's corpse. I crouched low. Tried to blend in with the shadows as well as the umbra could. I had heard stories that umbra could see perfectly in the darkness.

Time passed. Another soft step. Again from the direction of the corpse.

I held my breath.

Then it happened.

A naked silhouette of a woman appeared in the doorway.

I rushed. All my speed and anger burst forth, and I covered the five steps between us in moments. The instrument in my hand pierced her body even as I pushed her through the door and outside into the alley. Throwing my weight into the half-stab, half-tackle assault.

She cried out in pain and I heard her razor clatter across the pavement.

I pulled the sharp instrument out of her shadowy leg and growled, "For Thad," and stabbed again. My second strike was unsuccessful.

The umbra woman kneed me in the crotch and clawed at my face simultaneously. My third strike went wild and I heard the instrument snap. I rolled to one side, pain exploding where she had struck me. She rose and stepped back.

"You stabbed me," she gasped.

I rolled so I was looking up at her. Black shadowy blood seemed to leak from the wound in her upper thigh. It reminded me of the idling smokestacks on the city's monorails belching soot into the air.

Sirens sounded in the distance. I looked away from her for

a split second. The police. Again. She must have called them. That's what she was doing when I walked in. Setting up another scene. Another murder to pin on me. When I looked back up, she was gone, her razor lying in the dirty alley.

I groaned and sat up. Shaking, I stood. I couldn't remember the last time I had been in so many fights. This was getting ridiculous. My arm protested. My ribs ached. A sharp knot had formed above my crotch that made me huff for air.

I stumbled back to the doorway and flicked on the light, blinking at the sudden illumination.

The ghastly murder scene still remained, though now it looked all the more horrifying. The sharp pool of blood had been disturbed by the cat-and-mouse game between the umbra and myself. Bloody smears and footprints covered the floors, the walls.

My own hand prints. Smaller ones. Most likely the umbra's. I looked down at myself. I was covered in blood, Doctor Inox's blood. This was bad. If the police arrived, I'd be locked away forever.

I fled, heading north, toward the harbor. A few cephel heads bobbed from openings that led into the blue-lit level of the Sunk, their big eyes watching me as I hurried toward the nearest monorail station.

Witnesses.

Great.

I instinctively looked at my wrist to check the time, realizing my watch was still missing. It had been taken along with my money. It probably ticked away in some plastic bag in Lovat

Central doing no good to anyone, especially me.

I wondered how much longer I'd need to wait before I called Hagen.

Time was becoming more and more precious.

I thought about my options. I needed a change of clothes. I could loiter around Maynard Avenue, but that seemed foolish. I didn't know the north side as well as some.

West Lovat seemed my best option. It was a highly elevated warren on the western edge of the city.

A monorail ran from where I was to the warren's central area. I could go there. Keep low, and be far enough away from the city as to avoid trouble. "Go with your gut," my father's voice said, and my gut said West Lovat.

I had seen the killer. She wasn't some punk clad in a red jacket. She didn't have the bars and circle symbol on her shoulder or tattooed on her skin. She was professional.

The door to the old monorail opened and I stumbled inside. My body ached.

I wanted nothing more than the end to this nightmare.

ELEVEN

West Lovat sits on an island apart from the rest of the city. Its lowest level starts about where Level Two ends and Level Three begins in Lovat proper. It's far enough from the rest of the city that it keeps crime low; it also tends to be quieter. As a result the warren has become kind of a haven for the middle class and serves as a bedroom community for the city.

West Lovat.

My new hiding spot.

I leaned my head against the monorail window and watched buildings flash past. I felt sick, lost, and lonely. I was terrified. I had started to shake after collapsing into my seat. Too focused on fleeing, I had skipped buying a ticket. I hoped the conductor was feeling lazy and wouldn't pass through the car.

Covered in blood, bruised and scarred, I was likely to raise anyone's suspicions. I saw a few posters with my old face plastered on them. Killer. Wanted. Bounty. Two murders.

Flashes of the earlier events kept exploding in my mind

like firecrackers. She had taken the doctor's hands. Her hands! Sawed them off and hung them on her hip like they were some kind of sick trophy.

Overcome, I got sick on the seat next to me, my stomach ejecting my meager breakfast.

The murder scene. Emotions high. Fight or flight. I hadn't really processed what I was seeing then. Now it all rushed in.

Breathe. I told myself. *Breathe.*

I tried to force my hands to stop shaking but the memory of Doctor Inox's corpse—the stumps of her arms, the slash across her throat, the sheer brutality of it all—kept crashing into me like waves. It was horrifying.

The umbra had been so casual. The cock of her hip, the lightness in her honeyed laughter. That odd turn of her head. What had she called me? Guardian? What did that mean? I have never seen her before in my life. I could count the number of umbra I knew on one hand and a crazy, murderous vixen wasn't one of them.

Her eyes. They burned into my mind. Twin glowing coals blinking from inky blackness.

I shuddered. I got sick a second time, dry heaving. My bruised ribs complained.

Breathe. I repeated to myself. Just breathe.

A homeless kresh—the monorail car's only other occupant—moaned, looked down the car at me, and then rolled over, laying back down and falling asleep.

Bells clanged.

A recorded voice called out the stop.

The monorail doors opened.

We had arrived.

Before the kresh could stir again, I was gone.

A twenty-four hour pharmacy helped me clean up.

The human pharmacist was wary to talk to the bloodied and dirty man standing in his shop. I pulled out a wad of lira, paid for my necessities and asked for directions to the bathroom. He grunted, nervously handed me a key, and waved a hand toward the back, careful not to make eye contact. That was good. I'd rather he didn't recognize me.

I stared at myself in the dingy mirror and tried to settle my hammering heart. Blood covered my face, neck, shirt, and arms. I *looked* like a murderer. A damned mess.

Circumstantially, I would have arrested me.

Exhaustion was showing as dark circles under my eyes. The lines in my forehead and cheeks were more prominent. I needed a good night's rest. Preferably not in a pitch den, especially not one interrupted by the police, a crazed thug, or that umbra with her golden, glowing, coal-hot eyes.

Was that too much to ask? A single good night's rest?

I shaved, peeled off my old shirt and jacket, and washed myself in the sink. That done, I put fresh dressings on my gunshot wound, checking it carefully and hoping the stitches hadn't torn. They hadn't. Thank the Firsts for small blessings.

I dressed in clothes I had purchased in the pharmacy: a baggy white button-up shirt and a black canvas jacket with a hood.

I was still exhausted, but cleaned up, blood gone, in fresh clothes, I looked better. I looked normal. It eased me somewhat.

My jeans were still smeared with dark stains. More of Inox's blood. I really wished the pharmacy sold pants.

As I left the pharmacy I asked the proprietor for a recommendation for a place to stay. He frowned, disapproval written across his thick features, before rattling off a few hostels and hotels. He also recommended a noodle bar and a shop down the street that had good urchin.

I nodded.

I wasn't planning on going to any of them.

The way I figured it, the police were behind me and my hand prints were all over that scene. That alone would nail me. Who knows what the umbra had told them when she called it in. I most likely left a trail of Inox's blood; when the police caught up to my trail it would be nice to send them down a different road. I hadn't spotted a telephone in the pharmacy, but the guy behind the counter was obviously wary of me: he'd either be making a call after I left or sending a telegram.

Welcome to West Lovat.

I awoke the next morning in a shabby little hotel room; it was almost noon. I had slept, by my account, at least eleven hours. No problem thanks to half a bottle of vermouth. No nightmares. No police raids. No thugs. No umbra killer.

I felt better. Not perfect, but better.

I checked out of the room and telephoned Hagen.

"Hi Wal," said Hagen's voice through the receiver. "Glad you telephoned."

"Find anything?" I asked, hopeful.

"Y-yeah. I did," Hagen stammered, his voice drifting off. He sounded nervous. Silence poured from the receiver.

"Well?" I asked.

"L-look, I have to ask. Are you wanted? By the p-police?"

Now silence came from my end.

He stammered, "I s-saw your face come up on the monochrome last night. You shaved your head and cut off your beard, but the eyes were the same. Same as yours. I-I'm not an idiot. You're a wanted man, aren't you, Wal?"

I didn't speak. I didn't know what to say, to be honest. How far could I trust this guy? Thad hadn't liked him, but Thad hadn't really liked anyone.

Maybe that was a mark in this guy's favor.

Hagen spoke again, if anything to fill the silence. "L-look, I don't believe you killed those people. I don't believe you killed Mister Russel down the road, the musician, or that Bonesaw last night."

"Why?" I asked, finally speaking.

"This patch. My research has turned up something. It's loose threads, pardon the pun, but I could give you something to g-go on. Look, I don't really want to talk about this over the telephone. Can we meet? In person?"

In person? I thought about this. What if the police were using him? Bouchard was smart. On top of his game. If he had tracked me to Saint Olmstead it would have been easy to turn

Hagen Dubois. Especially for a random client like me. Still, I really needed to know what he had found.

I doubled down.

"Yeah, we can meet. I'm in West Lovat. Right now? Should I come to your sho—"

Hagen interrupted me, "You like aloo tika? There's a place over there. On the west side of the hill. Third Level. Er, I can't remember the cross street."

"I do. I can find it," I said. My stomach rumbled at the mention of the potato croquettes.

"It's on a busy strip. A nice public place. Should be safe."

Should be safe? I thought. His concern with safety was worrying. *What* did he find?

"Meet me there in an hour?"

It was busy, and very public. The shop was squeezed between two taverns that dominated the sidewalk. It had hardly enough room for two or three tables inside; a few other larger tables were scattered out front. A small speaker wailed the horn solo from the ancient Brother Miles tune, "I Waited for You." Fitting.

I arrived before Hagen and watched from across the street as he arrived. I wanted to be sure he wasn't followed or working with Bouchard. Just covering my bases.

The police can't catch what they can't find.

Hagen arrived alone, wearing khaki pants and a faded blue jacket with narrow lapels. He looked like a history professor. It fit his role as an antique dealer.

I watched from across the street as he ordered his food, took the little placard he was given, and found a seat out on the street in front of the restaurant.

I waited until his food came and then I walked up.

"Sorry I'm late. I walked here. Didn't realize it was so far," I lied.

Hagen shrugged. "You getting food?"

I nodded, and went inside. Ordered three of the potato croquettes. Taking my plastic placard, I returned to Hagen.

"I'm eager to hear what you found."

Hagen looked over his shoulder as he nodded. He slipped a hand into his jacket, pulling out my patch and sliding it across the table to me. He tapped it with a finger.

"That is a symbol of Pan."

"What?" I asked, confused.

"Are you a religious man?" Hagen asked.

"Not particularly."

"Read much?"

"No."

He made a face.

"Pan. It's a symbol of Pan," repeated Hagen, looking around. He was speaking in a low whisper.

"What's a Pan? Outside of the kitchen."

He shushed me and looked around. "Not so loud. Especially not now."

"Sorry," I said, leaning closer.

"Pan is a *who*, actually." Hagen explained, his voice soft. "A member of the pantheon of a pre-Alignment race of humans.

Was a god, albeit a minor one. God of..." he rolled his knuckles on the small table, the spurs clacking across the wood, "...shepherds. The wilds. Things like that. Some scholars think he was associated with male fertility. Ancient humans had gods for all manner of random things. Lightning. The night. Music. Aging."

"So this belongs to some god?"

Gods were a dime a dozen in post-Aligning Lovat. They came in all sizes, big and small, fat and thin, old and young, angry and kind, and with them came all manner of worshippers.

Hagen nodded and took a bite of fish, talking with his mouth full. "Yes, a god of a sort, as far as I can tell. He gets referenced a lot by many other names. Puck was a name that cropped up often. Sometimes I saw him referred to as The Black Goat. A few times he was called Cernunnos, though that seemed to fall out of vogue quickly, and once—" He pulled out a scrap of paper and studied it. "Once...ah, yes, bap-ho-met."

"Wait, black...goat?" I asked, that name sticking in my mind.

"Yes. Apparently this Pan was a satyr."

"What's a satyr?" I asked, dumbfounded. Hagen was spewing facts like bullets bursting from the barrel of a machine gun. I blinked, trying to process everything I was hearing.

"Half-man, half-goat."

"So, Lengish?" I had never been to the plains of Leng but I had heard stories of the goat men.

"Of a sort, though I don't think the connections are anything other than a coincidence. The Black Goat name was fairly common, though not with the originators of the worship of Pan. It predated their existence, then returned to prominence afterward."

"Is this Pan one of the Firsts?" I asked, wondering if he was one of the great old ones spoke of in legend.

We paused as my food arrived and I bit into the potato cake, munching hungrily. It was bland but my stomach didn't care.

After the waiter left, Hagen shrugged. "I don't know. Pre-Aligning texts are spotty. Tend to be more wordy and flowery than modern Strutten. It's hard to separate reality from fiction." He tapped the symbol. "Those bars represent a pan flute, or Pan's flute, a musical instrument named after him."

Pan. Pan's flute.

"So what's this symbol doing in Lovat?"

He looked around again. There was a sheen of sweat on his brow. A bit of his wild hair clung to his forehead and his eyes flicked around. He was clearly spooked.

"Where did you get this?" he asked, voice barely a whisper, his face deadly serious.

"I told you I pulled it—"

He shook his head. "No. No more stories. I understand you're trying to protect yourself, but I need to know, where did you get this?"

I stared at the antique dealer for a long moment. "I was attacked. Pulled it off the collar of the guy who attacked me, a maero. I had holed up in a pitch den to avoid the police, and he came looking for me."

"Have you seen it before?"

I nodded.

"How many times?" he asked.

I held up three fingers. "Three. Twice as a patch like this, once tattooed on a guy's neck."

"Tattoo," Hagen mumbled. "Of course a tattoo."

He nodded and ate in silence a moment. He finally looked up and spoke, his tone grim. "This isn't the safest information."

"I paid for it."

"I realize that, and I'll do what I can to explain what I found, but I feel like I should stress the dangers here. We're walking on perilous ground."

"You've followed the stories. I'm already in trouble. If you found something, I want to know. I need to know. I didn't..." I leaned closer. "I didn't kill those people. I've never killed anyone. I wouldn't. I couldn't. I didn't touch them, but whatever this is..." I tapped the patch, "I'm involved."

He nodded and glanced around, more beads of sweat formed on his brow, his voice quieted even more. I had to strain to hear him. "The symbol isn't Pan's. It's a symbol *of* Pan, but it's *not* Pan's. Do you understand the difference? It didn't decorate his temples; it was adopted, by someone else, in his name."

"I follow."

"I found a few books on the cults that sprung up after the Aligning. I believe Pan's flute is the symbol for an organization that refers to itself as the Children, maybe Pan's Children. I'm unsure of their connection to Pan, but they use his pipes as their symbol."

"So who are they?"

"Depends on what you want to believe. A club. A fraternal organization. A fanatical sect of Hasturianism. A cult. Everything I found was spotty, but records for the Children go back at least several hundred years.

"Early accounts were innocent enough. Feasts and festivals, that sort of thing. An offshoot, a minor deviation of the original organization. Sort of like the Reunified Church before the Aligning."

"So what happened?"

"Something changed. The early accounts were typical silly stuff: snake handlers, candles, incense, trying to raise the spirits of the Firsts, rumors of sacrifice in dark basements."

"Sacrifice?" I asked, thinking of the bizarre way Doctor Inox had been murdered.

"Nothing concrete. Those type of rumors come up often; most of the time it's just the writings of nervous people who see a demon behind every bush."

He ate another bite.

"Sounds dark," I said.

"Maybe I am just jaded. If you deal in religious artifacts for as long as I have it'll make you jaded towards this sort of stuff. Rumors of sacrifice are typical in old, dead religions. There were eras where whole civilizations were fascinated by the occult; writing books and making objects focused on it. You don't see it crop up so often nowadays."

"So these Children are in Lovat. Why? Why are they here?"

"Well, that's just it. They shouldn't be."

"Shouldn't be?"

"They were wiped out almost two centuries ago."

"Wait, wiped out? What? By who?" I asked.

"Well, I have two accounts. One account is a rival sect:

Black's Children. Probably a reference to the black goat name. The other is the Hasturians. I'd presume it was the latter. It seems the Children got brasher. They were trying to do more than call the spirit of some First. It seemed they were trying to bring one back from the dead. Resurrection. Dead rising again. Valley of dry bones. Dangerous stuff. We're not talking rumors of sacrifices. We're talking murders. *Actual* murders. In broad daylight. In public places. Public figures. All as some sacrifice to bring back this mythical figure. Went so far as to kill people in front of the authorities. Killing the authorities. They'd mutilate the bodies. Cut away bits and pieces. Acts of horrific terrorism. It started scaring the public."

I thought about Thad's lips, Fran's ears, Doctor Inox's hands. These butchers were after my friends. "Unfortunately it sounds familiar. I'm not sure how much you know, but the three murders involved missing body parts."

Hagen visibly shuddered.

"They left that out of the monochrome report," he said, pushing away his plate and turning an odd sheen of green.

"Who were they trying to bring back? Which First?" I asked.

Hagen looked around and shook his head nervously before whispering, "Some documents said it was Hali, some claimed it was some great mother figure. I never could peg down a name. It was all vague. Old texts. Dead languages.

"In those days the Children were still tangentially connected to the Hasturian church, and the Hasturian priesthood didn't take kindly to these associations. The priests branded the Children's practices heretical, and a hefty bounty was placed on all their heads." He paused and looked up at me seriously. "It *supposedly* worked. I couldn't find any more mentions of the Children after that incident." He tapped the patch. "Until now."

We both stared at the patch in silence. Pan. A black goat. A cult called the Children. Bizarre murders. An ancient god worshipped by an ancient culture at the center of it.

"What's the Pan connection?"

"I don't really understand that either. It's a loose association. I feel like it's the missing piece."

"So what's our next step?" I asked.

"Oh no. Oh no, no, no. If the Children are actually back, and it looks like they are, I'm out. I don't want to be involved with this. I don't deal with crazies. They were dangerous before, and they'll be even more dangerous now."

I looked at him, thinking. "Is there more?"

"I-I don't know. Look, I'm not interested in pursuing this any further," he said. "I'm out."

"Please, if there is anything else," I begged.

"Look, I told you what I found out. You take this information and do with it what you will. If it were me, I'd leave Lovat. These people are either copycats or *actual* Children cultists. I don't know which is more terrifying. But I assure you either would be dangerous. If they're responsible for these killings and somehow they're pinning them on you, then they're smarter than I would've thought. You have your work cut out for you."

The sight of the naked umbra flashed in my memory.

Hands in the plastic bag.

Wicked razor glinting.

I shuddered.

Hagen rose. "The most dangerous people are those who think they have something to die for." He rose, collecting the remains of his meal. "I wish you good luck. I hope this all works out. Be careful. Please. Don't contact me again."

I watched him leave, wondering where this left me.

TWELVE

P an.
The name rang in my mind, echoing like church bells as I wandered the quiet streets of West Lovat. Something was there. Something in the information, in that name. I had to find it.

Black Goat.

The clues were there, somewhere, between the rituals, hymns, passages, atrocities of yesteryear, and the pagan celebrations in clearings of long dead forests. I gnawed at my thumbnail as I walked and thought.

Pan.

I bought some starfish marinated in sunflower oil, grilled, and served over seasoned couscous. The food was bland, dry, and overcooked, but still I ate. Exhausted, I felt the need to recharge. I ate as I walked, moving along a quiet, empty road on Level Four. I could smell the salty scent of the sea waft from behind me. The intermingling smell of fish, salt, and sodden vegetation.

Black Goat.

Why was that sticking with me? Why did that name linger instead of the Pucks and Pans?

Hagen's report sat in my mind like caravan cargowains circled for an evening's laager. I mulled over it again and again. Trying to see a connection. Trying to pick through the layers of information. Symbols. Names. Dates. Cults. Rituals. I couldn't see the forest for the trees.

I'm no good at puzzles.

As a caravan master it's my job to focus on the trees, know what's happening in the now for my clients. The journey is important, but the dangers of the present, each stage of the caravan, that's what I am hired to take care of.

Something stuck with me, and it took a moment for it to rattle free.

My *clients*.

I felt a rush of adrenaline, like I was close to uncovering a critical piece.

Slumping on a nearby bench, I set my meager meal next to me. Across from my perch a pair of rats fought over the remains of an old shoe. I rubbed my forehead. I secretly envied Bouchard, a detective, a man trained to see both the forest and the trees; how easy would this have been for him?

Pan.

I threw the paper cup at the rats in anger; starfish and couscous exploded outward. The rats scuttled away before returning to pick over the remains. Who was Pan to me?

The Black Goat. There was something there. Something in that title.

The Black Goat.

Black.

Black.

The miles passed and the first stage of the journey was complete. I knew a Black—sort of.

Peter *Black.*

Partner at Wilem, Black & Bright. An employer. A client. The mysterious delivery. August's connection. The umbra calling me "Guardian." I did guard, in a way.

The threads were there but they were tenuous. I felt like a tightrope walker in the middle of his act, out above the crowd, rope between my toes, standing on my narrow braided line of salvation. A simple yet precarious path.

Could Peter Black have some connection to this?

It was the only lead I could see. I tried to run through everything. It started with Thad—no—it started with Fran Nickel. Killed the morning of my arrival. Then Thad. Then the Bonesaw. I was the only constant, connecting each of the victims.

I played through the last few days. My arrival in Lovat, the delivery of Black's cargo at the caravansara—from there I fetched my paycheck at Black's offices, then visited Thad. Moments after my visit, maybe right after, Thad was killed and from there...I had it. My cascade of problems flowed from that one pivot point; all trails returned to the delivery.

And who had put me in connection with Wilem, Black & Bright?

August Nickel. My friend. My business partner. A possible traitor. He had assured me of their honesty. Smiled, glad-handed, and patted my shoulder. The only one who knew where I was staying the night the maero assailant had attacked.

I knew what I had to do, and I didn't feel good about it.

I took the monorail back to Lovat proper. Making my way past uniformed patrol officers, head down, cap screwed low, hood up. Another face in the crowd, another nobody. I saw more wanted posters with my old face and I was glad I shaved off the beard. The rain had returned. I marched down Second Avenue, turning onto Hinds, readying myself to face my old friend.

August and I had met over ten years ago. I was working the shipyards and he was an assistant to a dimanian broker named Marius Nesbit. Nesbit had been a bit of a ball-breaker, and had liked sending August down to check on the shipments he had insured, making sure the stevedores handled his cargo properly. August showed up so often under Nesbit's orders that it wasn't long before he was coming out drinking with the roughnecks after a shift. We hit it off, and when I left the dock life for the road, August—now his own boss and a rising star in the commodities trade—had been incredibly supportive. He was quick to recommend my fledgling business to long-term clients of his own. He had always struck me as open, straight, and honest. Or so I thought.

I had been betrayed, sold out for some promise of coin, business, something. I knew it, felt it in my gut, and the thought sickened me. The closer I got to Comings & Goings, Ltd. the angrier I became.

It was the lights that slowed me.

I stared at the gathering crowd. Humans, dimanians, dauger, and even a few cephels and kresh formed a tight pack that stretched across Hinds Street and blocked passage through it.

Lovat Central police prowled the space beyond, shoulders hunched, clubs in hand, the officers looking eager for some fool to challenge their authority. I swallowed the lump in my throat and blended in with the rear of the crowd, taking in the scene.

Stern-faced ambulance men loaded a bloody sheet into the back of a white ambulance fourgon. Police milled about, taking pictures and scratching down notes on old flip pads. Lights flashed red and blue, spinning in their enclosed plastic casings, reflecting off buildings, signs, and the glass storefronts. A stuttering rainbow of intermixing colors. The neon signs for "Comings & Goings, Ltd." and "Sardini Market" seemed extra gaudy.

Mrs. Sardini.

I immediately panicked. They better not have touched her. I'll kill them. I'll kill August. I worried for the old woman. I rushed forward, panic overcoming my trepidation. I pushed through the crowd.

Did August betray her as well? Was she also dead?

I melted into the crowd, trying to overhear discussions between pedestrians and police.

"Waldo? Waldo, is that you?" came a creaky, old voice.

I froze, looking around for the source.

"Waldo," said the voice a second time.

I looked down and saw Mrs. Sardini smiling a sad smile. Her rheumy old eyes were wet and swollen, her thin lips drawn and turned down.

"It's just so sad. So sad. I'm sorry, Waldo."

I tried to catch my breath and tried to slow my heart rate. I was grateful that she was okay.

"Mrs. Sardini!" I said, nearly shouting.

"Oh, Waldo," she said, wrapping her hands around one of mine. I wished she'd quit saying my name so loudly. "It's so sad. So sad. I'm so sorry."

"What's sad? What happened?" I asked dumbly. But I knew. My stomach dropped.

"Oh. Oh!" She said. "Oh, Waldo! You don't know? My poor boy. My poor, poor boy. I'm so sorry."

I felt like I had been hit in the stomach.

"Know what?" I wheezed. "What don't I know?"

"August was *murdered*. Can you believe it? Poor August. Murdered! I went up to take him his lunch, right on the dot, one o'clock as he likes it. I saw him in his chair, and when I drew closer…" She let out a soft moan like air escaping a tube.

"What happened?" I asked, my stomach in knots. "Please, Mrs. Sardini, what happened to August?"

The old woman shook from sobs. "He's dead, Waldo. August is dead. There was so much blood."

She sobbed into my shirt.

"I didn't linger; I went downstairs and picked up that telephone August had installed for me. I never liked the vulgar things, too loud, too brash. But I placed a call to the police immediately." She paused and then dropped her voice to almost a whisper. I had to lean close to hear. "They took his tongue, Waldo. His tongue!

They cut it out. They cut it out!"

She cried and leaned against me. Shudders running up and down her thin frame, a feather compared to the weight that now bore down on my shoulders.

August was dead. It threw a wrench into my entire theory. If he had betrayed me, why was he killed? A coverup? Was he feeling guilty? Had he killed himself?

"But...Mrs. Sardini, how did he die?"

She stared up at me with eyes that had seen too many terrible things.

"Ch-choked," she managed through tears. "Choked on his own blood. They held him down, forced his head back, and slit his throat...."

The umbra...visions of her straight razor flashed through my memory.

"How do you know this?" I asked.

"The detectives told me. All I saw was the blood. There was so much blood. I dropped his lunch."

I wrapped my arms around her, unsure what else to do. There was a hole in my gut. I had been livid with August a moment earlier, but now all I wanted to do was cry. Another friend. Another loss.

August. Loud, boisterous August. Dead. It was heartbreaking.

Mrs. Sardini heaved massive sobs into my jacket, and I tried to comfort her as best I could. August was like a son to the old woman, and she like a mother to him. He protected her, let her run her business practically rent-free. This loss would be devastating to her.

I surveyed the crowd.

Blank faces from Level Three pushed against the police tape and recoiled as the officers threatened with a few well-placed smacks. I looked up to the edge where Level Four ended and saw faces from a crowd staring back down, gawking at the investigation going on below them.

I didn't recognize anyone. That was good. I was in the lion's den. Lovat PD officers were a heartbeat away. Clean-shaven, I felt confident it would take a well-trained eye to recognize me from the wanted posters, but at any moment someone could spot me. I decided I shouldn't linger much longer.

I was about to turn away and tell Mrs. Sardini goodbye when I noticed three figures in the crowd across the police line. A kresh, a human, and a dimanian. Wearing the rust red jacket of the Children, patches bearing the mark of Pan emblazoned on their sleeves. Pan's symbol.

As a kid I remember read a book about famous crimes where the writer—and I forget his name now—said that arsonists were often caught when they returned to the scene of a fire. Did murderers do that? Did they return to admire the chaos their brutal act created? The three Children stood near the police tape across the road from me, quietly laughing at jokes too distant for me to hear. Was the umbra also among the crowd?

"Mrs. Sardini," I said.

"Yes, Wal?" asked the old woman, pulling away and looking up at me.

"You ever seen those three? Over there?" I nodded in their direction.

She squinted in their direction and eventually pulled on the glasses that hung about her neck. "Who now?" she asked.

"Those three. Over there, near the police tape. Between the buildings. Red jackets."

She squinted again, and the moments ticked by slow as a cart in the mud. "Those boys? Of course, I don't know their names though. Friends of August and Robby. They rarely bought anything from me."

"How often did you see them?"

"Oh, they usually dropped in once or twice a week. Seemed like nice young men."

"Did you see them earlier?" I asked.

She shook her head. "I can't remember the last time I saw any of them. It was young Robby who came around the most."

"Robby who?"

"Robby...um, what was his name, Robby...Wilem. Yes, that's it. Robby Wilem."

Wilem.

Wilem, Black & Bright.

"Wilem? Who is Robby Wilem?"

"He's not over there right now. I don't know who he was; however, he had a similar jacket. I figured they were in a club together, maybe part of a jai alai team. He was the only one to introduce himself. Nice young fella, lots of tattoos—bit hot under the collar, though. He and August were always going at it."

Another mile passed. I was getting closer to the end of this trail.

"You going to be all right?" I asked Mrs. Sardini.

She nodded. "I was told to wait here until the police said I could leave. Detective Bouchard said he might have more questions."

Bouchard. My heart rate jumped.

"Bouchard is here?"

Mrs. Sardini smiled. "He said he was looking for you. I told him straight, I said to him, 'I have known Waldo Bell for years and he had nothing to do with these killings. He doesn't have it in him,' I said. 'If you were half as valuable to Lovat as you like to think, you'd have realized that by now.' He didn't say anything, just frowned at me. He seems like an unhappy man and he smells of whiskey. He asked when I had last seen you. I told him it had been a few days."

You never saw August's killers either. I thought, wondering if my gut was right and the umbra woman had killed August. It would have been easy for her to slip into Comings & Goings, Ltd. and kill August without Mrs. Sardini hearing or seeing anything.

"I need to run. It's too dangerous here for me." I paused. What if the umbra returned for her? Mrs. Sardini was connected to me as well, and I'd hate to see the old woman killed on my account. "You should leave the city. Do you have family anywhere?"

"I have a cousin down south in Destiny."

"Go to Destiny. Stay a few weeks. It's too dangerous here right now."

"But...my..."

"Please," I pleaded, interrupting her protests. "Something's not right. As soon as the detectives let you go, pack up and take the first monorail to Destiny."

"Okay, Waldo. If you think it's necessary."

I nodded. "Don't tell Bouchard you saw me. Okay?"

I gave the old woman a kiss on the cheek before backing out of the crowd. I hoped she would take my advice and actually leave the city.

Elizabeth Sardini smiled a sad smile and nodded. "Your secret is safe with me. You let me know next time you're coming, and I'll make your favorite cannelloni."

THIRTEEN

Betrayal is an awful feeling. It can be something as simple as catching someone in a lie, or something far more complex like catching your girl in bed with a close friend. It eats at you like rot in spoiled fruit.

I wasn't sure what had happened with August and the Children, and I probably never would be. I was certain, however, that he had given my location over to them; it was the only way they would have found me. Had he sold out poor Doctor Inox as well?

Why?

His own death muddled my feelings. Hard to hate someone after they're dead. It certainly left questions unanswered. Still, Lovat Central wanted me and the Children wanted my head, and it all came back to August and our deal with Peter Black.

A mixture of betrayal and pain was twisting around my heart like a python. I needed something to loosen it up. An ice-cold glass of vermouth sounded real good right now, maybe two. I wished I could have confronted him. It would have offered some sort of closure. Some answers. With August dead, I was left adrift, lost, stumbling through the trees and blind to the forest. I both mourned for him and cursed his name.

But I couldn't even begin to deal with that tangle of emotions. Not right now.

I considered my options. Returning to Bell Caravans was out of the question; with another murder the police would increase their search. I'm well-known in the caravansaras. If I returned to one of them I was sure I'd be caught.

The wild-haired, scruffy bearded picture of me that had circulated with Thad's death would be all over the monochromes by now. Four deaths, undoubtedly pinned on me. A broker. A doctor. A merchant. A musician.

Bouchard had to be livid. I pictured him shouting at slimy Detective Muffie, throwing paper cups of lukewarm coffee across the room. He would get his way. Patrols would increase. My old picture would circulate. They'd interview people who had known me. They'd stammer statements about never picturing me as a killer. Even with my clean-cut appearance, I knew that eventually—in a city of almost ninety-three million souls—someone would recognize me. It wasn't if, it was when. Just being in Lovat was playing with fire.

Where else could I go? I needed to clear my name and I could only do that in Lovat. That would be my first step. Clear my name, then stop whoever was committing these murders. I worried if Bell Caravans would ever recover. Eighty percent of my clients came from August.

Eighty percent.

Too many.

I could think about my business later. Name first, business later. I kept thinking about another one of my old man's sayings: "A man ain't nothing without his name."

The monorail hummed as it flew past various Third Level warrens on its way north. I was done telephoning and sending telegrams. I needed help. I needed my business partner. I needed Wensem dal Ibble.

I shrank in my seat and stared out the window, hat pulled low, hood still up. I rarely went north. Humans congregated in central, south, and in West Lovat. The North wasn't for us; it was for the younger races.

When the monorail slowed, a tinny announcer's voice said, "Reservoir. Doors open on the left." My heart skipped a beat. I had only set foot in Wensem's warren once before. Reservoir was a place for maero, maybe a handful of umbra, rarely humans. Keeping my head low, I shuffled off the monorail with the other passengers.

A maero woman with narrow eyes and long white hair brushed against my shoulder. I mumbled an apology and mistakenly made eye contact with her. She blinked in surprise. I felt her eyes on me as I moved away from her, and when I cast a glance over my shoulder I saw her standing on the platform staring in my direction. I looked away and pulled my hat down lower. Had she recognized me? I decided I'd make this a quick visit. Check on Wensem and get the hell out of here.

Reservoir was nice, but not in an annoying way, with its blue-collar atmosphere, simple maero architecture, and clean, quiet streets. A few umbra passed me as I hurriedly walked down the sidewalk, cloth wrapped around their limbs, giving them the appearance of ancient mummies wearing blue mechanic coveralls. It was hard not to react. They looked at me silently, their eyes glowing dots of blue and green. I relaxed a little; blue and green was good, unlike the eyes of my assailant in Doctor Inox's office. Her eyes were red-orange—red-orange and burning with hatred.

I found Wensem's place wedged between similar buildings down Eighth Avenue. Gray, plain, and lacking adornment of any kind, the neighborhood was a reflection of prototypical maero architecture. Maero believed in utilitarian homes, without frills or decorations. They didn't build them as reflections of themselves. Homes were shelter and the construction reflected that: simple, clean, unassuming.

The opposite of most humans. Despite looking superficially similar to humans, deep down, the maero were as unlike us as kresh or cephels.

I kicked open the gate that surrounded a dead front yard and stormed up to the door. Notices of a missed telegraph delivery and my faded message from the switchboard clung to the door. I was on edge; seeing my face adorning posters along Level Three hadn't helped either.

My knock was less than gentle. I pounded my fist against the plain steel of Wensem's front door. Boom! Boom! Boom! The knock echoed in the sparse interior.

"Wensem! Let me in!"

Boom! Boom! Boom! Nothing.

"Wensem!"

Boom! Boom! Boom!

"Wensem, open up!"

"He's gone, son."

I turned and saw a maero patriarch on the stoop next door. He looked ancient beyond belief, his face a map of canyons. He smiled an old smile as he rocked in a large rocker. He clutched a small sudoku paperback and a stubby pencil in his seven long maero fingers.

"G-Gone?" I stammered. It was the best I could do.

"Gone," he repeated with a nod. "Took his mate and that newborn son of his. Went to the hill country as per direction of the lama. Bonding ritual. Didn't say when they would be back. Though I reckon it'll be a week or so from now, maybe a bit more depending on how things go."

Of course. The Bonding. A primal ritual passed down from family to family and ordered by the maero's lama when the timing was deemed right. A family surviving alone in the wilds without the conveniences of modern post-Aligning life. Their hands, their wits, each other, nothing else—this was the trial of the Bonding. The father would build shelter, provide sustenance; the mother would head the household, protect the family, and the child...the child would eat, and smile, and grow. I knew it was an important maero custom, I just hadn't expected it so soon. That's what Wensem meant when he said he would be unreachable.

I stared in silence, my rage sputtering, lacking fuel. I pulled the missed notices from the door and stuffed them into my pocket. Better to not leave a trail.

The anger washed out of me. I was exhausted. I was hungry. I couldn't keep up this rush of emotions. I think I forgave August in that moment. Dwelling on his possible betrayal messed with my head. It muddled me. I had to think clearly. I needed to keep moving. The look that maero woman had given me when I had left the monorail was making me nervous.

I had few friends remaining in Lovat. Those who weren't killed were gone, and those remaining I could barely call friends. Staring out at the plain gray houses on Wensem's plain gray street, I tried to make sense of everything. I was out of options and I needed help. I began to run through who I knew in Lovat. Who I could go to for help, who I could trust. There was my company, but I hardly knew my crew off the trail and as their boss it was my job to take care of them, not the other way around. Dragging them into this wasn't right. There was an old professor from the university I knew, but we hadn't spoken in two decades. Mrs. Sardini was too old, and she had gone through enough. I kept returning to one person, one person who had more knowledge about the Children and this bizarre killing streak than I did, one person who had asked me to leave him out of this.

Hagen Dubois.

I had to go back to Saint Olmstead's Religious Antiques and see if Hagen would be willing to help me. If he refused, the least I could do was warn him of the danger he could be in, and of this weird connection that seemed to be linking me with the umbra's victims.

Saying goodbye to the old patriarch, I headed back to the

platform to take the monorail south. It wasn't far, and as I stepped onto the platform, a pair of trains heading in opposite directions slowed to a stop. I bought my ticket as their doors slid open. Riders poured out, filling the narrow space between the trains, and I stepped in line to board at the front of the train that would take me back to King Station.

I glanced quickly over my shoulder, taking in one final look at Reservoir and its inhabitants.

My breath caught in my throat.

Down the platform, hulking like a bear on its haunches, stood Detective Bouchard. His dark eyes darted around as he studied the crowd. It was clear he had just stepped off the opposite monorail. Clearer still he was looking for someone.

I had been made.

I was sure of it now. Bouchard was here for me.

Three more figures emerged from the monorail behind the detective. Two uniformed officers brandishing clubs, and an emaciated Detective Muffie, now sporting a thick bandage over his nose.

I had to hide.

I could feel my shoulder muscles tightening as I tried to make myself smaller. I hoped the crowd would protect me. I checked the line ahead of me and noted I was only five passengers away from boarding. So close. I pulled my hat down low and shuffled my feet. I was torn between pushing myself through the queue and avoiding a scene. Bouchard hadn't spotted me—not yet anyway—and I needed to keep it that way.

Bouchard turned and marched down the platform towards

where I stood, his long dun coat billowing behind him. I tried not to look. I tried to remain anonymous. This was too close. This was much too close. I needed to get out of here. Needed to hide. Needed to disappear.

Instead I shuffled, moving with the queue. Slow but edging ever closer to the monorail. Four people ahead of me. Then three.

The platform had grown crowded as people disembarked. Bouchard disappeared into the throng, but I could still see his swooping horns among the masses. They were moving in my direction.

Carter's cross, had he spotted me?

"Ticket, sir?"

"I, er...what?" I said, looking up into the face of the maero conductor. He smiled weakly at me and held out a seven-fingered hand, "Sir, your ticket."

Heart pounding, I quickly felt my pockets. Bouchard was closing in fast. He'd spot me, or one of his cronies would, if I wasn't on that train. I had to hurry.

"Sir, do you have a ticket?"

"Ah, here it is," I said with a smile, as I pulled it out of a back pocket and handed it over to the conductor.

He looked and it, then at me, then punched the paper. "Thank you, sir. Have a nice ride."

I moved into the car and collapsed in a seat near the window. I wanted to be able to keep an eye on the platform. Know if I needed to run. The train whistled and then began to roll. Outside, Bouchard marched past, his determined eyes avoiding my train altogether. He had missed me completely.

I breathed out heavily. The muscles in my back relaxed some-what. My hands began to shake so I balled them into fists.

That had been close. So close.

I was wary at the next few stops. Worried I would see an officer board and his head would turn in my direction.

No cops came.

I began to feel safer as more and more passengers boarded. I became anonymous in the crowd. No one paid attention to the guy who seemed to snooze in the seat, head down. My heart rate slowed as it became clear I had eluded capture. That had been damn lucky. I needed to be careful.

My anonymity narrowly retained, I took some time to mull over my current predicament, and I settled on three major things. First, I was wanted by Lovat Central for crimes I didn't commit and they clearly hadn't slowed their pursuit. Second, I believed these crimes were being perpetrated by some ancient and bizarre cult who called themselves The Children, lead by some creepy umbra woman. Third, this cult was being assisted; someone was pulling strings and covering up their actions and pointing the police at me. I was the scapegoat. My assault in the pitch den was too messy, my assailant too sloppy. The Children were clearly fanatics, not professionals like the Collectors. If they had really wanted to kill me, they'd have sent the umbra.

I needed answers, motive.

I needed to see beyond the trees.

Killing without motive only works if the killer is complete-ly and utterly insane. Everything the Children did smacked of purpose. They targeted specific people and took macabre trophies, presumably for some esoteric reason. This was different from the manic wildness of the random killing. This was a dark and deliberate evil.

A clock on the wall chimed two in the afternoon as I walked through the front door of Saint Olmstead. The ticking minutes sounding like cartridges dropping into the cylinder of a revolver. I moved among the shelves of religious bric-a-brac until I found myself face-to-face with Hagen Dubois.

"I told you I didn't want to be involved," Hagen said before I was able to open my mouth. "I asked you not to contact me again."

"Look, Hagen—" I began.

"Look, nothing! I don't need to get mixed up in your shit."

"There's been another murder. Another friend of mine," I spat. "I need your help."

"Who? Who was murdered?" He asked, his interest piqued.

"A commodities broker named August Nickel. A...a friend of mine...or he was, I think he may have been working with the Children. I think he may have sold me out to them."

"By the Firsts! You think *he* was *working* with *them*?"

"Yes, I saw a few of them at his office on multiple occasions. Look, I need help, but I am also worried you might be in danger. They've killed three of my friends, and a Bonesaw who helped me out. Someone I was hardly in contact with until all this began. I wouldn't think it'd be too much of a stretch if they came after you."

"After me?"

"Do you have somewhere you can go? Somewhere safe?"

"When did this happen? Mister Nickel's murder," asked Hagen, setting an armload of boxed candles down on the shelf. "When exactly?"

"Sometime early this morning. Before light."

He stared at me. Looking both tired and scared.

"Hagen, I didn't mean to drag you into this, but there's some connection to me. There's some reason they're after people I know. I got no one to turn to, so I came here. I know you didn't want to be pulled into this...."

"Mister Bell, I have a shop to run. I can't have wanted felons running in here every—"

He stopped abruptly as the door behind me chimed.

"Carter's cross," swore Hagen, taking a step back.

I turned.

An ugly human with a flat nose and almond-shaped eyes slipped around the door. His close-cropped hair exposed a lumpy head, and he had the thick neck and broad chest of a weightlifter. He sneered at us.

"This your shop?" he asked in accented Strutten.

"It is, welcome to Saint Olmstead's Religi—oh my..."

The human grinned wickedly as he reached into his rust red coat, pulling out a straight razor identical to the one I had seen in the umbra's hand. He began to chant as he sauntered toward us, "We are the thousand young. The Children of Pan. We are the ushers of sta—"

Not thinking, I lunged. Feeling my arm and ribs cry out as I crashed into the assailant, sending his knife spinning away. He grunted and I brought up a knee, slamming it into his stomach. He let out a wheeze. He pushed up on my chin with a palm and struck at my shoulder and chest with balled fists. My gunshot wound howled in pain and my broken rib cursed me.

"Let....me...go..." he growled through clenched teeth.

He was smaller than me, but solid. I lifted him and shoved him back down, a sickening crack sounding as his head slammed on the old tile floor. My assault was just making him angrier.

"The razor!" I shouted at Hagen. "Get his razor!"

"You're the Guardian!" said the attacker, his eyes growing wide. The ugly little man was slippery, and he wormed out of my grip and tried to crawl away. Leaping, I crashed onto his shoulders, forcing him back to the ground.

Hagen stepped back, grabbing the straight razor in the process. He held it out, awkwardly whipping it back and forth.

The attacker forced the words of his chant through gritted teeth, "We...are...the...thousand...young...the...childre—"

Straddling him, I lifted and shoved the attacker's head down into the tiled floor a second time; his chanting stopped. I repeated the motion again a third time, then a fourth. The tiles below his head were cracked and stained with blood. Hagen stopped me before the fifth.

"He's out. Wal, h-he's out. Wal, you knocked him out!" yelled Hagen.

I rolled off the man and leaned next to a shelf of statuettes. I kicked the unconscious Child of Pan in the ribs for good measure. Stupid son of a bitch.

I spoke through tattered breaths, "They won't stop, Hagen.

They'll send their assassin. I've seen what she can do. She's dangerous.

"It's a twisted little game and now you're connected. I wish you weren't—by the Firsts, I wish you weren't—but you are. Their assassin. I saw her. I fought her. Walked in as she was cutting off the hands of the Bonesaw I mentioned. She'll slip in, you'll never see her, by then it'll be too late. Come with me, go on your own, but just go. Lock up shop and leave. Leave until I can sort this out."

Hagen said nothing. He stared at the straight razor in his hands, and then looked at me.

"I'm sorry," I said, meaning it. "I really am."

"How do you plan on sorting this out?"

I spoke honestly, "I have no idea. I have some thin leads. Ideas mainly. I might know the identity of our Black Goat."

"You need help."

"I do," I admitted.

"If I help you...."

"I'll do my best to protect you," I said, interrupting. "You and yours. I promise. I've been fighting these assholes alone. Two of us would be stronger. I have to end this. I have to stop them. My name is tarnished, I've got nothing unless I can pin these killings on them."

"What is a man without his name?" said Hagen, as if quoting my old man.

"Something like that," I said. "In the end it doesn't matter about me anymore, it's much bigger than that. If Lovat Central locks me away the Children will still be out here. Out here killing innocent people and taking body parts."

Seconds passed, feeling like hours.

The assailant breathed deeply, completely unconscious. Blood dribbled from his nose, pooling around his ugly little face. I watched Hagen study the razor he held in his hand.

"We need to hide," he said. "My shop isn't safe anymore."

"Any ideas?"

"Saint Mark's," said Hagen. "I know a priestess there."

FOURTEEN

The Reunified Church is as old as anything in our ancient world. According to historians, the Aligning had been disastrous: civilizations had collapsed, governments had crumbled, cities had been destroyed. The pre-Aligning church hadn't weathered the upheaval well, and generations of disputes had weakened its foundations. In the years before the Aligning, the great religions of the world had become more and more fragmented.

There's an old saying about standing united but falling divided. There's a truth in that. The more and more fractured something gets, the weaker it becomes. I had a road priest once describe it to me as soft ice. It appears solid, but there's so many tiny fractures that the ice shatters when even the slightest pressure is applied.

It's a good metaphor for the earth, pre-Aligning. A majority of the world's population was decimated, and with it, so too were the faithful. Waters swallowed up cities, fires burned the mountains, and the Firsts themselves supposedly wreaked havoc over their dominion.

Denominations of millions became sects of thousands. Sects of thousands became fellowships of hundreds, and fellowships of hundreds were scattered like leaves before a storm.

Legend says Brother Ebenezer Alvord gathered the surviving priests together and sent them out as missionaries to the survivors. They were to traverse the world, reunite the broken, heal decimated sects of the church, and call the faithful home.

Whereas leaders before him were harsh in their order, Alvord spoke only of peace. The past was forgiven. Old rules that had driven wedges between the faiths were ignored. His kind manner and his tender touch worked, and the Reunified Church formed, uniting under a patchwork banner.

Saint Mark's was older than all that: older than the Reunified Church, older than Ebenezer Alvord, older than the Aligning. It was a relic.

It's the kind of building you wish you could see in the sunlight. A massive structure of right angles and sharp horizontal lines. Built on the solid ground of Broadway Hill, it extended from the floor of Level Four and through the roof and up into the floor of Level Five. It looked more like a fortress than a place of worship, standing tall even with the weight of five levels on its shoulders.

"My father was a priest," explained Hagen as we stood outside the structure. "Joined after our mother died. Raised my sister and me in the church."

"Is that how you got into the idol business?"

He grimaced. "My father wasn't pleased. He wanted me to be a priest and follow him in taking to the cloth, but I never heard the calling. Didn't care much for a life of service."

"Any particular reason?" I asked.

"Always seemed...ah...tedious. I'd rather choose my own direction." He sighed. "It was my sister who fulfilled his wishes. Took her vows when she was twenty, always the more obedient one. He was so proud, so very proud."

"So your sister's...?"

"She's the Reunified priestess I know," He said with a smile. "She's a professor for the seminary, working mainly as a historian—so much was lost during the Aligning. She teaches a few theology classes, 'training up future soldiers' as my father often says."

I flinched slightly at the word soldier. It wasn't far off, depending on who you talked to. Tensions had cooled between the Hasturian faith and the Reunified Church in the last decade, but I remembered hearing radio reports about battles between the two churches when I was a kid. Bombings. Murders. Assassinations. All-out assaults had erupted in those days.

The vestiges of a life lived under that constant state of fear still lingered on the cathedral's grounds. We passed through checkpoints and moved past gates built into thick walls under the watchful eye of angular guard towers where black-cloaked, stern-faced monks waited, rifles held in the crooks of their arms.

"They like their security," said Hagen.

We walked across a lawn of crushed rocks and passed an open parking lot that hadn't seen a functioning motor coach or fourgon in probably three generations. The front doors loomed before us. Reliefs of lion heads were carved into the facade and their lifeless eyes stared down on us in judgment.

Hagen knocked, the noise muffled by the massive door. I swallowed. I'm not a religious person. I avoid the Hasturians, don't go in much for the teachings of the Deepers, and I'm not one for all the ritual and the prayers of the Reunifieds. I do appreciate their trail chapels that dot the countryside between here and Syringa. The road priests who run those small parishes are often warm, kindly folk with a hot bowl of soup and a ladle of rustwine for a weary traveler. They don't tend to be the preaching types, and that suits me just fine.

Hagen knocked again, the taps sounding almost silent against the aged wood.

"Think they heard us?" I asked.

"They heard us," he said with a smile. Looking back at the checkpoints we had passed, he added, "They know we're here."

The big door swung inward silently on its ancient hinges. Standing just inside was a round little dauger priest. Beady eyes stared at us through the slits in his mask as he sized us up.

His mask was beautiful, not something one often sees among the dauger. Silver-inlaid with a gold filigree, it caught the light from a thousand small candles. Rare metals were uncommon in dauger masks; an expensive mask like this meant the bearer was a child or grandsire from one of the five precious families: the Golds, the Platinas, the Argentums of South Wold, the Osmiyums, or the Palladios of Casement. In all my days, I had never seen a member of the five families in Lovat, never seen a dauger in a mask so expensive, and I was surprised to find one here, a servant to the cloth.

"Can I help you?" asked the dauger. His voice placid. Almost bored.

"Yes, actually. Is Mother Samantha Dubois in?" Hagen asked. He shifted his small pack from one shoulder to another. Our rush from his shop had been hurried. Hagen had been grabbing small books and tomes, sticking them in his pockets and locking cases as he stuffed clean laundry atop pages of manuscripts. We had lost a whole hour by the time he locked the cage doors that secured his store.

"Can I ask who is calling?" asked the priest.

"Her brother—Hagen Dubois—and a friend."

The dauger turned his gaze to study my face. "He have a name?"

"He does, but he likes to keep it to himself," I stated.

The dauger's shoulders jerked back. He sucked in an offended gasp.

"Please just tell her we are here."

The dauger stared at me for a moment longer before he spoke. "One moment," he said, his hushed voice laced with disdain.

"Think he recognized me?"

"Perhaps, but he'd inform the other clergy before going to the police."

"How do you know?"

He chuckled. "Well, for one, I am in a family of clergy. I can promise you Reunifieds don't relish the idea of Lovat Central mucking around in church business any more than a shopkeep does. 'Bad for business,' as some might say."

I thought of Thad and smiled. I wondered what he would have thought of this place. Saint Mark's was a wonder, a building unlike anything I had ever seen before. Beautiful glass windows broke up the dark stone walls; above me the ancient wood ceiling—black from generations of candles burning in the nave—loomed like a thundercloud. On the floor was an inlaid tile labyrinth. I watched a few parishioners mill about until my musings were interrupted by the clack of heels on tile.

I looked up and inhaled quickly. One of the most beautiful dimanian women I had ever seen was walking across the nave toward us. She carried herself with pride and determination, head and shoulders back, chin jutting forward like the prow of a sailing ship. A nest of wild dark curls framed an oval face; at its center was a narrow nose and large dark eyes the color of burnt caramel. Her full lips—tinted a deep red—were curled into a smirk as she glided toward us. She wore the robes of a priest, but had foregone the gold belt; it fluttered behind her, exposing the far more normal clothing beneath. Tight trousers clung to shapely legs, and a white silk blouse was tucked in at the waist. She was definitely dimanian, but her features were subtle; no wild horn grew from her temples like her brother's, but small boney protrusions sprouted from either side of her chin and near each temple just above her cheekbones.

Carter's cross, she was beautiful. Was it wrong to lust after a priestess? And in a cathedral? I swallowed, feeling the heat rise along my brow.

"Big brother!" she said, her voice deeper than I had expected, throaty. "It's good to see you! What brings you to Broadway Hill?"

"Sam!" said Hagen. They embraced. When they broke apart Hagen drew back and, giving her an appraising once-over, said, "You look good. Have you lost weight?"

She punched him in the arm. "Hardly, you should see the tables the sisters set before us. All cheese, butter, and potatoes. I'm lucky I'm not the size of an ox."

They both laughed, hugged, and made small talk. Eventually she turned her dark brown eyes in my direction. I swallowed nervously, feeling as if she could probe into my thoughts. My very dirty thoughts.

"Who is this?" she asked with a smirk. A smirk that could melt ice. A tussle of her dark curls slumped from her forehead and into her face, but she blew it away. "Friend of yours?"

"Of a sort. Um, Mother Samantha Dubois, meet Caravan Master Waldo Bell."

"Call me Wal," I said, extending a hand. I could feel my palms sweating.

She stared at me, eyes betraying nothing. Eventually she placed her hand in mine and shook. Her grip was firm, her hand warm and soft. I noticed spurs of bone—similar to Hagen's but slightly smaller—running along her knuckles.

"Call me Sam," she said, matter-of-factly.

"Call me Wal," I repeated.

"You said that already."

"Er...right. Nice to meet you," I babbled.

Sam studied me, her eyes lingering on me a brief moment, leaving me feeling both nervous and giddy. Was I supposed to bow? Kiss her hand? I had no idea how to act with a priestess. After a heartbeat or two she turned back to her brother.

"What brings you to Saint Mark's?"

Hagen looked at me and then at his sister. "Trouble. A lot of trouble. Do you have a place we can talk privately?"

Sam's office was small but cozy. The desk she sat behind was dark, ancient, and gleamed with generations of careful oiling. A crucifix hung on a wall above a bookcase filled with various tomes and texts. Statuettes of saints and virgins stood on shelves all around the office in prominent places: silent witnesses to our conversation.

On lower shelves were glass domes holding bizarre antiques of a darker nature. In one I spied a mummified hand dipped in wax, candles on each finger. In another dome there was a twisted and deformed skull of a dimanian, the bone carved with all manner of occult symbols and strange writing. In a massive glass jar that sat between two dry, old tomes was what appeared to be a cephel hatchling preserved in a yellow liquid, tentacles curled tightly like huge fiddleheads. A menagerie of curios. In a lot of ways the decor reminded me of Hagen's shop, minus the price tags.

"This place feels familiar," I joked. "You two trade decorators?"

Samantha looked up at me from a set of papers she was studying on her desk and I deflated a little. "Not really. I do, however, happen to be one of Hagen's biggest clients. I'm a collector of sorts."

"These aren't Reunified statuary—not all of it at least," I said, tapping a jar holding what looked to be a petrified bok egg. "I'm no church man but I can't imagine the church is keen on keeping this sort of stuff on the grounds."

"They have all been deconsecrated as required. They're all important to my studies," she explained.

Hagen interrupted, "Sam is one of the church's leading authorities on ancient religions in Lovat. She also knows a great deal about active cults and sects operating in the territories. Most of these have to do with something in her studies or as an object lesson in one of her lectures."

I looked at the beautiful priestess that sat across from me with a deepening respect. "Why didn't you call her before?"

"Before? Before what, Wal? Before all this, you were just a guy who had walked into my shop and asked me to identify some patch. Before all this I had no idea who you were. You could have just been another one of the Children. Your face is all over the monochromes. I wanted to answer your questions and move on. Before all this, I didn't want anything to do with you."

"And now?" I asked.

"Now...now for better or worse...we're in this together. You stepped forward and saved me. If there's one thing I took away from the attack at my shop, it's that they tied me to you. I'm drawn in and it doesn't matter if I like it or not."

"Wait, attack? What attack? What are you talking about?" Samantha asked. Her eyes were wide.

"Well..." Hagen began.

Samantha folded her arms across her chest and stared at him coolly. Hagen gave a sheepish grin and then explained the story, starting with the first time I had walked into his shop and ending with us arriving at the door to Saint Marks.

"Sorry," I said, feeling ashamed. This whole ordeal was my fault. That, I could and would readily admit. There was little sense in denying it.

"I don't blame you, Wal. There's no way you could have known. You aren't crazy, I know that much. You're as lost as I am. We're now both being hunted and neither of us knows why. If anything, I feel bad for you because you're the one being blamed for these murders."

"Wait," Sam interrupted. "You're the guy on the monochrome? The Collector Killer?"

"The Collector Killer?" I asked, wrinkling my nose at the nickname. "That's the best they could do?"

"You don't look like him," said Sam. "He had a lot more hair and a—"

"I shaved. I'm 'him,' but I'm not 'him' if you catch my meaning."

"You didn't kill those people?"

"By the Firsts, no!" I swore, catching myself as it slipped out. "Damn. Sorry. Damn, er...darn, sorry for that."

Sam chuckled; it was warm and inviting. "Swearing by the Firsts means nothing here."

I looked at Hagen. "Look, if I knew my visit would have drawn them to you—"

"You didn't. Don't apologize. We have a lot to go over."

"Tell me your story," said Sam, turning her eyes to me.

Looking at her, I had to clamp down on my emotions. I felt like I could get lost in the dark pools of her eyes. It was a struggle to speak, but I eventually found my voice and told her my tale, allowing Hagen to interject here and there. She listened carefully as I laid everything out in detail: the murders, the Children, August's betrayal, the mysterious Black Goat. Everything.

I leaned back when I was finished. My mouth was dry.

Sam studied me and I felt both elated and nervous. She sat in silence for a long time before finally turning to her big brother.

"Pan, you said?"

He nodded. "I wasn't sure of the origin. Seemed ancient human from my limited materials."

"Why didn't you call me earlier? I've helped you out before."

Hagen smiled. "Didn't want to bother you. It seemed open and shut. Nothing that needed deep scrutiny from the church's lead historian in documented cults and sects."

She laughed. "Still, I wish you'd come to me. I might have some material we could look at, I'll check. First, you two look like you need a shower, a hot meal, a change of clothes, and a good night's sleep."

I must have perked up at this because Sam laughed, the noise sending tingles down my spine.

"That sounds like too much to ask," I said.

"Being polite will get you nowhere, Mister Bell. We have open beds in the rectory. You and Hagen are welcome to them.

I'll take you to the showers and have the brothers bring you a change of clothes. They won't be stylish, but they'll be clean."

I was overwhelmed by the generosity.

"Thanks," I stammered.

"You're a guest of the Reunified Church, think nothing of it. We'll hit the books tomorrow."

The shower was incredible. I felt like I was reborn as the hot water steamed pleasantly against my skin. I was careful to wash and clean my wounds; the bullet hole had torn open in my struggle in Hagen's shop, but it looked clean enough.

Suds from the lye soap sloshed the sweat and filth from nights spent in pitch dens and cheap hostels off my skin. When I finished, I stood before a mirror in the bathroom and shaved the stubble from my jaw. Then I redressed my wounds with the clean bandages the brothers of Saint Mark's had generously provided.

A stone-colored outfit of simple linen trousers and matching shirt was laid out for me. I watched as two monks took my clothes away to be washed. It felt silly to wear the monks' uniform, but it'd be a lie if I told you it wasn't nice to feel clean clothes against clean skin.

After we were refreshed, we ate in the dining hall in some lower level of the cathedral. The food tasted phenomenal. Rich roast with brown gravy and potatoes, whitefish poached with butter, and freshly baked bread still steaming as it was torn open. I felt as if I was walking on clouds.

I ate leisurely, laughing as I got to know both Hagen and Samantha. They spun stories about their childhood. How Samantha always got in trouble and Hagen was always spending time with his nose in a book. How disappointed their father had been with Hagen's decision and how he had grown to accept both his children's callings. They spoke kindly about their father, who was recently appointed Cardinal for a large parish in Destiny.

When neither Hagen nor I could eat anymore, Samantha led us to the dormitory for the monks. Row after row of single beds outfitted with white sheets and thick comforters covered the room. A few brothers snoozed lazily.

"Women aren't allowed inside," she explained. "Sheets are changed daily, so take whatever bed is open. Come find me in the morning."

Hagen kissed his sister on the cheek and disappeared into the gloom inside with a thank you.

Samantha and I were left alone in the hallway.

I smiled at her. "Thanks for all this. I mean it. I felt so lost these last two days. You and your brother's help has been—" I choked on the words.

"Don't mention it, Wal," she said, looking up at me with those dark eyes.

I felt like leaning down and kissing her, but fought off the urge. I had just met her, and she didn't seem to regard me as anything more than a charity case. It was probably just the stress making me feel infatuated over a little kindness.

Besides, she was a Reunified Priestess, and this was her cathedral. I was no scholar, but kissing her here felt improper, if not outright sinful.

"G-Goodnight," I stammered stupidly. What had I been thinking?

"See you in the morning."

I wondered if I heard a bit of disappointment in her voice, and that thought made it more than difficult to fall asleep. When I did fall asleep, I slept like the dead.

Both Hagen and I woke around mid-morning. We ate the last of the breakfast in the dining hall and walked the bustling corridors to Samantha's office. Students whispered to one another, monks strode by silently, and the Sisters of the Cross huddled in groups around foyers. Saint Mark's felt alive and vibrant despite its age.

Samantha was wearing her vestments as we entered. Apparently we had slept through the morning's services, but she had taken the time afterward to gather a seemingly endless number of texts, tomes, scrolls, and prophecies from her own and Saint Mark's libraries.

They stood in a pile on her desk, a model of Lovat's skyline formed from ancient texts.

"Good morning," she said in that intoxicating voice. "If I didn't know better, Wal, I'd have passed you off as one of my students."

I looked down at my stone-colored outfit, then back up at Sam, smiling awkwardly.

"What are all these?" asked Hagen, staring lustily at the books.

"Tomes, dear brother, old tomes. You'll love them."

"Pre-Aligning?" he asked, reaching for a small book the color of mud and the size of a sandwich.

"Almost all of them. I did a bit of research last night and pulled any references I could find on your Children, the Black Goat, and Pan. I figured we could spend the morning researching and seeing if we could come up with anything more. There's a lot here, as you can see, so we have our work cut out for us."

"I'll say," I said.

Sam smiled at me. It was everything I could do not to melt into my seat.

"You take this book," she said, handing me a yellowing book entitled *The Alabaster Realm*. "That one's a long shot, but it's a good starting point."

Hagen picked up another and Sam a third.

"So what do we do?" I asked.

"We read," said Hagen, tossing me a pad of paper and a pen. "If we find anything, we tell one another. Keep notes. Any mention of the keywords: the Children, Black Goat, Baphomet, Baal, Pan, Puck—write it down."

I rolled my eyes.

"None of that, caravan boy," said Samantha playfully. "We don't win the race by slacking off."

We dove into our studies, and I found it to be tedious and boring work. Page after page, chapter after chapter, word after word, I slogged through until my eyes felt like they would fall out of their sockets.

We had food brought to us and left it sitting untouched until it was cold. We drank buckets of coffee and continued to pour over tomes. We returned to the dormitory for a few hours of sleep, only to wake and head back to Samantha's office to crack open a new volume of *Alhazred's Treatise of Sana* or another of the *Nineteen Verses of Roland*.

We read, we took notes, we discussed until our eyes were red and our throats raw. This went on for three days. Three long days of tedious, neck-stiffening research. I'm not a researcher. I'm a caravaneer, a roader. I'm not keen on books in general; I'd rather learn what I need to learn from the trail. I found the process hard and I was growing more and more exhausted.

It wasn't until late the third day that we finally broke through our wall.

"I think I found something," Samantha said abruptly. She had been deep in an old leather-bound book with a bizarre twisted star shape on its worn spine. It jolted me out of some paragraph in a bestiary that was doing its best to put me to sleep. "I think I found a link to the Children." She paused and stared down at the pages before her. "...I...think."

She didn't sound too sure, but looked stunned. I rose and stood behind her. It was probably two or three in the morning. I yawned.

"What's the book?" asked Hagen.

"*Heredity & Lineage of the Firsts*, written by a Doctor Howard Softly in some previous age. According to Softly this is the most comprehensive listing of the family trees extending from the Firsts since the time of Alignment."

I looked down at a page of oddly twisted shapes. There didn't seem to be any order—no common lines of characters I was used to seeing in language. It wasn't anything I could read. "Looks like a bunch of scribbles."

"This is Aklo. An ancient language, long dead. I haven't seen it used in years."

"You can read it?"

"I wouldn't call my skills fluent, but I can translate some of it. Aklo is a bizarre language, no strict set of rules, so I find myself sorta bumbling around. It's not the easiest to read, and it's even harder to translate."

Hagen came around the desk and leaned over her shoulder.

"Aklo?" he said intrigued. "By the Firsts, I haven't seen an Aklo text in years. That's got to be worth a fortune."

"It's the church's. Came from the library," She explained, reading his mind. "Don't think about offering to buy it. It's the only copy we have, so I doubt the elders would be keen to part with it."

Hagen gave a sheepish smile.

"What's it say?" I asked, getting us back to the topic of our research. "What's the link?"

"Well, if my translation is correct, the Children are mentioned as direct descendants of a creature called Cybele—Cybill in Strutten. At their birth, according to this, there were a thousand of them. All their names are listed, and their sons and daughters, fourteen generations' worth. Goes on for pages and pages."

"So there're thousands of them?" I groaned.

"Well, this book is several hundred years old," Samantha said. "There could be far more than that or there could be far fewer. We have no idea."

"None of the Children I have seen look related. They've been everything from humans, to maero, to kresh—usually a family is of the same species. Carter's cross, the guys I saw outside of Coming & Goings were as good a mix as any."

"It's possible they have distant blood links to Cybill," said Hagen. "We know the races of earth all came from humans. Mostly."

"So if they are the sons and daughters—even metaphorically—of Cybill, why the connection to Pan? Why wear Pan's symbol when you're the Children of something else?"

Samantha chewed on the end of her little finger, turned back a few pages, and studied the Aklo script. I went back to my chair and left her to her translating.

After a few moments she jabbed a finger down on the page. "The father!"

Hagen jumped and looked up at me.

"What?" I said.

"The father! There are two characters here. One is the father and Cybill is the mother. I switched two of the marks around an—"

"I don't understand? Spell it out for me." I was back on my feet, leaning forward across her desk. From my vantage point I could see down her shirt. I fought to keep from staring at the round tops of her breasts.

She looked up, caught my wandering eyes, and rolled her own. I felt stupid again. Reading into that kindness of hers as some sort of sexual attraction. My head was a mess.

Hagen was oblivious. "The text is confusing. I thought it was just a mistake. Sometimes Softly refers to Cybill with the feminine pronoun, and other times he uses the masculine form. I wonder if in his own way Softly was describing both the mother and the father."

"I'm even more confused," I said, abandoning my breast-watching perch for the comfort of my chair.

"Yeah," said Samantha. She looked down at the page again and read, "So all the generations of Cybill who came to earth after the Aligning of the stars were brought forth, united by he with the thousand young—"

"Thousand young," said Hagen. Interrupting her, he snapped his fingers as if remembering something. "I knew that sounded familiar. That's what the attacker in my shop had chanted. Thousand young, Children of Pan."

"But these aren't Pan's children. These are Cybill's. Are you sure there's a connection?" I asked.

"The text is very specific: the thousand young. The Children," said Samantha.

"Is Pan in that book?" I asked.

She shrugged and flipped through the pages. "I didn't see him, wait...ah yeah here he is, sort of."

"What do you mean?"

"Well, he's not labeled as Pan; instead he's labeled as Puck."

"The name is interchangeable," said Hagen. "I saw that in my own research. You may also see him listed as a bunch of other things. Baphomet. The Black Goat."

Samantha flipped back in the old tome. "Yeah, the goat thing. Cybill is also referred to as a goat. Yes, right here, the Black Goat who bore a thousand young. Wait, here she's referred to as a ram. That's the mother and father thing I was talking about. Softly isn't clear."

"Black goat," I repeated. Letting the word hang on my tongue.

"I'd wager my entire shop that's a reference to Pan," said Hagen, a smile breaking through his beard.

"So Cybill is the lover of Pan, maybe this Black Goat, and the Mother of the Children. The Children who seem very devoted to their father," I began. "I still don't understand how it ties into these murders or ties into me."

Samantha flipped between the pages listing Cybill's children and the pages of Pan's. "There're some divergences but they are minor: names misspelled, missing family members, that sort of thing, but both lists are pretty much the same. I'm going to go out on a limb, but I think Pan might be our father and Cybill the mother. Both are called goats, and Pan is definitely male."

"Hagen had dug up a lot of information on that after I left his shop." I looked up at him.

"Yeah, it wasn't much," he admitted.

"When you first told me about the whole Black Goat thing my former employer, Wilem, Black & Bright, was the only connection I could make."

"I remember you mentioning them." Samantha said. "Do you think there's a connection? Black is a common enough surname."

"It's all I have. August told me both Wilem and Bright were dead. That leaves Black. Only Black." A thought struck me, "You know what? I'm wrong. It doesn't leave only Black. When I ran into August's tenant, Mrs. Sardini, I asked her about a group of guys I could swear were part of the Children. She mentioned a Robby Wilem. Said they looked like a bunch of Robby's friends."

"A Robby Wilem, you hadn't mentioned a Robby Wilem," said Samantha.

"I forgot," I said, feeling like I was onto something. "Does the church keep any city records here? Births, obits, that sort of thing?"

She shook her head, "No. You'd need to go to the library for that sort of stuff."

I frowned. I was still spooked by my close call on the monorail platform a few days earlier. Stepping outside Saint Mark's wasn't the safest decision I could make right now.

"It's probably best you don't poke your head out," Hagen said. "Not right now."

"I agree with Hagen," said Sam, "I can go. What is it you think we should be looking for?"

"Robby's father. I want to know if there is a Wilem family connection to the Children."

"Wal, what makes you think there will be a connection?"

I shrugged, "I don't know. It just feels like this is too much of a coincidence. Robby Wilem hanging out with the Children, August's connection to Wilem, Black, and Bright, and somehow all this starting after I finished a run for that particular organization."

"I'll pull what I can," said Samantha, rising from her chair and pulling a coat off a wall hook. "You two stretch your legs and we'll meet back here in a few hours."

"Dr. Raymond Wilem, forty-eight, Lovat, died at his home last night from complications relating to thrombosis. Dr. Wilem was one of the three founding partners of the import and export firm Wilem, Black & Bright where he has worked for sixteen years. He was a member of Carcosa Grove Hasturian Church and the Lovatine Rotary Club. He enjoyed gardening, cribbage, and liked to think of himself as an amateur historian. He is survived by his son, his wife Helen Machen-Wilem, and his business partner Peter Black. Funeral services will be held... blah, blah, blah, blah." I stopped reading and looked up from the obituary. "Is this it?"

"I did a cross check on Wilem, Black, & Bright," said Samantha, "It didn't turn up anything much. Any searches I did on the Rotary Club only returned a boring list of public minutes."

"Any lead on the name of the son?" I asked.

She shook her head. "Not from the obit."

"What about Carcosa Grove?" asked Hagen.

She pulled out a single sheet of paper. "That turned up something."

"Oh?" I asked.

She laid out a clipping of a photograph taken from what looked to be a church newsletter on her desk. I picked it up, squinting at the poorly copied clipping. It showed two blurry men, a portly human and what I guessed was a handsome dimanian standing side by side in a park, arms around each other's shoulders. In his other arm, the dimanian held what appeared to be a baby. Below the photograph, the caption read, "New father Ray Wilem, son Robby, and Peter Black, godfather, enjoy the lamp light of mid afternoon at the Carcosa Grove church picnic."

Robby.

We were getting close. I could feel it. Robby Wilem had to be near thirty now, but he still had a father figure in his life, his godfather Peter Black. Was Black really our Black Goat? Was he the leader of the Children pulling his godson's strings, or was Robby acting alone? Either way there was something here, some connection. Coincidences can only be ignored when they are random. All these little coincidences were knotted together. Something was going on, something that tied into these murders. The ritual of it all. The timing.

What *had* I brought back with me from Syringa? What *was* in that crate? Why had that delivery started a chain reaction of murders throughout Lovat?

We had a trail, but it left us with as many questions as it had answers.

I knew what I needed to do.

"I need to go have a talk with Mister Black."

FIFTEEN

The doorman stood before the Hotel Arcadia like a gar-
goyle in a white calf-length jacket. I had forgotten about
the doorman. There would be no way I could get around him.
No way I could slip past his stern gaze and the iron hand that
wrapped around the handle of the hotel's entrance.

It had only been my letter that had gotten me past him on
my last visit. Fresh from the trail, covered in the dust of the road,
it was clear without the letter he would have never let me past.
Looking down at the clothes I was wearing now, it was obvious
to me that he would have the same reaction. My old jeans were
washed but still faded and stained. The shirt I had borrowed
from the rectory was too large and too plain to belong to a tenant
of the Hotel Arcadia. The jacket I had picked up in West Lovat
had started to fray, and the edge of my ball cap was stained from
sweat. It was ratty attire that wouldn't help get me past the front
door, let alone higher into the building.

My options were limited. I needed to somehow trick the

bastard into letting me inside. I considered bribery, but I was running out of the money August had loaned me. Forgery might work, but the doorman was clearly not an idiot, and I didn't have a way to forge credentials anyway. A direct assault passed through my mind and was pushed away like dust in a windstorm. He was twice my size, and I was already wounded; it would be a suicidal charge.

So I found myself sitting across from the Hotel Arcadia, staring at the hustle and bustle of the entrance, and wondering how I would ever get inside when my answer came. Literally. It arrived at the entrance, rolling to a stop on fat rubber wheels. It was enormous, stretched out, bigger than any cargowain I had ever seen. While the driver was clearly visible in the cockpit, blackened windows hid the occupants in the rear.

A motor coach such as that, in a city like Lovat, was the epitome of extravagance. Few roads curled between the levels, and those that did were usually choked with pedestrians or impassable from years of neglect. It was possible that this coach hadn't left Level Seven in hundreds of years. Which made its use that much more excessive.

The driver, a short human in a smart uniform, stepped out and crossed behind it, pulling open a door at the rear of the vehicle opposite of where I stood. A plan burst into my mind like a gunshot.

Edging forward and keeping myself low, I came up to the door on the left side of the coach, listening as the riders each exited in a nice line. I slowly undid the latch. Only two of the passengers remained inside: twin boys spending most of their energy trying to push past one another to follow their siblings and parents up to the open door of the Hotel Arcadia. I slipped in behind them, leaving the door behind me open.

The father—a tall, lanky man in his early sixties—handed a wad of lira to the doorman and began making small talk. The two boys I shadowed finally came to an agreement, bounding from the stretched motor coach as I slipped out behind them, apologizing to the driver who had almost shut the door on me. He stared at me with confusion and began to speak, his voice growing louder behind me as I hurried my pace, careful to stay with my adopted family, my ticket inside.

If the doorman noticed me, he didn't say anything. He was probably too distracted by the rich guy chatting him up. I passed through the passage and into the lobby unmolested.

The acquisition of the lift token was easier. The girl behind the ancient counter didn't even look up, just slid a plastic disk at me with an annoyed sigh and went back to her novel.

Jamming the token into the slot, I hoped it would break the mechanism inside to allow anyone to use the elevators freely. Damn the hassle of the tokens. Sadly, it didn't seem to have an effect. The shiny doors slid open and I stepped inside, punched the button marked fifty-one, and let the slow ride fuel my anger. The last time I had been in this elevator, Wensem had been standing next to me. Now I was alone. Alone with my thoughts.

There was no paycheck to pick up at the end of my ride, no hope for a warm meal afterwards, no month off exploring Lovat's culinary treasures as I had planned. This was a much different visit. This time it would be just me, Peter Black, and my arsenal of questions.

Samantha and Hagen hadn't been pleased with my decision. Hagen thought I was being rash, and Samantha had agreed, adding that a violent confrontation wouldn't help my cause. Before we had all turned in for the night they had warned me of the dangers. I was convinced last night, but my mind had spun. I hadn't slept. Questions kept snapping through my mind, and by morning I had stopped caring about the risks. I was convinced that Black was just as involved as his godson.

Keep a distance between yourself and other travelers.

"Travelers" in this situation could be Black. I didn't care. It was worth the risk. If Peter Black wanted a war, he was going to get one, and I was going to bring it to his doorstep. I wasn't going to be threatened. I was the type of man who would stand before my aggressor. I wanted to meet the individual who was playing with my life, look into his eyes, and tell him that we were onto him. We were circling, hunting him, and we weren't afraid of him, his umbra assassin, or his devoted army of thugs.

"What if you're recognized?" Hagen had asked me. "Your face is all over the city."

"Then I run, I hide. I've been running since this whole damn thing started. I can do it a few more times if I have to."

Hagen had just stared at me, confused.

"Eventually you won't be able to escape," Samantha said. "Your luck will eventually run out. You've seen how tenacious his followers have been, attacking you in the middle of the day, during a police raid, walking into Hagen's shop."

"It's a risk I have to take," I explained. "I need to see him."

They didn't understand. They wanted to remain at Saint Mark's, continue the research, build a case. To them, going after Black was foolish. Hagen felt it would drive Robby Wilem underground or expose us to Black, so we'd never be able to find either of them again. Samantha thought the connections were too thin; if we revealed too much, it would allow him time to prepare an adequate alibi.

I argued about his arrogance, the brashness of the murders.

"He's playing with us, like a cat with a mouse." They didn't buy it.

The lift dinged as I passed another floor. My breath came out in hot puffs as I rose. As the lift moved closer and closer to the fifty-first floor my courage began to falter.

What if Samantha and Hagen were right? What if this was foolish, what if there was an army of Children inside the doors of Black's offices waiting for me? What if Black used this visit against me? If he was connected he'd never lift a finger, would never do anything to clear my name. Now—so close to my destination—I was wondering if Hagen and Sam hadn't been right, if maybe I should have stayed at Saint Mark's.

The lift made the decision for me as it slowed and opened its ancient doors.

It was mid-morning, and being so high above the scrape and span, I found myself squinting at the bright, unobstructed sunlight that shone through the windows at the end of the hall. I stepped out of the elevator for the second time and made my way to the frosted door with the hand-painted letters that read:

Wilem, Black & Bright.

I took a deep breath, summoned whatever fragment of courage I could muster, and pushed the door open.

The same smartly decorated waiting area held the same square leather furniture. The same detailed etchings still hung in their extravagant frames. The receptionist still sat behind her richly appointed desk. Big wooden doors were set into the wood-paneled walls, leading to offices and hallways. One behind the receptionist's desk was marked with a golden plaque that read: "Peter Black, Partner."

"Can I help you?" asked the receptionist. The bored dauger wearing the reflective mask with the cobalt blue sheen. She had her hair in a tight bun on the back of her head and wore a pant suit of cobalt that matched her mask.

"Is Mister Black in?" I demanded.

"Do you have an appointment?" she asked, cocking her head to one side like a spaniel.

"Is he in?"

"You'll need an appointment, sir."

I pushed past the desk, seeing red.

"Sir! Sir! SIR! You can't just barge in here like that. You can't—! Sir! I'll call security! I'll call, you'll end up in jail!"

Ignoring her, I pushed open the heavy door that lead to Black's office. I was ready to face my antagonist: the man who had turned my simple life into a living hell.

"Mister Black, I need answers and I need them now," I demanded, not waiting to see if he was inside.

"Mister Black, I tried to stop him and—"

"Where is Robby Wilem? What's your connection with him and with the Children? Who's the umbra who tried to kill me? Why me? Why my friends? Why *you*?" I fired off my questions like I was pulling the trigger of a gun; as my chamber emptied and the room grew quiet, I realized how loud my voice had grown.

"He just rushed past me," said the receptionist from over my shoulder. "I can call security."

"It's okay, Nancy," said a rumbly baritone as I stepped into the office. It danced with music. I had been expecting a cold impassive voice, a mastermind, not something like that.

Peter Black sat behind a desk twice as big as the receptionist's desk, in a room twice as big as the waiting area. Expensive paintings lined the walls, ending in a huge floor to ceiling window that looked out on the archipelago and the distant mountains that grew from the biggest island in the chain. It was a beautiful office with a grand view, and it had the rare aroma of oiled leather, old wood, and fresh flowers.

Peter Black was dimanian. Two horns sprouted from his temples and curled back through the white hair on top of his head. Bright green eyes regarded me with cool intelligence. He was handsome for an older guy, wore a sharp goatee that had at one time been black but was now stained with silver.

Black smiled at me, a warm welcoming smile. He motioned to one of the couches that ran parallel to his own desk.

"Please, Mister Bell, sit. You are Waldo Bell, right?"

I was taken aback.

"Mister Black, are you sure this is okay? I can call security," the receptionist offered.

"It is okay," Black nodded, lifting a hand. "Please, Nancy, close the door. There's a good girl."

He watched the receptionist depart before rolling out from behind his desk. I inhaled sharply. Black was bound to a wheelchair. A rust-colored blanket rested across his lap and slippers peaked out from under the blanket. He wore a suit jacket of deep green but beneath was only an undershirt. I watched as he rolled over to a bar that sat on the right of the office.

"I'm afraid I'm not as spry as I once was," he stated, seeing my gaze focus on his wheelchair. "I caught a bandit's bullet thirty years ago. Can I get you anything?"

He held up bottles of brown liquor.

"I'm fine," I admitted, feeling surprised by his politeness. "I have some questions for you."

He ignored me. "I had a friend once tell me, never refuse another man's liquor. He claimed it was bad for one's health."

A threat?

"Even at..." I checked the clock on the wall behind him, "... nine in the morning?"

Black smiled and shrugged, rolling himself next to a small table.

"I was hoping you'd say yes so I could pour myself one. Same friend also told me to never drink alone. Both bits of advice I try to live by. Yes, sir. Oh, by the way, I never got a chance to personally thank you for your work on the Big Ninety. The Syringa to

Lovat run can be dangerous during the mid-summer melt. How were the mountains?"

I studied Peter Black, trying to read him and coming up blank. I could describe him as bland, but that wasn't it. No, I'd say he seemed…genuine. Like what you saw in him was what you got.

Doubt began to creep into my mind. Was I wrong? Maybe Black wasn't caught up in this at all. He didn't look like a First; he looked like a tired old dimanian. Pot-bellied and world-worn. Covered with wrinkles and liver spots, not blood. It wasn't what I had expected.

"They…were, they were fine," I stammered, confused as to what to say.

"I am sorry I wasn't around to greet you when you picked up your payment. I was in Destiny. Closed a few deals with a cargo captain. You ever seen the inside of a big cargo ship? They're a sight to behold."

"No, I never have."

"Well, they used to be a sight in Lovat. Ships today aren't the size of ships of legend. As big as a building, some claim, as wide as a city block. Cephels say their bones are common in the Sunk, but who believes a cephel? They tell tales taller than those legends of the Firsts." He paused, and seemed to size me up. An odd glint in his eye I couldn't place. "I'm a bit surprised to see you here. Was there something wrong with the payment? I trust it was adequate." He chuckled. "Did you get some forged lira? I swear those forgeries are becoming more and more common."

I smiled, but stayed alert. "No, the payment and the bonus

were both quite generous. I'm just a bit confused. I ran into some trouble and it made it difficult for me to come down to the Arcadia. I spoke with August—August Nickel—and he put me in touch with your gate, a Zilla? He said she would get me in touch with you."

"Gate? Young man, I don't operate with a gate. That's outfit work."

"You sure? August seemed pretty sure it was the best way to get ahold of you."

"I think if I employed a gate, I would certainly know about it." Black laughed, then thought about the comment. "I suppose Nancy is a bit of a gate. Maybe August meant her; let me telephone him and we can sort this out."

He made a move to roll back to his desk, but I leaned forward. "I'm afraid that would be impossible. August was found murdered in his office about three days ago."

"Oh, dear me." Black grabbed his chest and blinked. "August? Who would want to kill poor August?"

I studied his face, looked for a crack in the concerned façade. Black looked like a shocked old dimanian, his eyes watering, his mouth hanging open. Going in I had been so sure he was tied to this, so sure he was a part of this conspiracy. Then something, a twinkle in his eyes? A quick upturn at the side of his mouth? I wasn't sure if I had seen anything…but it was hard to shake the feeling I hadn't.

"The police think it was that Collector Killer," I explained carefully. Waiting for a reaction.

"That crazy from the papers?"

"One and the same."

"Oh, dear me," Black sighed. If this was an act, Black was very good. "Poor August. Poor, poor August."

"Mister Black, I am here because of him, in part. He put us in communication, and all this crazy stuff has been happening since your delivery. First, the police are trying to arrest me, and they need you to confirm I was here and on the trail working for you—would you be willing to do that?"

"I can do that."

Relief flooded my body. At least a part of this ordeal could end. I'd have my name back.

"You just need to call a Detective Bouchard. I have his number somewhere."

"We could do it right now."

I felt around in my pockets, realizing the number I had for the detective was written on a scrap of paper in the clothes the Reunified brothers had taken to be cleaned.

"I seem to have misplaced it," I admitted.

"I can call later. I have a few friends at Lovat Central. What were the other things you wanted to see me about?"

"Well," I began. "August. Before he was found dead it seemed he was dealing with a cult who calls itself the Children of Pan or the Children, and it seems like they might be connected to you, and if not you, then your godson, Robby Wilem."

"Oh?" said Black.

"Yeah, in particular your godson."

"Robby?"

I nodded.

"Robby hasn't been in Lovat in years. He left shortly after his father passed. Followed some mystic off into the wild. I haven't talked to him in ten, no, twelve years."

I tried to get a read off of him. It was impossible to tell if the old guy was lying. I wondered if maybe Mrs. Sardini was wrong. If the three thugs she had pointed out to me weren't someone else. What had she said, "It was young Robby who came around the most."

"You sure he's not in town?"

"I-I mean, he might be," Black seemed to stumble over the explanation. "If he is, he hasn't reached out to me. You think he's connected to these cultists?"

I spread my hands, and asked my next question. "You ever met or worked with any of the Children?"

"The Children of Pan? Who is Pan?" He shook his head. "No. Never heard of a group with that name. Sounds silly. I'm in Rotary though."

He chuckled weakly.

"It's far from Rotary, I'm afraid. You sure you haven't heard of them?"

"Young man, I am sixty-four years old and bound to this chair. My dealings are with tradesmen and their ilk, not cults. Damn the Firsts, at least not intentionally." He narrowed his eyes. "You're not one of them Purity Movement types, are you? I don't go for cults, but I think they should be left well enough alone. People should be able to believe whatever they believe and practice what they want to practice."

"I'm not with the Movement, no."

"Good. Blight on our society. Spewing hate from that so-called church of theirs."

I nodded, agreeing with Black. "I have one other question if you don't mind."

"Mind? Why would I mind?" Black snorted. "My wife always asked me if she could ask me a question. Always got on my nerves. All the asking. Just say what's on your mind, son. Quit asking all the damn time."

A wife. I tilted my head—could this be Cybill? Black stared back at me with his ivy gaze.

"I didn't realize you're married."

"Was. Was married. Forty-three years. Was hoping for fifty. Charlotte passed two years ago." He smiled sadly, holding up his left hand. A thick tattoo ran around his ring finger. Odd, usually dimanians got their tattoos removed when they divorced or when a spouse died, leaving a scar. Leaving the tattoo would signify he was still married. The old fellow touched the mark gingerly. "She was a gem of a woman, a true gem. Heart bigger than all of Lovat. You don't see that today, not anymore."

He didn't strike me as a mastermind, but he could be lying. He had answers but they weren't solid. He hadn't spoken to Robby in years. He still wore a marriage tattoo despite being a widower. Those weren't solid leads. It was hard to see him as anything more than a tired old widower, wheelchair-bound, who spent his days playing at importing and exporting from his tower office. It was hard to imagine him ordering the murder of anyone, much less having the murderer cut away body parts. I had no idea where this left me.

"Is there something else, or did you just come to grill me?" Black smiled, teasing.

"I'm sorry, I was just confused," I confessed. "I'll leave you in peace. Thanks for this impromptu meeting. I hope this doesn't taint any future business dealings between us."

"No, no, no, I am glad you stopped by. I really appreciate the work you and your company put in with my caravan. Wilem, Black & Bright will definitely be working with Bell Caravans again."

Black leaned forward and extended a liver-spotted hand in my direction. I shook it, meeting his green gaze. He had a surprisingly strong handshake for an old dimanian.

"Sorry for bothering you," I apologized.

Black waved away the apology. "It was good to meet you in person. I felt awful when I missed you last week. Where is your partner?"

"Ah," I said. "Wensem is maero, just had a kid. His first. Apparently he had to go in the forest and do maero things."

"Ah, the Bonding ritual. I see," Black said, rolling beside me as I walked to the door. "Any idea when he will return?"

Why did he care? I opened my mouth to ask, but Black interrupted me, "I always wanted children. Charlotte couldn't have them, unfortunately. I'd love to meet Wensem and his little tyke."

I smiled, but didn't say anything. Something wasn't right about the question.

When we paused by the door, Black reached out and put a hand on my arm. "Nancy won't forgive you anytime soon, even if I talk to her. She's a stubborn one."

"Well, I was a touch rude, bursting in here," I admitted.

"If she had her way I'd never be disturbed. Interruptions are a part of business, I tell her. Does she listen, no, she just continually forces people into her appointment book. I just want to warn you, expect a cold reception going forward."

I smiled. "I appreciate the warning. It was a pleasure working for you, Mister Black."

"Pleasure is all mine, son," he said.

I opened the door and stepped through. My mind was now a jumbled mess of knots. I had been so sure Black was my man. So sure he was some personification of Pan, but looking at the old dimanian in his wheelchair, doubt had crept into my mind.

"Oh my last question," I said, leaning partially out of the door. "What was in the crate?"

Black smiled, the crow's feet around his bright eyes crinkling. "Antiques."

SIXTEEN

My conversation with Peter Black left me more than confused. He didn't seem like the mastermind I had assumed
he was, made me wonder just how poor my sleuthing had been.
Still, why the question about Wensem? It would be a good ploy:
pretend to be the kindly old man to throw investigators off the
trail, but that sort of thing only happens in monochrome serials.

August's death didn't help ease the confusion. If Black wasn't
our guy, then the trail pointed to Robby Wilem; but if Black
was to be believed, Wilem wasn't in the city. So why was August
dead? He had been another victim. Another target of the umbra
and her straight razor. I wondered how she fit in with all of this.
Was *she* the mastermind? I knew next to nothing about her.

Pulling up my collar and screwing down my cap, I pushed out
of the lift doors and into the Arcadia's lobby. This was the part I
was wary about. I had no idea if receptionist Nancy had alerted
security or if she had called the police like she had threatened.
For all I knew I would face a small army of uniformed officers or

angry security guards. Either way, I expected it would end badly.

Instead I was greeted by the echoes of bustling people milling about in the half-empty lobby. I let out a relieved sigh and leaned against a nearby pillar, catching my breath.

"Can I help you, sir?" asked a human bellhop in a white uniform.

I said nothing, pushing off the pillar and moving toward the door like I belonged there, leaving the bellhop staring at my back.

Striding through the big double doors and past the doorman, I made sure to keep my head down and my face blocked by either the bill of my cap or the height of my collar. Just another nobody keeping to himself, on his way somewhere, no one of interest.

I took a left outside the Arcadia's doors, heading south and east toward King Station. I played my meeting with Black over and over in my mind. It all seemed wrong.

The streets were sleepy this early on a weekend and only a few people milled about. I passed by a couple conversing and ducked around a bicyclist studying a map. Lost in thought, I wasn't paying attention. I let my guard down. I had been so nervous exiting the lift and striding into the lobby that when I got outside I felt free. That mistake—and with my mind more focused on my meeting with Black—was why I bumped into Detective Carl Bouchard .

Bouncing off his gut, I looked up, my eyes widening as I recognized the detective.

"Watch where you're going you—Bell!" Bouchard shouted, taking a step back and blinking at me. Confusion gave way to cold anger.

"Carter's cross," I swore, easing backward.

"You," he growled. He thrust out his big, meaty palms in an awkward attempt to grab me. Out in the open like this I was quicker than the old detective. Slipping under his outstretched arm, I burst into a sprint.

Saint Mark's would eventually be my destination, but leading Bouchard to the cathedral would be a huge mistake—I'd have to lose him first.

The police can't catch what they can't find.

"Stop! Bell!"

My feet slapped against the pavement. I was wondering which direction I should head as I took the first corner. I didn't know Pergola Square, I didn't understand its streets, and I certainly didn't know Level Seven. It was like dropping a greenhorn on the Big Ninety and telling them to go to Syringa.

"Stop! Lovat P.D.!" Bouchard screamed. "Stop!"

It only encouraged me to pick up speed; my ribs protested with each stride, but I tried to push it out of my mind. A little pain was better than the alternative. If I was caught, this was all over. I'd be jailed, and seeing the hate in Bouchard's eyes, I doubted a trial would be in my future. I ran harder.

Bouchard was shouting, screaming from behind. I could hear his shoes slap against the clean sidewalks of Level Seven as his big legs pumped after me.

I ducked under a cart and crossed the street. Bouchard was on my heels, his heavy breath sounding like a massive bellows.

I gave a cursory glance over my shoulder and saw him

struggling to keep up. His face was red, his teeth bared like a wild animal, his eyes wide. His coat flapped behind him like wings.

I spun and turned down a street to my left. Windows, staircases, and bodies rushed past. Bouchard let out a furious grunt and followed. A crash echoed from behind me, then a curse and a shout, but I didn't indulge in a look back. Seconds mattered.

A sense of déjà vu overwhelmed me. Buildings blurred. The dauger, dimanian, and human citizens of Lovat who called this area of the city home froze in place and watched me run, the big detective hot on my trail.

"Stop that man!" Bouchard bellowed. "Lovat Central! Stop! That! Man!"

A few citizens made weak attempts to grab my jacket but I was able to slap them away. One fruit vendor tried to be a hero and jumped in my way, but I bowled through him, knocking him into a pile of his produce.

I turned down a narrow alley between two gray brick buildings. It was darker than the street, with fewer lights hung from the ceiling above, but it gave just enough visibility to see where I was going. I leapt over a barrel and jumped off a crate. My ribs jolted with the impact.

Checking Bouchard's distance, I was grateful to see he was slipping behind. I wanted to let out a whoop of victory, but better to save that for an actual escape.

The alley before me widened and turned left. Wide-eyed tenants stared at me through windows, a few pulling their shutters.

I followed the alley left, knowing that if I could make it to the next street I would be home free. Bouchard was too far behind and wouldn't be able to pursue me much longer. I would be able to lose him.

There was no next street.

As I careened around the corner my alley ended. A small railing blocking the path gave over to empty air. I slid to a stop. Level Six opened up below me, the tops of old buildings and the movement of citizens far below filled my vision. A few old pipes crossed the empty space, carrying power, water, and air to various locations within the city.

Another alley seemed to continue hundreds of feet across the expanse. If the two paths were ever meant to connect, those plans had been long abandoned and forgotten. The other side taunted me, beyond reach. Many stories below was the roof of a Level Six building. Air circulators and gravel covered its crown, along with the occasional shanty made of wooden crates and sheet metal. Bouchard's breathing echoed from around the corner, sounding like an enraged bear.

I had nowhere to go.

This is it, I thought. *It's over, it ends here.*

Turning around, I backed up against the railing, feeling the cold metal through my jacket. I waited. Wondering for a scant second how this would play out. Would he throw me over? Shoot me? Arrest me? Beat me to a pulp?

Bouchard burst around the corner like a cannonball, crashing into some garbage cans and sending a big centipede the size of my arm fleeing under a pile of trash. He slowed and came to a stop when he saw me. A bright grin cracked the smoldering expression on his red face.

Bouchard began to laugh—a deep, exhausted, choking laugh—that burst between gasps for air. He doubled over, hands on his knees. He forced himself to take a few breaths before standing up and glowering at me, his words coming out in airy huffs.

"I don't like running, Bell. You made me run."

"Sorry," I apologized, my voice remorseless.

"You'll pay for it. I'll see that you pay for it. You broke Muffie's nose, you know?"

"It needed breaking." I snapped. Bouchard chuckled sourly and pulled a revolver from inside his coat.

"Yeah, probably. Expect he'll want to return the favor. He likes to play a little rough, that Muffie."

"Why are you doing in Pergola Square, anyway?" I blurted.

"If you must know...Peter Black of Wilem, Black & Bright telephoned, ah...yeah. That's right," he said, watching my reaction. "I figured you knew him. He wanted to speak to me...about you actually." Bouchard grinned a toothy smile.

I closed my eyes and rubbed my forehead. Black had promised to call Bouchard, promised to clear up the misunderstanding; meeting him on the street was just poor luck. If I had left a few minutes earlier, or lingered at the hotel a little longer, maybe catching a quick meal, everything between us would be settled.

Bouchard's laugh died out and his expression changed to anger. "All right. This has gone on long enough, Bell. You're under arrest for the murders and mutilations of Thaddeus Russel, Fran Nickel, Doctor Eliza Inox, August Nickel, and Lilly Westmarch." He paused. "And Firsts know how many others."

The last name he mentioned sounded familiar. I tried to dredge it up from the cobwebs of my memory. Lilly Westmarch. Westmarch. I had known a Westmarch, both August and I had. Old Man Westmarch worked as a foreman down on the docks. Was this Lilly related to my old boss? The memory welled up. She was his daughter. I hadn't seen her in years. My stomach dropped as the reality of what he said set in. Lilly was dead. Another murder. Another acquaintance. Another connection to me.

"I didn't kill anyone," I said, trying to sound calm.

"You took his tongue!" He shouted, spittle flying from his flabby lips. "His tongue, you son of a bitch! You took Lilly's eyes! Every one of your murder scenes I walk into just gets sicker and sicker. You're a screwed up bastard, Bell. A sick, sick, screwed up bastard."

"I didn't kill anyone," I repeated.

"I have your bloody handprints all over the Doctor's office."

"I was there, but I didn't kill her," I said.

Bouchard edged closer; the swooping horns that ran along his bald head looked wicked in the dim light, more wicked still was the snubnose revolver firmly grasped in his hand. "Why did you do it? Why take their body parts? Is this some sick sex thing? IS THAT IT?"

I needed to get out of here. I had to escape. I couldn't let myself get caught. I couldn't. It wasn't over. Bouchard could lock me away, but the killings wouldn't stop. This wasn't the end. The umbra would kill more.

Looking around the alley, I searched for an exit, something, anything. A fire escape, a door, a drain pipe.

Bouchard watched me, silent, his breath returning to normal, the red fading from his face. "There's no escape. There's no way out. This is it, Bell. This is how it ends. Level Seven, Pergola Park, in a dead end you thought was a way out. The chase is over, you bastard, and you lost." He paused, and looked at his gun and then back at me. "You know, a part of me doesn't even want to take you in. It'd be much easier to just put a slug in your head right here, maybe two, nah...three. Maybe one for each of your victims," Bouchard snarled, leveling the gun at my head. "No one will care. I can see the headline, 'Collector Killer Killed.' The monochrome reporters will bust a nut over the news. I'll be a hero. 'Hero Cop in Alley Shootout.'"

I glanced over the edge of the railing. There was no way I could leap across the chasm, but I could fall. I tried to judge the distance between this opening and the roofs and buildings below. Two stories? Three? Four? Could I survive?

"Still looking for that exit?" asked Bouchard with a chuckle, waggling his gun. "We can end it right here. Let me know if you're going to try it. A gunshot would be a lot less painful than bleeding to death from a fall."

He wasn't more than a few paces away now. A pair of steel handcuffs were pulled from the inside of his frayed sport coat. They twinkled in the dim light.

"I want to shoot you, Bell. Especially after seeing what you did in Westmarch's studio, seeing her body lying among her paintings, but I go by the book. I'm not a dirty cop. I'm going to bring you in."

Carter's cross, what else had that umbra done to Lilly?

"I didn't do it, Detective."

"Bullshit."

"I haven't seen Lilly in years. I worked with her dad, and she dated August for a while. I know you don't believe me, but it doesn't make it any less true." I filled my lungs with a deep breath and judged the distance again. It was high, dangerously so, far enough it could break my legs, maybe even kill me. It was this or rotting away in a cell like a caged animal. I couldn't deal with that. Not again, not while that umbra, Pan, or the Children stalked the streets. If I was too slow Bouchard would be able to grab me, but if I was too fast I could land wrong and it'd be over.

"I got enough evidence to say you did."

"It's wrong. It's planted. It's—"

Now or never.

"NO BELL—!"

I threw myself backwards, slipping over the railing and twisting in the air.

Level Six's roof structure flashed past me, and the lights from the alley disappeared. I caught a utility pipe with my stomach halfway down, forcing the air from my lungs. I scrambled against the smooth surface, trying to gain purchase but I lost my grip and slid off, dropping further below.

Everything moved in slow motion. I could hear Bouchard shouting from somewhere above me. The roar of air filled my ears, his words were slow and drawn out.

The building below rushed up at me, and I landed on the balls of my feet. Pain exploded upward through my legs, my chest, and down my arms like an electric current.

I pitched forward into a roll, carried with the momentum, and landed on my back. My ribs screamed at me, and my legs felt numb, my fingers tingled from the impact.

I breathed.

Far above me and upside down I could see Bouchard staring, moon faced, angry. He was spitting and cursing. Waving his gun but careful not to shoot. Who knew what was in this building, and that snubnose of his would easily punch through the roof.

The layer of gravel was thicker than I had expected. Softer. I was sure it had helped absorb some of my fall. I breathed again. Feeling pain in my chest, on both sides of my ribcage now.

When I tried to move my arms I was grateful to see they still worked. I looked down and tried to move my feet; they moved, but something was broken or fractured. Waves of pain exploded upward. The world pulsed in and out, a gray fog at the corner of my vision. I was fading between consciousness and unconsciousness. I needed to get out of here. Bouchard would find a way down. Find this roof. Find me.

I struggled to stand, rolled to my knees and tried to get my feet under me. My right knee felt like it was on fire. Sharp pain rushed up both sides of my body, exploding behind my eyes.

Gravity proved too strong and my knees too weak. I collapsed again, the gray returning to my vision, darkening, then going black.

SEVENTEEN

Hey, friend! Hey! You all right?"

I blinked and tried to force my world to come into focus. Everything was so blurry, like someone rubbed lard over my eyes. I felt a nudge on my shoulder. I tried to move.

"Friend, you took a hell of a spill. You all right? You okay?"

I shot up. Realization of the touch, my fall, Bouchard reaching for me—it all exploded into my mind. The world roared. My right leg screamed in pain. I had expected to be in a cell or to see Bouchard standing opposite of me, his fat revolver pointing at my forehead, the cave-like barrel yawning.

Looking around, my neck cracked and popped through the stiffness. I was still on the rooftop and Bouchard was nowhere to be found. I looked up from where I had dropped, expecting to see his wide face leering down. He was gone. Only empty air and the distant ceiling of Level Six were above me.

"Hey, hey, you all right?" I turned and saw a squat anur looking at me intently. He was wearing brown rags and a dumpy hat.

One of the rooftop squatters. His big black eyes blinked as he studied me.

"I think so," I managed. Pain reverberated through my body. I looked down at my legs and wiggled my left foot. It responded. When I tried to wiggle my right the pain almost forced me to black out a second time. I noticed my right leg was twisted violently to the right just below the knee. I wondered if I had broken it.

"Why did you do that, friend? The jump?" asked the anur. I studied his face, my vision still swimming. His brow was knitted in concern, as much as any anur's brow could be. He seemed reasonable enough. Hell, on a more elevated level like Level Six—and in his shabby condition—we were kindred spirits.

"Police trouble."

That set him off.

"Oh friend, oh friend, oh friend," the anur repeated. "Deeper ain't going to help you with them. Deeper can't, not now. Not now. Not now." His voice moved from concern to panic and he jumped around in little hops. He struck his fists up and down as if he was playing invisible drums. "You gotta get out of here, friend. I can't have them finding me up here. They'll kick me off. Kick me out. Back to the Sunk. Back down below."

"Okay, okay." I tried to stand but a wave of pain erupted from my right leg and drove me backward. My back popped as I landed on my ass. "Look, help me up and I'll get out of here."

"Again," urged the anur, grabbing ahold of my hands and hauling me upwards. This time I was careful not to put any pressure on my right leg. I looked down at my right foot; it was wrenched to the left, the knee lumpy and swollen beneath my jeans.

My left leg bore my weight fine, and for that I was grateful. I was hobbled but not immobile.

How much time had passed between my fall and my waking? A minute? Ten minutes? An hour?

Bouchard was no idiot. He had probably immediately moved to alert Lovat Central. Who knows how long that would have taken though, because he'd have to find a telephone, or at the very least one of the new police call boxes slowly scattering their way throughout the city.

"Friend! Here, friend, a gift. A gift. Here, take this board," said the anur, dragging an old piece of timber about his height toward me. "A crutch, see. A crutch! Use it as a crutch."

He stuck one end under an arm and waggled the board about, demonstrating.

Taking the board, I followed suit, sticking it under my arm. As a crutch it was poor—uncomfortable—but in the absence of anything better, it'd have to do. My new anur friend was right: I needed to get out of here. Bouchard wouldn't just let me fall. Level Six would be crawling with Lovat's finest before long.

"Good luck, friend. Good luck!" said the anur, his wide mouth frowning and his dark eyes blinking as I found the door to the stairwell and began my hobble back to Saint Mark's.

I barely remember the return trip. It was a blur of misery and frustration and hysteria. My heart hammered and my knee screamed in pain, drowning out the constant drone from the bullet hole in my arms and the bruises on my ribs. I collapsed in exhaustion a few times, falling onto benches, slumping against buildings in dirty alleys as police rickshaws and scooters moved past. I did my best to make myself look inconspicuous.

Awkward lift rides felt the same after a while. I would clamber aboard, barely escaping the closing of the doors, and then lean against them hoping I'd catch myself before they opened. Stairs were my bane: difficult to manage and slow, and eventually I was forced to abandon my makeshift crutch in order to descend a particularly steep flight. The agony in my leg didn't ease, and my head was further muddled from the pain and shock.

When I found myself dragging my body toward the doors of Saint Mark's, I remember I was still regretting the loss of my crutch. Then shapes, shadowed blurs of figures, moved from behind the cathedral's walls, looking like umbra.

Seeing those forms, something in me panicked.

I don't remember passing out again, but I did.

"You look like hell," said Samantha.

I was lying on a hospital bed, my lower half covered by a white sheet. I wasn't sure where I was in the cathedral. Some old room, underground from the look if it. It had once been painted white, but that white had aged and stained over the centuries to the color of worn leather. A few rusted pieces of equipment hummed and buzzed in the corner, tubes hanging off of the metal arms like vines. A counter framed with shelves occupied the wall to my left.

Samantha had rushed into the room. Dressed nothing like

the priestess she was, she had her hair pulled back in a messy bun, and wore old cotton trousers and a baggy T-shirt that hung off one shoulder. She looked like she was getting ready to paint a room or work a hammer.

Dark circles were under her eyes, hinting at a lack of sleep. She approached my bed, her expression changing from concern to shock as she took me in. I smiled a loopy smile. My shame barely covered, I felt embarrassed. My skin darkened as I blushed.

"Hagen said you had been hurt, but he didn't say how bad," she said, reaching out and placing a warm hand on my shoulder. My skin tingled under her touch. "Are you all right? You're all bruises and scrapes."

She sat on a stool that had been placed next to my bed.

"I'll be okay," I said, nodding toward my leg. Pain bunched around my knee with every heartbeat. I breathed out a long, slow breath. My head pounded. My ribs ached. But...I was safe. I was safe in the cathedral. Not out on the streets where Bouchard could snatch me up. The tension that had been built in my haphazard flight from Level Six's rooftops to the cathedral grounds slowly seeped out of me. I could feel myself relaxing.

"Carter's cross!" Samantha swore, looking down at my knee and calf. They were deep purple, the muscles swollen around them. She reached to touch the knee, but hesitated, her fingers hovering over the wound. I was grateful for that.

"What happened to your leg?" she gasped.

I shrugged and stumbled over the words, "Had a bit of a fall. I think it might be broken."

"A bit of a fall? You think it *might* be broken?" Samantha repeated, her eyebrows rising.

I pushed myself up on my elbows so I could see better myself. My sides ached with pain. I winced.

"Easy...easy...lie back, Wal. Look at you. Did Black do this? We told you not to go, it wasn't time. We weren't prepared. You weren't prepared. By the Firsts, Wal, you could have killed yourself!"

A homely monk, human by the look of him—though it was hard to tell with his lanky gray hair and the long gray beard covering most of his face—shuffled in.

"Mister Bell's leg is in bad shape. Mind taking a look at it, brother?" asked Samantha, her voice taking on an authoritative tone. It was a tone I hadn't heard before. I liked it.

The monk poked and prodded at me, circling my bed like a buzzard. I wasn't the most congenial patient, and his light touches often caused me to wince or pull away. A few times I cried out in pain.

"Easy...easy...." Samantha would say, as the monk would hum and haw and rub his bulbous nose, studying me with a pair of pale, beady gray eyes that stared out from under shaggy eyebrows.

"When were you shot in the arm, son?" asked the monk.

"Week and a half ago," I paused, thinking about it, trying to count the days. "Maybe...."

"Well, the wound is clean, not gone to rot. Better than most gunshot wounds I see in the city. It looks like you have a few bruised ribs. Three on the left and one more on the right."

Samantha raised an eyebrow at me and I did my best to shrug. I wish I hadn't: it hurt.

"What about his leg?" asked Samantha.

"My best guess is a dislocation at the knee, which is causing him considerable pain. Also the swelling." The monk finished his appraisal and stood at the foot of my bed. I felt like a thoroughbred.

"Can you fix it or do you have to put me down?" I joked.

The monk didn't seem amused. "I can reset the knee, but it'll hurt. Hurt like hell. Could hurt for some time. We'll need to make sure you have a solid pulse in your leg before you try to walk on it. Also we'd need to make sure there was no damage to your nerves. I'll want to splint it. It'd be best if you stayed off it for a few weeks. Took it easy. Relaxed. I've seen injuries like that reoccur when fools don't listen to advice from doctors."

The faces of Fran, Thad, and August danced their way through my mind. I didn't have the time to stay off my feet. The killer was still out there, taking body parts, destroying lives—my own included. I had to stop her.

"Just fix it," I said.

The monk nodded and instructed Sam to move behind me and hook her arms under my armpits. She drew close and I could feel her breasts push against my back, and her cheek brushed against mine as her head lowered. The small spurs from her chin lightly brushed against my jawline. It made me shiver.

"Don't get any ideas," she teased with a whisper. For once, I was glad I was in so much pain, naked and covered only by a thin sheet: the last thing I needed was my body to betray me even further.

I chuckled, as the monk grabbed my leg by the ankle and yanked.

Third time is a charm, I suppose.

When I came to, I was still lying on the bed in the monkery. I was wearing pants again. The right leg was rolled up above the knee, which was encased in a metal cage to keep it from bending. Thick bandages covered most of my chest and the dressing on my arm was fresh as well.

Hagen loomed over me. His wild horn splayed out from his forehead like a gnarled tree branch.

"He's awake," he stated and I blearily looked around the room. Samantha came over.

"How's the leg?" she asked.

I thought about it. My stomach rumbled.

"Sore," I rasped out, my throat dry. "I'm hungry. I'm starving."

"Can you move?"

I took a few deep breaths to clear my head and wondered the same thing. I was sore, but I felt like I could move. I nodded.

"Good. We have a lot to talk about," said Hagen.

"Shirt?" I asked.

Hagen handed me a fresh monk's tunic. I sat up slowly and pulled it on, wincing, and decided not to button it up.

"Would it be a cliché to say I told you so?" Hagen asked.

"Yes, but your sister beat you to it," I said and rubbed my face, feeling stubble scratch back at the palms of my hands.

Hagen frowned at Samantha as I slipped off the bed. Gingerly putting out my left foot and then barely touching the right to the ground. The knee protested but with the metal splint it took the weight with considerably less pain than before.

"Crutch?" asked Hagen, holding out a padded wooden crutch that looked older than my father. Still, it was a real crutch, better than the board I'd used earlier. I took it.

"When's the last time you ate?" asked Samantha.

"When did I leave for Black's?"

"Three days ago."

"Well, it's been three days," I said. My stomach rumbled in agreement.

"I'll get some food from the cafeteria," Samantha began. "Meet you two in my office. We can catch Wal up to speed with what we know."

I was handed a plate of meatloaf, mashed potatoes with a thick black gravy and some long green vegetables that reminded me of green beans but tasted like the sea. When asked if I wanted something to drink I nodded.

"Vermouth," I requested. "By the Firsts, I could use a glass of vermouth, with ice."

Samantha's eyebrows rose a fraction, but she nodded and moved to a shelf holding her liquor cabinet. I was thankful that Reunifieds weren't a dry faith like the Curwenites. Couldn't abide that now. I needed something to clear my head. Something strong.

Samantha placed the glass before me, the ice tinkling. I took a long drink, tasting the sharp flavor and letting the alcohol soothe me.

"So," I began, after eating about half the food on the plate in silence. "I don't think it's Peter Black. I think any connection of his is coincidence. He was asking some weird questions about Wensem, but I don't think a few invasive questions is enough to convict a guy. If anything I think Robby Wilem is our best lead. Tenuous as that is."

"Really? Not Black?" Hagen asked, surprised. He looked from me to his sister. A puzzled look crossed both their faces. "Who did this to you then?"

I told them.

Hagen slumped in the chair behind his sister's desk. "Bouchard? The detective? Carter's cross, Wal, you could have been killed."

"I was good as dead if I let him take me in. Lovat Central doesn't like escapees, and do you think this killer would be worried about the police? Whoever that umbra is, she's not concerned with authority."

"...And you're sure it's not Black?" asked Samantha.

I shook my head. "Bouchard said Black had called him, but I had asked him to. I think Bouchard was coming down to question him when he ran into me. Black is a wheelchair-bound dimanian. Two horns." I tapped my forehead. "Sorta swoop back kind of like Bouchard's along his skull and then curl back around. He was more kindly grandfather than anything else, and was pleasant actually. More polite with me than I was with him—"

Hagen dropped an open book on the desk's surface. It was

as old as the desk, bound in soft leather, the edges of the thick, yellowing pages twisted and fraying. An etching as old as time itself was displayed across the open pages. The artist had done a considerable job and the years had been kind as most of the details were still visible.

A half-man, half-goat was portrayed dancing through the trees. He was naked; human from the waist up, but his legs were a pair of furry goat legs. A long, almost comical penis hung between them, seemingly swaying with the motion of his dancing, very human and looking out of place between the hairy, animal legs.

Two horns sprouted from the figure's forehead and wrapped back through a tangle of black hair as wild as the thickets he moved through; an eight-barred flute was clasped in his hands and held to his lips. Behind him a string of naked children followed, faces frozen in wide, manic grins as they danced along, twisting through the trees until they disappeared.

The face was familiar. A black goatee, a warm welcoming smile, eyes that sparkled. I considered my initial reaction. He looked like Black, but how much of this etching was Peter Black, and how much of it was influenced by my meeting?

"That's Pan," said Hagen.

"I gathered that much."

"The Black Goat," explained Samantha.

"Okay."

Hagen laid down a photograph of the Wilem's and Black taken from the church newsletter. He tapped Black and then tapped the illustration in the book. My heart felt like it seized in my chest.

Even with the poor quality of the photograph the face of Peter Black was clear. The grin the same. The sharp eyes identical.

"The Black Goat with the Thousand young," I said. "This from that *Lineage* book?"

Hagen shook his head. "I found this in something else entirely. *The Codex Obscurum*. Book of Darkness."

"Ominous."

"Ancient scholars had a flair for the melodramatic," said Samantha, coming over and sitting in the chair next to me. "However, this was a very helpful book, lots of details about the Firsts. Pan is the husband to Cybill. Softly's records were right."

"So we have confirmed connections from Black to Pan, and Pan to Cybill. What about the Children? What about the murders?"

Hagen flipped to a bookmark placed further back in the book. It was another engraving, only this was more hideous. White and immense, like a tower of flesh, it rose above a dark forest. A massive beak—the mouth of a cephel—jutted from the flesh near the top, surrounded by a swarm of globular gray eyes with hourglass pupils. Around the mouth were thousands of small arm-like things that were drawn as if they were flailing about. Spindly legs, like that of a spider but as tall as a building, extended from the lower half of the body and massive tentacles rose away like the branches of a tree. It was revolting. Terrifying.

At the base of the creature was a small figure, arms upraised, a silhouette of the figure in the previous engraving. Pan. A massive bonfire burned at the base of the creature, and smoke swirled up and around. The bodies of children were scattered about the forest floor. Unlike the previous image, none of these children were dancing.

"Cybill."

"Are you kidding?" I asked, looking at Hagen and then at Samantha. The meatloaf in my stomach churned. "That's the wife of Pan?"

"Lovely, isn't she?"

"What is she?"

"A First," said Samantha, "one of them."

Hagen nodded, "She is referred to as an 'Awakener' or in other texts, a 'Kindler.'"

I set my plate of food aside.

"It wasn't easy to find this link. She's not labeled as Cybill or Cybele," Hagen began. "The Aklo translation doesn't work in Strutten; it needs to be read with a Cephan translation, comes out to Shub something—it's gibberish. But we know it's her. We cross referenced and double checked, even brought in Sister Jaeli—she's a cephel—to confirm our suspicions."

"Okay," I said slowly. "They're the same person. What does all this mean?"

"The Awakener is the being who brought the Aligning the first time. She wakes the Firsts from their slumber within the stars—"

"Or the earth," added Hagen.

"Right, or the earth," agreed Samantha.

"Okay...so?"

The Dubois were clearly frustrated with my confusion.

Samantha spoke first, "According to the Codex Obscurum,

Cybill should be awakened within the fire following a ritual using parts gathered from eight souls by either the blessed executioner or the father. It's horrid stuff, but it's matching the order of the murders: ears from a musician, lips from a merchant, hands of a samaritan, tongue of a supplicant."

"Eyes of an artist," I said, remembering what Bouchard had told me about Lily Westmarch.

"Right, how'd you—"

I interrupted, "Bouchard told me there had been another one."

"There're three more. Feet of a traveler. Pipes of a newborn. Heart of the Guardian."

Heart of the Guardian.

The umbra had called me Guardian. My skin broke out in goosebumps.

Hagen produced another tome and showed it to me. The language on the cover was similar to Aklo but it wasn't anything I could read.

"This reads, *Rituals of the Firsts, A Guidebook.*"

"A how-to occult guide," I said.

"Exactly. It's where we got this information from, some ritual called the 'Calling of the Mother by the Father and their Young.'"

"These eight parts can be taken at any time but must be connected to one another, all tracing it back to one person: the Guardian," Samantha explained.

"Cybill has an avatar. A huge thing, sorta like an altar, but carved with her likeness in stone. It's mentioned in both the

Codex Obscurum and *A Guidebook.* It's supposedly a sacred object, but it's never to be at rest. Her followers are instructed to move it around constantly as a form of protection. Usually someone goes before the avatar. They're referred to as the Guardian. It's the Guardian's duty to make sure the avatar arrives at the destination safely."

"Like a caravan master," I said coolly. Another mile passed in this journey, and my mysterious destination became more and more clear.

Samantha nodded. "Transported anything massive lately?"

EIGHTEEN

The water from the tap ran amber from iron and it reminded me of blood. I pushed the thoughts from my mind. Lathering up my hands, I quickly rubbed the soap onto my face, working at the layers of sweat and grime. The discussion had left me feeling like I needed to cleanse myself.

Lathering done, I brought up handfuls of the tepid water and splashed it against my face rinsing off the suds.

I looked up at the mirror. Water dripped off my eyebrows and chin. I hardly recognized myself.

My mother would be displeased. It was normal for me to come off the trail thin. Eating tack, the occasional small mammal and drinking stream water can only sustain a man for a time. Bell Caravans did all right but we didn't have the money to pay for a decent chuckwain. Downtime between caravan runs was when I would regain my weight. I'd eat and rest and store up reserves for the next run: my own form of hibernation. This trip, however, I had lost that opportunity.

Shutting off the water, I hobbled my way out of the bathroom and back down the hall toward Samantha's office. The old crutch pressed into my armpit, but was more comfortable than the board the anur had given me on the Level Six rooftop. I was grateful for it. The crutch did little to ease the pain in my ribs, but less pain was preferable to the alternative.

I moved slowly. The weight of the news Hagen and Samantha had given me made every step tedious. I felt like I was pushing through mud. Pieces had fallen together. The miles were behind me, my journey was almost complete. Peter Black. His act had distracted me from the truth, a magician waving one hand while the other works his illusion. He was the damned mastermind behind all of this.

I shouldered my way through the office's door and guided myself back to one of Samantha's guest chairs. Hagen still sat in his sister's chair behind the ancient desk and Samantha had taken up residence in the guest chair next to mine. Neither moved. I could feel their eyes on me. The looks of concern, a flash of sadness, a small breath indicating pity. Ignoring them, I slumped into the chair.

Silence hung in the air between us. The truth was there, palpable, tangible, and weighing us all down. None of us wanted to speak. If we did, that truth would become a reality, and we all knew it. It infuriated me.

My mind ran through the ingredients required for Cybill's macabre ritual. I ignored the mark placed upon me, settling on another ingredient. *Pipes of a newborn.* I shuddered, my mind playing images of the scene. Seeing the assassin, with her straight razor and fiery gaze that brimmed with malevolence, bursting through the door. Ready and willing to murder a child. A *child*. A shudder tickled its way down my spine. I only knew of one child who was connected to me: Waldo dal Wensem. My business partner's newborn son.

My head hurt. I tried to rub the pain away. Now I understood why Black was asking about Wensem. Why he feigned interest in Little Waldo.

Glowing red eyes burning hot as coals flashed in my memory. The answer came before the question. I knew the truth. The umbra would have no qualms going after a child. She was a fanatic, a true believer.

When I finally spoke my voice sounded like a bullhorn in the stillness of the room. "Black tricked me. He tricked me into being his *Guardian*." The word tasted like bile on my tongue and a disgusted laugh burst from my lips. "The son of a bitch."

"You couldn't have known," Samantha said, leaning over and placing a hand on my arm. "Wal, you couldn't. It was a psychopath's plan. There's no doubt they selected you on a whim."

"My partner," I said, staring toward the chair where Hagen sat but not really looking at anything. "My partner just had a child. A newborn. Named him after me. Waldo dal Wensem." My smile was weak, and the thought of the umbra assassin overwhelmed any warmth I got from the memory.

"Didn't your partner head off into the wilds? Isn't he in the process of the Bonding?" asked Hagen. "If he's away, maybe it will buy us time."

"He left the day we got back I think. I went to see him before

I came to your shop for the last time. He wasn't home, but I was told by his neighbor he would be due back in a week. That was—" I thought about it, mentally calculating the days, "—about a week ago. Black asked about him. Asked when he was coming back."

"Carter's cross," Hagen swore. The curse had an awful inevitableness to it.

That heavy silence settled back between the three of us, thick as fog. The muted, ghostly sound of a clock and distant voices down the hall was the only noise. I shifted my body, careful not to jolt my right knee.

I hated myself even as I asked, "Let's say they get what they need. Let's say they kill the last three of us. What happens then?"

Hagen leaned on the desk with both his elbows. "Depends who you believe. Some say nothing. Others...well...."

"Well?"

"The legends say the Awakener knows where the silver key resides—whatever that is. With that silver key...she brings forth... wait..." Hagen paused, grabbing a piece of paper, "...I wrote this down, 'the opening of the gate. The awakening of the Firsts. The eventual re-Aligning. The blessed return.'" He looked up and saw me staring at him blankly. "In layman's terms, Cybill will unlock some metaphorical door that will awaken all of the Firsts—"

Samantha interrupted, "—All hell will break loose. Literally. I'm sure you know the legends. Millions dying. The lands forever changing. All of that. Probably more. How accurate that all is...." Samantha shrugged. "The first Aligning was a long time ago."

"We can't let it happen, Sam. Even if the ritual is bunk, we can't let them kill more people." Hagen looked at me, his face stalwart and serious. "We can't let it happen. The police won't do anything. By the Firsts, they have their hands full enough as it is."

I agreed with a nod, "Staying here does no good. I need to see if Wensem and Little Waldo are okay. At the very least I need to warn them.

"Black's a few steps ahead of us. He saw me coming and played me like his flute. He knows we're onto him. Knew I was coming, anticipated how to manipulate me." I paused, thinking through the last few weeks. "Suppose I've been easily manipulated from the start."

"You aren't in any position to fight," said Samantha.

I shrugged and gave a hollow chuckle. "What choice do I have? Call Bouchard?"

"We have evidence."

Shaking my head I said, "No, we don't. We have circumstantial evidence at best. Most of it from ancient tomes, connections made on paper. Bouchard isn't a scholar so he's not going to pay them any mind. What does he care about the stone avatar thing? From his perspective all I delivered was a big, old rock. He's not going to see this as some great battle. He doesn't even know the Children exist. Lovat Central has me at three of the crime scenes. Three. Fingerprints, hand prints, with connections to all the victims. If any commissioner looked at that evidence, he'd think it was solid police work. I'd be locked away and the key would be thrown in the Sunk." I paused. "If they didn't kill me first."

Heavy silence—our old companion—settled back between us. I worried about Wensem, his wife Kitasha, and little Waldo. Horrific scenes played through my head, leaving me disgusted by my imagination. I felt sick. The pain in my body was a distant roar. I couldn't bear doing nothing. I was closer to Wensem and his family than anyone else from my crew. He was like a brother, his wife like a sister. Carter's cross, he named his son after me. Having their deaths—even one of their deaths—on my hands would be too much to endure.

"I need a gun," I stated, my words carrying a bit of finality with them. Fishing into my jeans I pulled out what remaining lira I had left, counting it slowly. More than enough for one.

"I beg pardon?" asked Samantha, looking at me, eyes wide.

I didn't respond; instead I carefully folded my remaining bills and slipped them back into my pocket. I wondered if it would be enough to buy two guns and a few boxes of shells. I'd have to go deep. Find a place out from under Lovat Central's ever-watchful eye. The location of a merchant materialized from my memory.

"I know a place," I explained. "Level Two, below your shop, Hagen, in King's Station. Clean weapons. No trail, it'd be perfect. We can check on your shop on the way. Make sure it's okay."

Hagen perked up at this. Clearly his concern for his business had been building, though he had been silent on the subject.

"I can't believe you are actually thinking of arming yourself," Samantha crossed her arms defiantly. I didn't respond and she continued, "And you're just going along with this, Hagen? Father raised us better. Don't fall into the mistakes of the past. Remember the fighting between the Reunifieds and the Hasturians?

It went on and on and on and never ended. Each side trading body for body, blood for blood."

Hagen rose and I moved to follow suit.

"This isn't a monochrome serial! In real life things don't always clean up so easily. What do you think you're going to do? You going to burst into Wilem, Black & Bright, guns blazing and get your revenge on Peter Black? There're hundreds of the Children. Maybe thousands! You kill one and they'll all be after you. Then what? Another and another? The more you kill, the more bodies in Lovat Central will lay at your feet! You may not be a killer now, Waldo Bell, but don't let Black turn you into one."

"What do you want us to do? Lie low?" I shot back. "Wait for the assassin to come and visit? She seems more than capable of slipping past the monks guarding Saint Mark's. Do you expect me to watch her murder more of my friends? I've seen what she can do. I've seen how she behaves. She's a cold, bloodthirsty murderer. I'm sorry, but I can't just sit still surrounded by books. These won't protect us, Sam."

Trying to rise, I lifted myself out of my chair. I moved too quickly and the pain from my leg sent me back down. Seeing my struggle, Samantha tried to use it against me.

"Look at you. You can hardly walk. If the assassin comes and you're out on the street, she'll flay you alive. Rip your heart out of your chest and finish off the rest of the victims before you're done bleeding to death." She was almost pleading, "You can't run anymore, Wal. You can't fight! You're out of this. You're in serious need of medical treatment, more than what you can get from the cathedral or a second rate Bonesaw."

The anger in her face was clear. She was concerned for her brother, maybe even concerned for me. A part of me wanted to give in—it really did—but something else drove me on. Stupidity? At the time I'd like to have thought it was selflessness.

"You coming?" I asked Hagen, as I tried to ignore Samantha's dark gaze. I could feel her eyes burning into me. Hagen stepped around the desk. "Help me out of this damn chair."

"I can't believe you're going along with this."

"The man's right, Sam. We need *something*. The church won't provide us with weapons and if we hide here too long we'll bring the Children down on top of you all. So yeah, I'm going along with him."

Samantha huffed angrily and returned to her own chair. I spared a glance and saw her staring at me, her eyes burning with fury.

Hagen and I did our best to ignore her as he helped me to my feet, but her dark eyes continued to burn as the door to her office closed behind us.

NINETEEN

Hagen paid for our tickets on the monorail, which was good, because with our recent purchase of weaponry, I was out of lira. I kept my collar up and my hat pulled low as we boarded a crowded middle car that smelled like curry and wet dog. Finding a pair of empty seats I slumped and kept my head low like a snoozing passenger.

When a conductor asked us for our tickets and inquired after me, Hagen did a bang up job, making up a story on the spot about me just getting out of the hospital and returning home to Reservoir. If the conductor was interested, she sure didn't show it; she nodded and punched our tickets, then moved on before Hagen was barely into his story.

We had acquired two heavy .45s that the dauger who ran the shop referred to as "Judges." My gun hung in the pocket of my jacket making me feel off balance. I never liked carrying pistols, they made me nervous. There was something too personal about handguns—they were so in-your-face, so brutal. I much preferred a rifle, but in the tight enclosed spaces of the city a rifle doesn't do much good.

Samantha had been less than happy. After we had checked in on Hagen's shop (it was fine), he had wanted to return to Saint Mark's before we headed north. It wasn't the best decision. Samantha had some time to dwell on our choice to buy the guns, and she was quite angry with the two of us. She refused to speak with me. I left Hagen to face her tirade, choosing to sit out in the hallway. I was doing my best to ignore the muffled argument coming through the walls. Get out of my head a little. Find a silver lining to this…whatever this was. It didn't help. My mind was still rattled with all that I had seen, all that I had experienced.

A short while later Hagen emerged from the recesses of Samantha's lair looking the worse for wear. When I asked him how it went, he mumbled a few words, none of which I could make out. I figured it was better to let the moment pass, so we took a slow, winding path to the monorail station nearest Saint Mark's.

The scenery out the monorail window changed as it had before. Buildings as tall as their level's ceiling gave way to small, plain houses with square roofs and stumpy porches broken up by cross streets and narrow alleyways.

"Reservoir. Doors open on the left," said the announcement as the monorail's door rattled open.

Hagen stood and helped me out of my seat, following me as I hobbled off the platform, leaning heavily on my crutch and trying not to put pressure on my damaged leg.

Night was falling, and the lamps overhead had dimmed to

their twilight setting, a few winking off altogether. I instinctively checked around for the maero woman who had recognized me before, but no one seemed to care about a human and a dimanian this late at night. The streets were quiet with only a few people milling about. We passed a few maero carrying jai alai equipment and a large dauger wrapped in the heavy coat of a welder, arms full of heavy shopping bags. He nodded at us as he passed, whistling a Saint Ellington tune.

"It's quiet."

I nodded. "Reservoir's a working class warren. Good, honest, blue-collar people. They need to be up early tomorrow. My guess is the loudest things around here are kids and pets."

"Never made it up here before," said Hagen, turning to me. "How you doing?"

"My knee hurts, my chest hurts, and my arm, which happens to have been shot, is actually feeling much better—except when I move it—oh, and I have a headache. That's new."

Hagen frowned. "Need a hand?"

"Nah, I got it. Just move slower, would you?"

Pausing at the corner of the street we took care to make sure the police hadn't set up a watch. No cops milled about, but we waited all the same. When we were sure the street was abandoned we made our way up to Wensem's front doorstep. No light poured out from the window, and the old codger from next door who had been rocking on his front porch during my last visit was absent from his chair.

I laughed quietly to myself.

"What is it?" Hagen asked.

"This whole...I dunno, this whole thing. Whatever it is, I keep feeling like it's looping circles. From Bouchard to this; this is the second time I've stood on Wensem's porch."

"Déjà vu?"

"Something like that." I grinned, not really believing I was here yet again.

After we knocked on the door a light flicked on inside. Something in my heart fluttered to life. Some glimmer of hope. I could hear movement, and the muffled crying of an infant spinning to life like a siren.

The door opened and my partner stood before me, unchanged. Same dopey expression, same crooked jaw, same kind eyes, same towering frame with the hunched shoulders.

"Wal! Wal? Carter's cross, you look like hell. Who's that with you?"

"Hi, Wensem. Can we come in?"

"Sure, sure, what time is it?"

Hagen told him.

"We aren't usually in bed this early, just with the little one and spending all day traveling home, we figured we'd take advantage of the lull and crash. Little Wal likes to wake us up before dawn, figured we'd try to beat him to it." He smiled, then called over his shoulder. "Kit, it's just Wal and a friend of his."

Kitasha emerged, a wide smile across her own long features, a small bundle in her arms. Pausing, she looked from me to Wensem and then back to me, shock playing across her face.

"Wal, you look terrible," she said, her voice as soft and light as I remembered it. "And who is this?"

I made the introductions, "This is my friend, Hagen Dubois. He sells religious artifacts out of his shop in King's Station. Offered to come with me when I said I wanted to visit you. Hagen, meet Wensem dal Ibble, and Kitasha wen Gresna, and their little son, Waldo dal Wensem."

"What happened?" asked Kitasha.

"I'll be okay. The leg, well it's just a little trouble that I should have sorted out soon."

She frowned at me.

"It's nothing," I assured her with my best smile. "Really. Honest. Now let me see that darling little maero who stole my name."

Kitasha's frown flipped and she beamed a smile that only a mother can wear as she whisked to where I stood. She was lighter on her feet than my business partner. Where Wensem plodded, she was graceful; her lithe form and long limbs made her movements seem sure and confident, like a dancer.

Kitasha placed the bundle in my arms before I could protest, and I hobbled back to one of the few chairs in the sparsely decorated central room. I stared down in wonder at Wensem's baby boy.

Waldo dal Wensem—my namesake—stared up at me. The maero boy looked much like a human baby, only extended. Longer arms, longer legs: thinner than most human children with the slightly more narrow head and features of his race. He reached up with his seven-fingered hands and grabbed at my nose, giggling in a baby's babble. His bright blue eyes studied my foreign features.

"By the Firsts—Wensem, Kit—he's beautiful."

Wensem beamed and put his arm around his mate. Kitasha was slightly shorter than her husband, and far better looking. It was clear the Bonding had exhausted her, weariness had settled into her large blue eyes, and her normally pristine and sculpted hair was worn in a thick braid that hung halfway down her back. Yet, despite her exhaustion, her soft smile made clear how much pride she had in her little son. Seeing this baby in my arms and how happy she and Wensem were made me feel like an intruder.

"How did it go?" I asked, my whole reason for being at their house in the first place washed away. "The Bonding I mean?"

Wensem laughed. "When did you learn about the Bonding?"

I explained, telling Wensem about my earlier visit and my meeting with his neighbor.

The smile on Wensem's face betrayed his words. "Ol' Bridge can't keep his damned mouth shut, not surprising he blathered. Probably told half the warren."

Little Waldo started to cry and Kitasha moved over to scoop him out of my arms.

"He's getting hungry, I'd imagine," she said in her soft, almost imperceptible voice. "I'll feed him and leave you three to talk." She paused and looked at me. "Wal, you sure you're okay?"

I nodded and smiled.

"If you don't mind, I'll excuse myself as well. I'm exhausted, running around the woods with these two is hard work. It was good to see you, Wal, and nice to meet you, Hagen."

"You too, Kit," I said, watching her disappear into a back room.

"Nice to meet you," Hagen echoed.

"I meant what I said, you look like hell," said Wensem, taking a seat in another empty chair. The sparse decor caused our voices to echo off the walls. Maero weren't much for decor, didn't see the need for it. "What brings you here tonight in such a panic? Don't think I didn't notice."

"You read the papers? Heard the news?" I asked.

Wensem rolled his eyes. "You ever have a kid?" He paused and chuckled, "One that you know about? I got back and went to bed. I haven't touched the radio or flicked through the papers. What is it?"

Hagen interjected, "You're looking at public enemy number one, Mister Ibble."

Wensem grinned, leaned forward, and rubbed his face with his massive hand. "First, it's Wensem, Mister Ibble is only if you want to be all formal. Second, there's no way Wal can be public anything, except maybe public glutton."

"Hagen's right," I said. My voice flat.

Wensem's laugh choked to a stop. He tilted his head and looked at me, his face twisting into displeasure. "What?"

"There's been trouble. I was arrested."

Wensem looked like I was pulling one over on him—probably from a life of me pulling one over on him every chance I could get.

"After we split I went and saw Thaddeus. Wanted to sell those spectacles I picked up on the Big Ninety. He was killed shortly after my visit. Him and a bunch of others. A lot of people."

The shock in Wensem's face was obvious. He hadn't been as

close to Thad as I was, but he still considered the anur a friend. "Maybe you need to start at the beginning."

I did, telling him everything that had led me to his doorstep. Wensem sat in silence for some time staring at an empty spot on the floor. I let him stew. Wensem was smart but he wasn't quick to act. Every motion of his was intentional; he thought out his actions six, sometimes seven moves in advance like a master go player. Where I tended to be more hot headed, Wensem was the slow burn. After a few moments Wensem looked up at me.

His own eyes had faded over the years, looking more steel than bright blue. He shook his head. "How in the hell, Wal?"

I shrugged.

"I have a kid now. A son."

"I know."

"If August was alive, I'd probably kill him."

"We don't know how involved August was, I'm not sure he knew what he was getting into," Hagen said.

"Look, I just need you to corroborate my story. It should keep Bouchard and the police off my back. Even for a little while. It's impossible for me to move around freely."

"Wal, I've been gone for two weeks. I can vouch for you with Thad and with the musician, but these others..." his voice trailed off.

"There's something else," I blurted out, wishing I didn't have to.

Wensem's features turned darker.

"I think they're after you. It's connections to me. All the victims. I dated Fran. Was friends with Thad. The doctor helped me out. These were people I knew. Friends. Family. They need my heart, and two more—" I winced, "—pieces."

"Feet and throat," said Hagen.

"We're guessing from you and...Little Wal."

Wensem rose, his eyes widening, and he ran his long fingers through his stringy hair as he paced back and forth through the room.

"You needed to know. I couldn't have anything happen to Kit, Little Wal, or you."

Wensem didn't speak. He shook with rage, fighting with himself to quell it. I could see Hagen pull back, unsure of what to expect. I knew we were safe. Wensem's temper was perfectly under control. He knew we weren't to blame for this, and he was just dealing with information overload. I held up my hand toward Hagen and nodded, he eased somewhat.

"You have a gun?" I asked after Wensem had stopped pacing and slumped against a wall by his front door. He shook his head.

I pulled the Judge from my coat pocket and held it out. "I picked this up. For you. I meant what I said, I've seen enough death. I can't have Black get to you as well. Take this. Just in case."

Wensem stood and moved closer, reaching down and pausing, his seven digit hand hovering above the firearm.

"Take it," I insisted.

He reached down and gingerly picked it up.

"Heavy," he observed.

"Called a Judge," I began, pulling out a box of .45 slugs from my pocket. "The gun shop owner said it shoots both these and some kind of modified buck shot."

"Bizarre."

"I guess. The shells are .45s. They pack a big punch. Use it only if you need to. Don't let Lovat Central catch you with it either."

"Is it hot?"

I shrugged. "It wasn't cheap."

"Is it clean?"

"We were assured it was," added Hagen.

"I'm not leaving you unarmed am I?"

I shook my head. "We bought two."

Wensem resumed his position on his chair. His emotions were clear again. His face was as placid as an alpine lake during a summer dawn.

"I don't know when this will end," I admitted.

"Do you need help?"

"Maybe. I'm still trying to figure this out. I could use a good word in with Bouchard. I won't turn myself in, but it'd be nice to not be public enemy number one."

"How dangerous are these people, these...Children?"

Hagen leaned forward. "They've killed five. They've cut off body parts and walked away, pinning it all on Wal here. I'd say that makes them very dangerous."

"Why pin the murders on him?"

"I honestly don't think it was intentional, merely a side effect of Wal's involvement. It creates the perfect distraction. Wal is running around and the spotlight is on him not on the actions of the Children."

I chimed in, "The Children are passionate but clumsy. I've thrown down with them a few times. It's the umbra you have to worry about. She's the real killer."

"The assassin."

I nodded.

"We're going to head back to Saint Mark's tonight," I said. "Hunker down and lie low."

"You sure it's safe?" asked Wensem. "You can stay here."

I nodded. "I don't want to expose you and your family anymore than I already have. I'll try to figure this out, and if I need you I'll send a telegraph. For now stay alert and stay alive."

"We will," said Wensem.

"The cathedral has a telephone." I gave him the number on a scrap of paper. "Ring me tomorrow. Ask for Samantha Dubois, Hagen's sister. She'll connect you with me. We need to get some communication going between us. Make sure the other is okay."

Wensem and I embraced and he and Hagen shook hands.

"Pleasure to meet you, Wensem."

"You too."

"We'll talk tomorrow," I confirmed, and Wensem nodded.

I stepped out of the house and into the quickly cooling street. Hagen stood next to me and we both listened in silence as Wensem locked the door behind us. I didn't know what to think, confusion and guilt ran through my brain. I felt responsible. It was probably selfish, but seeing the kid that bore my name and seeing the happiness in Kitasha's face and the sun-bright pride in Wensem's smile had crushed me. Visions of the shadow assassin with her red eyes danced through my head, waving that wicked, straight razor in figure eights.

Hagen and I shivered against the night air. It may have been the dead center of summer, but nights in Lovat cooled quickly, a testament to the circulation built within the floors and ceilings of the levels. I pulled my jacket close and Hagen and I hobbled down the street toward the monorail platform.

"Good people," Hagen stated.

"You can see why I was worried. I love all three of them. Wensem is like my brother. I'd die for them, any of them."

Hagen nodded in understanding but didn't say anything.

"Here, hold up, let me catch my breath." I eased down onto an old bench and waited until my leg quit throbbing.

"You okay?" asked Hagen.

Nodding, I said, "I'm tired. This whole ordeal."

He gave me a weak smile. "I understand."

"No," I spat. "No. You don't. You don't. This is on me. I brought this down on all of us. Look, I'm sorry, Hagen. I'm sorry for you and I'm sorry for Sam. I didn't want to drag you into this, I didn't want to drag Wensem and his family into this, if I had known…"

I could feel my eyes well up. Embarrassment flushed my cheeks.

Hagen held up a hand, silencing me. "No. Play the martyr all you want, but this doesn't fall on your doorstep. This lies solidly at the feet of Peter Black." He chuckled. "Maybe his hooves."

I laughed. The joke wasn't that funny, but emotions overwhelmed me and I laughed. It felt good. Honest. Real. I needed more of that right now.

"Sam's pissed, isn't she?"

"She doesn't like guns."

"Think she'll forgive me? Forgive us?"

"Us? I pinned this all on you," Hagen said with a grin.

"Carter's cross," I swore. "Let's get back to St. Mark's. I'll see if I can't get your sister drunk on the sacramental wine."

"You know you aren't too beat up for me to slap around," said Hagen, offering me a hand. I took it and he pulled me to my feet. "That is my little sister you're talking about."

"You don't think I'd make a decent brother-in-law?"

"I might kill you before Black does." Hagen laughed.

We turned a corner and moved off of Wensem's street and into a darkened alley with dim lights. Holly crawled up the walls of buildings, the dim light and shadows making it look like it was moving. The air smelled of summer marigolds. A few rats scurried at our feet, eager to get out of the way. The plaintive, desperate howl of a tomcat echoed between the buildings.

We moved slowly. Silently watching the silhouettes of the inhabitants through their lit curtains in the windows around us: shadow plays of mundane, yet strangely appealing lives. The flicker of monochromes in the homes that could afford them. The muffled sounds of radios playing jazz from those that could not. Good folk. Honest folk going about their business. Living their lives.

We took the monorail to Frink Park, our attempt at being clever and following the advice of hardboiled detectives from the radio serials for losing potential tails. We moved away from the monorail platform and lost ourselves in an alley, winding our way through Broadway Hill's narrow, twisting streets.

The food booths that had greeted me when I arrived in the city were closed. The lights were dim. The faint memory of the smell of cooked meat and grease was overwhelmed by the cloying scent of dampness. If this were a weekend, drunks would be stumbling about seeking purchase on one of the booth's stools; but in the middle of the week, in the late night or early morning, things were quiet.

"I want this to be over," I admitted as we made our way down a narrow alley. My stomach rumbled as I thought about the food. Pierogi sounded good.

Hagen smiled and placed a hand on my shoulder. A friendly gesture. Agreement. Companionship. I looked over at him, my own smile faltering as the scent of summer marigolds filled my nose a second time.

It's a funny thing, detective serials. The truth is, despite our best efforts, we didn't know how to lose tails. We couldn't figure out how to be discreet. A wild-haired dimanian walking down a quiet alley with a hobbled up caravan master is hardly an inconspicuous pair.

Hagen's face went from a friendly expression to one of dead surprise that sent a cold chill down my spine. My skin turned to goose pimples. I followed his eyes as he focused on something over my shoulder. I moved but was too slow to react.

My world became blackness.

A bag of dyed hopsack was pulled tightly against my face. I tried to see through the loose knitting, but before I could gain awareness, my crutch was kicked free. I dropped, landing on my knee—my hurt knee.

I screamed.

Everything seemed fuzzy, felt fuzzy. Sounds. Smells. It was as if I was underwater, hearing noises far above me. It felt like the cloying dampness—always persistent in Lovat—had flooded over me.

Hagen's own shouts sounded distant. A gurgling, muffled choke as they ended.

My knee burned fire as my mouth was filled with rough, choking fabric.

TWENTY

The weight of the hopsack was pulled from my head but it didn't do my eyes any good. It was pitch black, wherever we were.

Time was muddled. I had lost track of it, lost track of everything. We had struggled against the invisible assailants but there had been too many and they had gotten the jump on us. Any chance I had to react had been ripped from me as pain flooded the recesses of my body.

My wounded knee, my ribs, even the gunshot in my arm had all had their moment in the spotlight, each a bright spot of pain flaring up in the darkness behind the musty scent that lingered in the hopsack. The pulls, pushes, shoves, pokes, kicks, and punches drummed against me as I was half carried, half dragged to this black abyss.

My kidnappers didn't speak, but they weren't silent. A shuffle here, a gust of air there as a body breezed past, a muffled grunt from behind me, a hacking cough. I struggled, but my hands were tightly bound behind my back by a cord. The knot grew tighter, and I could feel my hands numbing. I tried to remember when I had been bound, but couldn't; my abduction was a murky tangle of memories.

I tried to figure out my surroundings. In the distance water dripped, with a hollow ringing sound like the tolling of a clock. Nearer, the sound of boots crunching on gravel. Even closer was the sucking slurp as mud pulled at someone's heel.

Through it all, I smelled the heady stink of vegetation, the cloying bouquet of dampness. I caught a brief whiff of something sweeter, but through the fog of my mind, I couldn't place it. A flower. Some sort of flower. Then it was gone.

Lost, I was lost. Even with all these clues I couldn't get my bearings. That realization was devastating. It was like I was missing an essential part of what made me who I am. My sense of direction is a part of my trade, something I'm proud of. I lead with confidence and people follow. It's what makes me a good caravan master.

But here...here...wherever I was, something was missing.

I was lost, not just to the world, but to myself.

Someone collapsed next to me, the loudest sound in this bleak, lightless void. Hagen, probably. He grunted and the sound echoed with a hollowness that seemed to absorb more than it reflected. My mind raced, trying to catch what had reflected the noise—brick, cement, stone? I couldn't be sure.

"Hagen!" I said. "Hey Hagen. You okay?"

No answer.

"Shut up," someone ordered.

Moving my head, I looked over my shoulder, hoping for some glimmer of light. Realizing how much I missed it, how much I normally took it for granted. In the blackest nights on the trail there is always light. Even down along the Sunk, the sodium lamps hiss and pop, keeping the lowest portions of Lovat lit. Here, it was impossible to tell. I didn't know if the walls were nearby or hundreds of feet away. I felt closed in, trapped in utter blackness. For all I knew I could be on Level Two or on Level Nine, hidden away in some windowless back room in one of the towers.

It hit me like a runaway ox, what was missing from this scene. There was no way I was in the city—it wasn't possible. The dripping water had led me down the wrong trail.

Even in its driest summer, Lovat is always dripping. There's always a leak, always a flood from somewhere above in the more elevated levels, but beyond those drips was always the buzz... and the buzz was missing.

Caravaneers talk of the silence of the road, but it's a misconception, because the road is never truly silent. Even at its most still, in the early morning hours or late at night, the world still rushes with life. Grass sings with the breeze, branches sway and creak, cicadas buzz in hot passion, night birds call out claiming territory, and coyote packs roaming the hills howl telegraphs to one another.

Lovat is also never quiet. It hums like some great hive. Something is always awake, either above you or below you. Traffic, pedestrians, pets, vendors, music, the sounds of millions upon millions of souls living together, stacked atop one another and always, endlessly, generating noise. It never ceases: a white noise. The city. Alive.

Here in the black pit there was nothing.

It unnerved me. My heart began to beat louder. I was somewhere else, and somewhere very foreign.

This was wrong. This silence. This was very wrong.

My panic increased. My heart thrummed in my chest, loud enough it was probably audible to whomever—whatever—was circling Hagen and me now. A hand pushed me back down as I moved to rise, struggling with my bonds.

Laughter.

It exploded in the silence of the space. Raw. Unabashed. Cruel.

A red glow appeared in the distance. So subtle I could barely make it out. I blinked, my eyes trying to focus on the fuzzy glow, unsure if it was actually there. It glided in soft bobs toward me, increasing in brightness as it moved closer. As it neared, it separated into two distinct shapes.

It was impossible to do anything but stare at the two pinpricks of red light—any light was glorious to me. Something beyond the murk.

I couldn't look away from the eyes of the umbra. The eyes of the killer. I shifted back as they drew closer, drawing yet more laughter from my captors.

"Look how our Guardian cowers," came a voice from somewhere over my shoulder.

The glowing red eyes stopped a few feet away, hovering like stab wound slits in the blackness as they leered.

"Lights." Another voice. Male. Deep. Like an earthquake. "Lights."

The sound of filaments bursting and hissing within their glass globes overwhelmed the muffled quiet of the space. Lanterns. My dilated eyes burned, and I was forced to close them despite my hunger for light.

Eventually—I don't know how long—my eyes slowly opened. I did my best, following my habit of taking in my surroundings while my eyes grew accustomed to the influx of light.

What had once been a black, lightless void became an enormous run-down tunnel. The place was huge, vast, and overwhelming. The ceiling disappeared above us, obscured by darkness the meager pool of light failed to penetrate. Chunks of concrete had collapsed from its roof in eons past and squatted like rubbled cairns across the floor. Each was the size of a cargowain but looked minuscule in comparison to the tunnel's structure. The walls I could see were caked with grime, dirt, and mud. Black moss and pale, almost translucent vines crawled up the side nearest us. I looked down, my knees deep in cold, wet mud. A sickly mist hung above the floor like a death shroud, slowly creeping away from the light of the lanterns.

Breathing out, I looked up into the faces of my captors.

They continued to circle me like a pack of hungry wolves. Eyes wild with that die-for-the-cause stare I had seen on the few I had encountered before. The marks were recognizable: patches, tattoos, jewelry, scars; all in the shape of the flute. Pan's flute. Peter Black's flute.

These were the Children.

"I thought there'd be more of you," I managed to gasp out.

A few sneered, but none chose to respond directly. Instead they just laughed. More mocking laughter. They reminded me of Detective Muffie's cocksure arrogance while I was behind the bars of the cell.

Swallowing the lump in my throat, I watched the pack. Careful to follow faces with my eyes but not to turn my head. It was an old habit when facing down a wild animal. Never show fear, stay calm.

Hagen moaned and slumped to one side, causing me to look over. I was horrified; his face was a mess. Blood dribbled from his nose and mouth, both his eyes were swollen shut, the single wild horn that grew from the side of his temple had been snapped off, leaving a broken spur surrounded by inflamed flesh.

"Was that a growl?" chuckled a feminine voice. Not the umbra. Another.

I started counting. One. Two. Both humans, one of them a woman with an underbite. Three. A maero, huge, muscular, bigger in every way than Wensem, his massive seven-fingered hands splaying and clenching. Four and Five were dauger, their masks painted black, heresy in the dauger community. Six, Seven, and Eight rounded out the pack and all were dimanian. Six was rail thin with large spurs along his arms. The one whom I numbered Seven was enormous, a heavy pendulum of a gut moving before him and two thick horns sprouting from his head. He had been the one who spoke with the deep earthquake voice. Eight was ugly, with squat features and heavy brows that hung above dark, violent eyes.

"Zilla ain't happy," said the big dimanian. He nodded to the umbra.

It all made sense. Zilla! The gate! Peter Black's gate! I wanted to respond. Say something harsh and snappy, but the pain that currently danced through my body prevented me from doing anything more than wheeze out a guttural grunt. I might have even drooled a bit.

Time passed. The pack circled. The umbra—Zilla—stood like a statue.

"The gate," I finally forced out.

The umbra grimaced. She was as naked as she had been when we tussled in Doctor Inox's office. Her feminine shape edged with an eye-maddening softness that made me mistrust my senses. Her body was like some bleeding wound in reality. A shadow. A form. Yet I had stabbed her. Felt her skin—or whatever her equivalent of skin was—break before the surgical instrument I had wielded. I could see my handiwork through a bandage around her thigh. A spot of dark blue where her blood had seeped through. My mark.

"The gate," I repeated, more forceful this time. She grimaced a second time. It was something in her eyes. The murky ink of her face was unreadable, but her eyes...they gave her away.

"August mentioned your name. Said he'd put me in touch with you. I telephoned. You never answered." My throat hurt as I spoke.

Zilla, the umbra, stood silently.

"You proud of this? This barbarity?" I spat.

She never answered. Just looked at me with those red eyes

and blank, faceless expression. More laughter ruptured around me.

"Is this it? Is this how it ends? All these weeks. All this time? Just to kill me here?" It sounded so stupid. What you'd expect a frightened victim to say. I was buying time. She knew it. I knew it. In disgust at my own behavior, I spat at the Umbra's feet, missing by inches. My saliva was tinged red with my blood.

"Here in the tunnel? No, of course not...but soon. Yes, soon," the big dimanian promised. "We are building toward the crescendo. Yes. The crescendo. The end for you, and yet the beginning for us all. It's what we have been working toward all these weeks, these months, these long years. All pieces are in place. All *parts* gathered," he paused and looked over at the umbra, watching Zilla shift slightly.

Hagen coughed next to me. The sound was painful. Blood trickled from his swollen lips.

I tried to shuffle close to him, but before I could move one of the humans stepped around behind me.

"Let's remain where we are, sound good?"

Ignoring him, I looked over at Hagen. "Hey, Hagen. Hagen!"

He stirred, his face turning in my direction. His wild hair caked with mud, his face half covered by blood. He looked awful.

"You okay?" I asked.

Hagen nodded, painfully. I hoped he still carried his gun.

I looked back at Zilla, the umbra, Peter Black's gate. She stared right back at me.

It was the earthquake who spoke: "We have the maero, your partner. The lanky fellow. We have his shit kid too. Took them right after you left. We were wonderin' where they had gone. Nice of you to lead our siblings there."

His stomach quaked with laughter.

My heart sank. Wensem. Little Waldo. I glared knives at the umbra expecting a reaction. Zilla remained silent, passive. The red craters in the shadow of her face watched me. I tried to read them as I had before. Tried to catch a glimpse of emotion. They remained apathetic.

I hoped Kitasha was okay.

My nervous shifting got me a slap across the back of the head from the human behind me. Zilla stepped back, drawing her straight razor from somewhere and holding it casually at her side, the blade still folded in the handle.

We stared at each other like ancient gunfighters, each trying to get a read off the other. She tilted her head to one side, the motion oddly innocent for someone whose hands dripped with the blood of my friends. Shadows rolled lazily off her shoulders like inky black smoke.

The razor clicked open, the edge reflecting the lantern light around me.

TWENTY-ONE

Chanting started up from somewhere behind our captors. Too low to make out and droning like the buzz of an angry nest of wasps. For some reason it comforted me, even in that moment. It was something else, some other noise. As if Lovat had gone silent and was suddenly waking back up.

My head was wrenched backward by someone, and I felt a knee jam into my spine. I arched back in pain, feeling my ribs protest, making me want to double over. There was no way to escape. The hold secured me in place and my neck became a tight arc.

Staring down the length of my face, I could still see Zilla. She didn't say a thing, she just watched me like some alpha predator waiting for the right moment to strike. She casually held the razor at her side. Her hateful red gaze focused on my face, her eyes meeting my own. After a moment, she began to approach in a slow, methodical saunter.

The chanting droned on.

This is it, I thought. *This is how it ends.*

Time ticked by in laden seconds, every moment feeling like an hour. I wondered how close I was to Wensem and his son. I hoped Wensem would find a way to escape, and if not I hoped their own deaths would be painless. My mind raced with thoughts of Thad, of August, of the other victims. Was this how they died? Under the hellish gaze of Zilla with some thug holding them down, necks arced, waiting for the bite of a straight razor?

Zilla squatted down, straddling my extended thighs. Her eyes focused intently on my face, and the shadowy cloud of her form seemed to suck the warmth from my body like a mosquito. I felt the cool blade touch my neck. I shivered and she grinned.

We stared at one another for a moment. My heart hammered with adrenaline. I wanted to kick out, claw out those glowing eyes, and knee the bitch in the crotch. Fighting was what my body wanted, but at the same time in its current condition, I knew it couldn't. I was trapped. I hated being trapped.

This is it.

I screamed. Closing my eyes I belted out a powerful, lung-splitting scream that rose from my stomach and exploded from my lips like a geyser. I shouted with as much force as I could muster in my final moment. It filled my ears, covered my world. It drowned out the snickers from my captors and the drone of chanting from deeper down the tunnel. My shout of defiance.

It would be my last act.

Never let it be said that Waldo Emerson Bell went down quietly.

The razor bucked and I felt it bite into my neck.

The end, I thought.

It didn't come.

I opened my eyes as Zilla slumped. Her weight settled heavily on my lap. She stared at me, dumbly, her face inches from my own. Her head tilted to one side, as if she was studying me again, before slumping further askew. Her eyes began to fade, the coal-hot red becoming the burgundy of blood and then congealing to blackness. The straight razor tumbled down my chest, settling on my crotch.

Inky shadow spilled out from a bullet hole in the side of her head, drifting away.

Zilla was dead.

Shot.

The tunnel crashed as more gun shots rang out. The grip that had held me in place released, and my captor fell in the mud to my left, an exit wound in his chest where his heart had been. Panic struck the survivors. They turned and sprinted into the darkness behind them. More shots followed their retreat, driving one of the fleeing dimanians to the ground.

Zilla's body was arching backwards as gravity pulled her down. The stream of shadow rose from the bullet hole like smoke from a campfire. I tried to roll her off, but with my hands bound behind me and the mud pulling at me the process was next to impossible.

"Wal! Hagen!" echoed Samantha's voice. My heart jumped with recognition. She knelt down in the mud between the two of us: our rescuer. One of the Judges was grasped in her hand. "Thank God. Thank God you're alive."

"Samantha! By the Firsts, Sam!" I declared in surprise. "Where'd you get the gun?"

"Hagen left it, before you set out for your partner's," she explained. "He insisted I keep it in case the Children snuck past Saint Mark's security."

"Carter's cross, I'm glad you're here. You saved our lives. You saved my life. Here, untie us." I gestured with my head towards Hagen's bonds. I couldn't stop smiling. My heart sang. I looked at the weapon gripped in her hand. "I thought you didn't like guns?"

She dropped the firearm in my lap untying her brother and I before responding, "I don't."

Freed from my bonds, I shoved Zilla off my lap, and then struggled to get my legs under me. My knee protested the bending, but, after a little pain, I was able to pull myself into a crouch, my hurt leg extended to one side. Sam had gathered Hagen next to her, laying his head in her lap. He was making noises but wasn't fully conscious yet. She looked worried.

"How's he?"

"He'll live."

"Will that horn of his grow back?" I asked.

"Let's hope not." She smiled a weak smile up at me.

I checked the gun for ammunition. The cylinder was empty. I held it up and Samantha tossed me a half-empty box of shells she pulled from inside her coat. I reloaded the pistol and slipped the box into a jacket pocket.

"You need to get out of here," I insisted.

Samantha opened her mouth to protest, but I shook my

head. "Hagen is hurt; if you leave him here, one of them could find him. We can't have that. Not again. No more deaths on me. Get yourselves out of here."

Sam closed her mouth, but her eyes stayed with mine.

"How'd you find us?" I asked, shoving the Judge into another jacket pocket and putting all my weight on my good leg. I tried not to think of the pain in the rest of my body.

"I waited for a while. Worried about Hagen..." she said, pausing and looking at her brother before looking up at me and adding, "...and you.

"I waited two hours, then I made up my mind. I took the gun and a box of shells, and went to look for you. I didn't know where to start so I headed to the monorail. I saw you two disembark and was going to call out, but I realized how stupid that would be, with you wanted by Lovat Central. So I followed you. You don't move fast, so I figured I'd eventually catch you. They jumped you before I could catch up."

"By the Firsts," I swore. "I'm glad we were delayed. If they caught us before you were out and about, we would both be dead right now." I looked around the tunnel and rubbed at my neck absently; my fingers came away bloody. "Where are we?"

"An old tunnel. We're below the Sunk. The old Humes tunnel, I think."

"The Humes tunnel? I thought parts of this had collapsed eons ago and the rest had flooded. Last I heard, it was home to cephel gangs, maybe a couple of angry bok."

"The elevator they took is old as dirt, built right above the Sunk between two empty abandoned buildings. I was surprised it still worked. The sign above it said "Tunnel Access," and they didn't seem concerned about drowning, so I followed." She waved her hand, indicating the tunnel we were now in. "Elevator is the opposite way those Children ran."

Hagen stirred, the less swollen of his eyes widening slightly. "Uhghhh."

"Take it easy, big brother," said Samantha, patting back some of his wild hair.

"Get him out of here. They have Wensem and his kid; time has to be running out. I have to go," I said.

Sam nodded, and Hagen looked up at me. His lips moved but no sound came out.

I leaned close and looked at him. "Hang in there, Hagen. Sam has you, she's going to get you out."

He reached up and touched my face, his lips still moving.

"I'll see you when I see you, buddy," I added, pushing up into a standing position with my good leg and turning to head deeper into the tunnel.

"Wal," called Sam, her voice stopping me. I turned and looked over my shoulder at her.

"Be careful," she said, her dark eyes flashing. "Please."

Words didn't come, so I just nodded, allowing myself one last look at Samantha's face. Her eyes. Her smile. The way her hair fell across her forehead. The nubs of horns that sprouted along her cheeks. I memorized them.

Turning, I hobbled off into the darkness leaving Samantha and Hagen behind me, and wondering if I'd ever see the two of them again.

TWENTY-TWO

Pierogi.

My stomach rumbled. It was absurd that—now of all times—I was back to craving pierogi. I stifled a laugh. The darkness had quickly swallowed me up as I followed the footsteps of the frightened, fleeing Children. I didn't know who could be lurking.

Here I was, hobbling down a slimy tunnel below the Sunk in an abandoned corner of Lovat with several bruised ribs, a damaged arm, a bum knee, and having just barely missed getting killed; yet all my mind could focus on was stuffed dumplings?

It was probably for the best. I think better when I'm hungry.

In an effort to keep my mind occupied I tried to remember my last meal and came up short. That's odd for me. I played through the meals I had eaten since arriving in Lovat. Chicken skewers. The disastrous bao yu. Mrs. Sardini's pasta. Random snacks from carts. Then it hit me. Meatloaf in Samantha's office, that had been the most recent, but how recently was that?

Hours? A day? It was before the guns, before Hagen and I went to Reservoir and met up with Wensem, before this tunnel.

Would things have turned out differently if I hadn't given away the other gun? If I had been armed, would I have been able to stop the Children when they came to take Hagen and me?

The thought vanished.

I *really* wanted pierogi.

Darkness was my constant companion. After some time I looked over my shoulder and realized I couldn't make out even a subtle glow from the puddle of light. The tunnel began a soft slope upwards and I shuffled my feet, hoping the motion would avoid snags. It didn't work. I tripped over something low and hard in the darkness and caught myself just in time. The floor was dry. Gone was the muck and the mud. I ran my fingers over the surface and it felt like sandstone or smooth granite.

The less rational part of me wished I had brought along one of the lamps. It would have made this whole ordeal a bit easier—easier, yes, but it would also give me away.

The fleeing Children Samantha had scared off had undoubtedly reunited with their chanting companions. For all I knew I'd be meeting a fresh gang of them halfway, armed to the teeth and looking for blood...and my heart.

Before pushing myself upwards again, I felt around, my fingers bumping into the object that had tripped me. A cold metal rail was built into the floor of the tunnel, not one but a pair. The metal was rough and rusted from the centuries, but still recognizable by touch as tracks.

I kept my bad leg along the inside of one rail to give me

some guidance. I continued this way for a while. Listening for the chanting and yearning to see some light.

Thoughts of Wensem and Little Wal drove me onward. No more killings. I was determined to stop these bastards. Peter Black's maneuverings to make me the trigger in his grand scheme would end here.

My hurt knee banged into something hard that gonged low and loud in the tunnel. I dropped to the floor, seeing explosions of stars in my vision. I gripped my knee and rolled on the hard dry ground, biting my cheek to keep myself from screaming out as I waited for the pain to ease. My stomach twisted in knots. I huffed short quick breaths.

When my knee eventually stopped howling, I felt blindly for what had sent me careening to the ground. A large metal box on wheels sat in the center of the chamber, filled with some sort of rough stone. Rail cars, of a sort at least. Intended to haul out the refuse as the diggers continued building their tunnel deep below the warrens of the previous city.

I was losing count of how many times I had struggled to my feet recently, but I repeated the motions yet again and pushed my way along; hands held out blindly as I stepped, swung my bad leg, and stepped again. It felt like hours before I began to see the outline of my hands; my heart hammered a beat and I forced down a loud whoop. Light! Precious light from somewhere ahead! I had to pull myself back. Light, yes, but I could also hear voices up ahead, some stern, a few panicked, one loudly bellowing.

A gunshot.

It echoed around and behind me, rolling like thunder, engulfing me in its ripple of sound. More shouts and some screams of pain followed.

More rail cars emerged from the gloom, black shadows large and lumpy, gradually becoming visible. Metal rusted to almost nothing, wheels forever locked. I stayed as low as my bum leg would let me. Scurrying between cars at an awkward, bent gait. My hands came away red with rust as I pushed from cart to cart and moved from one hiding spot to the next. They had to assume someone was coming after them. I met no Children in the tunnel, which meant they had either fled down some passage unknown to me, or they were waiting with others. However many were at the apex of the tunnel—fifteen or five thousand—they would all know Zilla was dead.

The light up ahead intensified as I came to the slope's crest. It emanated from a massive bonfire on the tunnel's floor. The shadowed darkness behind me kept me hidden and safe. I smirked at this—a sentient shadow had nearly killed me. Now shadows protected me.

Head low, I edged closer, moving as silently as my leg would allow. From a distance, I probably resembled a goose with a broken leg struggling to walk, I pushed and rolled and shuffled, trying to keep pressure off my knee.

I could hear a multitude of voices over the crackle of the bonfire. Many of the rail cars that had lined the center of the old tunnel had been moved to huge piles to either side. The cleared carts turned the space into an enormous amphitheater the size of the Hotel Arcadia's lobby.

People dressed in burgundy moved about, but the chanting had stopped. The massive crate I had left in the caravansara sat to one side of the makeshift space. It was presided over by about ten figures in dusky red robes and squat birettas, and an eleventh I couldn't make out.

Ducking behind a cart a decent way from the edge, I tried to count the number of people I could see. It was mostly Children, and neither Wensem or Little Waldo were among them. The final count was probably fifty, maybe sixty if I was being generous. A decent gathering, but not the "ten-thousand young" a part of me had expected.

They came in various shapes, sizes, and races but they all wore the ruddy red of Children. Pan's flute sewn onto their arms, tattooed onto their necks and faces, scarred into their naked chests. Six bodies lay in a line on the floor, blood pooling around their heads. I recognized them as my escaped captors. Clearly their retreat hadn't won them any sympathy from the rest of the cultists.

A few of the bigger and burlier of the group stood near the edge of the amphitheater, rifles, clubs, and knives held white-knuckled in their meaty hands. The one closest to me picked his nose as he peered out into the gloom where I now hid.

Behind the gathered figures rose a huge machine, several stories tall, a gargantuan cylinder lying on its side. It emerged from the gloom like the prow of a ship cutting through a fog and occupied the entirety of the far end of the tunnel. The tracks I had been following ran through the middle of the cleared space, under the bonfire, and emerged from the other side before disappearing into the machine's belly.

I had come to the end of the tunnel and had found the tunneling machine. It had seen better days. I could imagine it during its heyday, before the Aligning, when its crew worked through its various floors building the tunnel around them as the machine chewed through the earth.

The scaffolding that wove through and around the great machine was rusted and collapsed at points, and vines wove in and out of rusted metal walls like worms through soil, covering extended steel beams that looked on the verge of collapse.

This made sense to me, the gathering here in the end of a tunnel beneath the city. I knew little about the Firsts; my knowledge was child-like compared to the lore Hagen and Samantha knew. I remembered my uncles trying to scare me with tales of the Sleeper; they spoke of his dwelling place deep within the earth. A fat monstrosity that required pale servitors to bring it food like a gluttonous ant queen, its will enacted by sentient blobs of goo. The tales had always fascinated me more than they frightened me. The creature sounded more helpless than scary.

Yes, this place made sense.

A dwelling under the Sunk, hundreds of feet in the bedrock. Away from the buzz of Lovat. It made perfect sense. This tunnel, as immense as it was, was the perfect birthing room for a monstrosity. The perfect lair. I could see Children dragging victims down below to sacrifice them before their god.

Inching even closer, I tried to avoid the gaze of the nearest thug as I tried to catch a glimpse of Wensem or his son, but saw neither. A few figures moved among the rusted catwalks of the great drilling machine, but I didn't see my partner among them.

Had the Children already dispatched them? The thought sickened me. My mind turning into a bonfire, blazing with hatred. Should I rush into the throng? I had only five shots in the Judge, but it was clear that whatever had happened here earlier had been interrupted. Most of the Children seemed to be waiting for something.

Then *he* appeared.

Peter Black.

Pan.

A lanky maero with a small face pushed the old man in his wheelchair. It was him. Two dark horns rose from his head through a mane of greying hair. He still wore the suit jacket I had seen before and was still shirtless underneath. A blanket still lay across his lap.

It was all I could do not to rush the bastard. A short distance from the crate, the maero stopped pushing and bent down to whisper something in Peter Black's ear. The old man smiled that patron's smile and then patted the hand of the maero before pushing himself up and out of the chair.

Peter Black rose and walked to the bonfire.

TWENTY-THREE

Gone was the weak grandfatherly act I had seen at Black's offices, as much a lie as his supposed disability. He moved at a strut. Chest out. His green eyes sparkled wickedly. A grin was plastered on his face, splitting his silver goatee in two. His lower half was goat, his legs bending back from the knees and then jutting forward. His feet were black cloven hooves that matched his horns.

Beneath his open coat he was naked, and seemingly proud of the fact. He strutted with the arrogance of a teenage boy. His prick—absurdly proportioned—dangled between his legs, half-obscured in the long tangles of black hair that covered his lower half.

Peter Black—Puck, Pan, Black Goat, Baphomet, whatever name he went by—was in his element, and I hated him for it.

With a theatrical turn, he spun to face the crowd. Arms extended, his coat flapping behind him like a cape. His back to the bonfire, he raised his hands, silencing the group surrounding him. "My friends! My family! My Children!"

The cultists cheered with wanton abandon. All I wanted to do was shoot him. Instead, and maybe to my credit, I waited. My goals were still very clear in my mind: make sure Wensem and Little Waldo were all right. If Wensem and his son were okay, then I would focus on rescuing them before I killed Peter Black. If Wensem was dead...I honestly didn't know what I would do. I hated the possibility. I'd likely try to massacre the lot of them.

"My Thousand Young!" Black continued. "I apologize for the delay. Things were underway, and I know it is frustrating when plans don't run smoothly. We know this is a fallible world. A world without direction. Without leadership. It rusts around us just as this machine behind us rusts away. But..." he paused, and a hush descended over the throng. "We know we can restore it to perfection!"

They loved him for it.

"It seems while we have had to make a few more sacrifices this night, things are straightening out. I can assure you the Mother will be most gracious even with these delays. She understands better than any of us, better than myself, how rusted this world is; her own family, her mother and father, her brothers and sisters, and her aunts and uncles have been driven back. Forced into dreams. They slumber in deep and distant places."

He let the words hang. Watching the crowd.

"But..." he finally said, his voice almost a whisper, letting the cultists hang off the cliff of his words, "This is only temporary. The stars are right once again and they can reawaken! Their bones were dried up, but now my Children, now, they can LIVE AGAIN!"

The crowd roared.

After a time Black hushed them. "My Cybill will reward us for our sacrifices. Reward us and rain blessings down upon us. Secret knowledge. Life eternal. Power. POWER! Believe me, my Children, when I say she will be most thankful. She will reward each and every one of you for your service!"

He grinned the sadistic grin of a madman and again waited until the cheers died down before continuing his speech. He was good at this.

"There was an incident with the Guardian."

Boos.

"Now, now, those responsible have faced the repercussions of their failure," Black said, motioning to the corpses. The crowd turned on the bodies, hacking with blades, kicking with feet, punching with balled fists. Black watched them with pride as he spoke, "Rest assured, he will be captured. There are, after all, only so many places he could go."

Laughter now. The crowd smiled up at their leader and nodded with blood-spattered faces.

I shrank back. The irrational part of my mind was wondering if Peter Black knew I was here, right now. Wondering if this whole show was for me.

"These are the sacrifices the Mother wants. The substances to awaken her!" Black turned and looked over his shoulder, calling out, "Talc! Hübner!"

Two thick dauger stepped out from the crowd. One wore a mask of dark black material while the other wore a pale white one. Both carried shotguns. Both looked twice my size.

"Fetch our Guardian. Fetch him and bring him here. The hour is almost upon us and he is—after all—our guest of honor."

The room erupted into more cheers. A few Children tore their clothes, and knives and hatchets stained with blood were waved about. I shuddered and sank behind the cart, trying to calm my nerves and stop the pounding in my chest.

When I could look again, I saw the two thugs advance from Black and pass through the crowd. Talc and Hübner moved like seasoned killers, soldiers ready to die for their cause. Their knotted arms of muscle flexed with each step, and the dull lights of the tunnel caused their skin to gleam. Tattoos of skulls and fire and dark writing I couldn't read wove their way up exposed flesh. Fanatics. Two killers as dedicated to this madness as Zilla. Did Black really have thousands like these at his disposal or was that just a tale? A few days ago I would have dismissed that notion, but now...I wasn't so sure.

Carefully watching around the edge of the cart I followed Talc and Hübner as they moved away from the crowd, disappearing into the half-lit murk beyond the circle of light. I wondered if Samantha had been able to take Hagen back to Saint Mark's. I couldn't be sure. Hagen had been in a bad state when I had left them, and as tough as Samantha was, Hagen outweighed her. She was going to have a tough time getting him up and into the elevator. The Judge shifted in my waistband, reminding me of its presence, urging me to do what my rational mind wanted to avoid.

No more innocent deaths.

Not on me.

Not at my feet.

Talc and Hübner wouldn't make it to Sam and Hagen. They couldn't.

One last glance at the circle of cultists and I assured myself that Wensem wasn't to be found. Head down and trying to be as silent as my leg would allow I slipped away from my vantage point and began picking through the labyrinth of waist-high carts as Black dove back into his speech with the fervor of a politician.

The going was faster than the coming. The thugs who had been watching the shadows as I had approached had turned and joined the crowd, ignoring the possibility of attack. Black's loud, echoing voice and the cheers from the Children covered up the sounds of my shuffling. I was able to relax a bit as I limped after the two masked dauger.

Neither Talc nor Hübner were moving very fast. They made small talk and picked through the overturned carts, shotguns held relaxed at their waists. They were both tall for dauger—nearly as big as Wensem—and both had thick shoulders and wide upper bodies. Both probably lifted weights and worked as doormen or bouncers when they weren't helping a bloodthirsty cult hunt me down.

I edged closer, grateful for their slow pace.

"How long you think we got?" the one with the darker mask asked.

"Well, they still have to fetch that maero and his kid from the belly of the tunneler. He wasn't coming easy, mind you. Broke Nightingale's neck and Smith probably won't walk ever again."

"Carter's cross."

Pale mask nodded. "I have no idea how the hell they got him down here. Why they didn't just do him in his house?"

"I don't know the exact reasons. Something to do with the ritual. Father was talking about it with the priests. After those cravens showed up."

"So they brought him here?"

"They did, before the Guardian actually. He's been trouble ever since. Was tied up by the bonfire before he broke his bonds, threw the priest holding his son into the fire, and disappeared into the tunneler."

"Which was how Nightingale was killed and Smith was hurt?"

"Yeah. He wouldn't come out. Father eventually sent Bent and Dornan in after him. They should be able to talk sense into that lump of a head. By the Firsts, I hate maero."

My foot banged against an empty cart and the dauger with the darker mask spun around, bringing the shotgun up to his shoulder. I dropped down, prostrate on the cold floor of the tunnel.

"What is it?" asked a voice.

"I heard something," said the other. I couldn't tell which. If it wasn't for the masks, I'd have a difficult time telling them apart.

"Hear what? The roar of the siblings? Father's speech? I'm angry we're missing it."

"We have a job to do. An important one. If we pull it off we'll do what Zilla and her crew never could. There should be rewards in that."

"I'll tell you what, blessed or not, I am glad that shadow bitch is dead. She was nothing but trouble. If she hadn't screwed it up we wouldn't be tramping after the Guardian like this."

"She was a priestess," the other said, his voice a rasp of shocked reverence.

"I don't care if she was the bloody Mother herself. She was cocky and arrogant. Everything was a show. It all had to be done just right. Remember when we worked for ol' Palladios? Two shots to the back of the skull. Leave the gun. Maybe clear out a register. Walk away. Lovat Central would be left scratching their heads."

A chuckle, then, "Yeah. I miss those days."

Silence settled between them and they withdrew, and I began to follow. Their forms grew more and more murky as the darkness swallowed us. Eventually one of them broke the silence, "Palladios was different. Those jobs didn't have the ramifications this does…or the rewards. Besides, none of the Precious Families are Father."

"Look, I know Father is upset by her loss, but I say we're better off without the umbra. The way she did that painter. Carter's cross, Talc. What a mess."

The conversation had brought both dauger to a stop. Behind me, the crowd cheered as Black made some point I couldn't hear. I pulled the Judge from my jeans and held it close. Making sure all chambers were loaded. I'd only get one chance at this. Both of these dauger were armed, and their masks gave them some protection. I couldn't afford to miss.

They kept talking as I eased from behind a cart and crawled

along the floor, dragging my hurt leg behind me. I moved around behind the one with the pale mask, Talc I believed, and paused for a moment. Both were too engaged in conversation to notice.

"What about the trinket man? The one they brought down with the Guardian."

"A liability. Yes, I know. What about him? You heard the report. There was some shooting, no one knows who, but at least two were killed. After the siblings brought the word to the body, Father immediately killed the power to the elevator. Odds are he's stuck down here as well."

Their conversation had given me enough time to edge closer to the dauger with the pale mask. Only one cart sat between him and myself. I pulled my good leg underneath me and coiled it like a spring, ready to push up at a moment's notice.

"There's an unknown here," said Pale Mask.

The darker masked one crossed his arms and looked annoyed. "What's the unknown?"

"Who was shooting? I thought we had taken the Guardian and his friend unarmed and brought them bound, as custom dictate—"

The crowd exploded behind us, shaking the tunnel with its roar. Pale Mask never finished his sentence. Summoning all my strength, I pushed up on my good leg and leveled the Judge at the back of the dauger's head, pulling the trigger without a second thought.

"Talc! Look ou—" the darker mask—the one named Hübner—shouted.

The Judge issued its sentence.

Fire belched from the barrel.

Hübner's warning caught in his throat as blood spattered across his mask. He fired his own weapon, but Talc's position between us saved me from the brunt of the spread. Talc seemed to collapse in two, falling like cut timber as I moved forward.

My knee screamed and I ignored it.

Hübner fired again, but I was behind the spread of his shotgun and the blast erupted in my wake. I was so close, I could see his blue eyes staring at me from behind his mask, feel the heat from his breath. He towered above me, staring down in confused horror as I shoved the Judge up under his chin, hearing the barrel scrape against his mask and feeling it meet soft flesh.

"Wait. I ca—"

I squeezed the trigger.

Hübner's black mask flashed red as the bullet tore its way into his skull. He dropped to the tunnel floor as the crowd quieted. The sound of my gun blast seemed to echo around me. A fading reminder of what I had done.

I had killed two people. Reality burst into flame around me. I exhaled all the breath out of my lungs in one long huff.

Two dead. Two. Two lives.

I collapsed to the ground. Staring at the Judge still grasped in my fingers. It looked so wrong, felt so foreign. My hands shook. My body shook. My intestines clenched.

I have had my share of tussles. A fistfight here, a drunken brawl there, a disagreement every now and again. I had killed a cougar once as it sprinted toward one of my customers' cattle, fangs bared. I had seen people die around me. I had even drawn iron on the trail, fired my weapon into the air as a warning. But never had I killed a person.

Never.

"This was what had to happen," I growled to myself, partly ashamed and partly relieved at my own reaction. "It was them or Samantha. Them or Hagen. Them or you. Black murders innocents. These men were killers. They admitted as much as they walked. They would have gladly butchered you and your friends."

I had brought this abomination into Lovat. An abomination that marked a trail of death throughout my city. It was on me to finish it. I knew there would be more bodies before this was all over.

I breathed.

I wondered if killing ever got any easier.

Samantha and Hagen should still be alive, and the two dauger had said Wensem was too. Wensem would protect his son, he wouldn't let them take him. That meant Little Waldo was probably still alive as well.

My mind hardened around what I had to do. Protect my friends. Stop Black. Stop these killings. Stop the Children.

I reloaded the Judge and grabbed one of the corpses' shotguns, looting fresh shells from the other fallen thug until my pockets bulged. I slipped rounds into the shotgun's magazine. The Judge had five shots, but I was slow on the reload. It wasn't much of a backup plan.

Moving was difficult enough, and I was making it harder by carrying a shotgun, but I could use all the armament I could get.

I took a deep breath. I had to get back.

Black's horned shadow played out on the ceiling of the tunnel as I carefully made my way back to my hiding spot. The scent of burning flesh and the metallic smell of blood seemed to cling to me. Shouts of "Mother! Mother!" and "Io Pan!" flooded over me as I moved, Black masterly building his crowd, kindling that religious fervor that burned inside each of his zealots. He was a seasoned orator, waiting patiently as cheers rose, a wide grin plastered on his handsome face. He was igniting the crowd as he spoke more words to build them up. He waited until the cheering was about to stop before raising his right arm, and turning in a showman's flourish, revealed the scene that emerged from within the belly of the ancient machine.

A gasp caught in my throat as Wensem walked out from within the tunneler, slightly stooped as to not crack his head on a rusted girder that dangled too low. A bundle was clutched tightly in his arms. Behind him followed two burly figures, human and dimanian, dressed identically to Talc and Hubner, and armed with long knives strapped to longer poles. They jabbed at his backside, forcing him forward.

My partner's face was bruised and bloody, his massive seven-fingered hands scratched and covered in blood. More blood was smeared around his crooked mouth and drew dark stains across the yellowed undershirt he wore.

He wasn't defeated—he didn't move like a broken man, but like a defiant one. His crooked jaw was set. His eyes burned hotter than Zilla's ever did. He looked ready to snap anyone in two, even with Little Waldo clutched in his arms. Unlike me, Wensem was a slow burn. It's what made us good business partners.

It took a lot to force his emotions, so it was rare Wensem became upset. He was the guy who would allow himself to be pushed, and pushed, and pushed until finally he would break, and when he broke, hell followed.

"The feet of the Traveler!" Black shouted with a flourish toward Wensem.

Cheers.

"The pipes of the Newborn."

Little Waldo—taking after his namesake—let out a loud baby's scream. His fat little arms pumped angrily at the heavy air. He wanted food. He wanted his mother.

Laughter.

I could see Wensem tense. More cheers. Shouts of "Io Pan! Io Pan! Goat god! Satyr god!" followed. A few Children danced.

Wensem was stopped a few strides away from Peter Black. Out of arm's length but close enough that the two of them could read the expressions in each other's eyes. Wensem glared trails of hate at Black. The two burly Children with makeshift spears stood behind on either side, weapons at the ready, eyes twitching and nervous—as if recognizing Wensem was a lit powder keg.

The blood around his mouth didn't fit. His face wasn't swollen. I wondered if one of the Children in this gathered throng was missing a chunk of flesh. I had seen Wensem bite into an opponent before, and it was never a pretty sight. With his crooked jaw, he could never bite anything clean off, always had to tear.

I shuddered.

Black turned from the maero and looked at the crowd, continuing his homily: "My friends, this is an auspicious occasion.

The *re*-Aligning, as it were, and yes, we are its architects. We have heard the stories of those who had come before us, but now, now it is our time. Yes, the Mother, my dear Cybill, will usher our new world into fruition. She will bring the high priest and awaken the old ones. The *Firsts*. Yes, I have sired our movement. But it is so much more than me. So much more than the Mother. It's *you*."

Screams of delighted joy.

I felt sick.

"We couldn't have done this without your love. Your worship."

The cheers exploded in a rush. The sound louder than any gunshot in this empty, echoing place. Black motioned to the ten robed men standing near the crate. The brand of Wilem, Black & Bright was still burned into its side.

"Our Mother!"

Children produced crowbars and pried off the wood that surrounded the object held within. Boards fell away, shedding like a molting exoskeleton. Inside sat the object I had guided from Syringa's gates to Lovat's door. It was a stone carving. A massive idol. And it was horrific.

Long and narrow, it was carved in the shape of what I could only assume was Cybill. I was shocked at the strangeness of it. Undulating like badly set clay, hundreds of globular eyes emerged from the surface at one end and cascaded across the sides like engorged ticks. They grew smaller near the middle and faded before meeting at the opposite end.

The lower half was composed of fat, chiseled tentacles and

odd, spindly appendages in relief that reminded me of the legs of harvestmen spiders. More tentacles moved up the side, sculpted as if they were tangled and knotted together like stone intestines. On the top of the slab, surrounded by a swarm of eyes, a jagged, parrot-like beak beveled out from the rock, wide open as if Cybill was shouting at the tunnel's ceiling. Around the mouth were carved hundreds of smaller limbs like some fleshy beard. A lolling tongue was carved upward, as if beckoning to pull objects inside.

It was a terrifying idol. An ancient cult's vision of a First.

"To the fire!" Black screamed, his face red with manic effort. The chanting began again. Rhythmic. In a harsh, guttural language I didn't understand.

I peeked from my hiding place. Robed Children next to the stone drew poles through tentacles carved along the top of the object that served as brackets. They all lifted, struggling under the weight of the thing, and moved in plodding unison, half-dragging, half-carrying the idol to the bonfire. I didn't envy them. I had seen the weight of the thing break two axles and crack three cargowain wheels.

The idol-bearers eased the stone into the center of the fire and withdrew their poles, retreating to the enclosing circle of chanting figures. A few of them had to beat out flames that had crept up their long robes.

"Come, breath, from the four winds, and breathe into this slain avatar, that she may live." Black chanted and then laughed, pulling a bulging hopsack stained black from under his abandoned wheelchair. It dripped blood. I edged closer, hiding behind the nearest row of carts and watching the procession through the breaks in the crowd.

Black moved *into* the fire. He seemed so unafraid of the flames, so unworried about the possibility of damage. The hair on his body burned away but his flesh remained unsinged. I expected to smell the scent of burning hair, but instead I got a whiff of wildflowers. Marigolds.

Black stopped, standing atop the blaze, above the stone, with his arms outstretched.

The crowd drew closer.

Even I leaned forward.

Black reached into the rough sack and pulled out a pair of eyes, cut from the head of Lilly Westmarch. That poor girl. He held them aloft.

"The eyes of an artist!"

He shoved the parts down into the gaping maw carved into the stone. The crowd cheered.

He repeated the process.

"The hands of a healer!"

Again more cheers.

"The tongue of a supplicant!"

I watched, horrified, as Black fed August's tongue to the stone.

"The ears of a musician!"

I thought of Fran. My breathing rasped against my gritted teeth.

"The lips of a merchant."

The shriveled piece of flesh Black had drawn from the hopsack didn't remind me of Thad. I wasn't sure if I had expected it to. If it was something like my friend's head, it would have sent me over the edge. This, this was unfamiliar.

The scent of burning flesh began to fill the tunnel. At first I thought it was Black. Then I realized what it was: the body parts—the trophies taken by Zilla—were now cooking inside the stone idol.

I was waiting for my moment to strike, watching intently from behind my overturned rail car. Fear and anger bubbled under my skin, ready to burst. I'd like to say it was wits and skill, but it was probably only exhaustion keeping me in my place. If I acted too early the Children would overwhelm me, but if I timed it right, I could send them into a panic.

Black laughed atop the burning pyre. He tossed the sack aside.

"Now!" he shouted. "I am sure Brother Talc and Brother Hübner will be here soon with the Guardian! But..." he said, pausing and turning, looking down from his post at Wensem and screaming baby Waldo. "...we're missing two other vital ingredients before we get to the Guardian's heart. What shall we do with you two?"

He waggled a finger toward Little Waldo.

The baby screamed.

"Cut them!" shouted a female voice.

"Burn them!" came a male's.

Shouts mushroomed upwards, carried with the smoke. Each claiming a better way to murder Wensem and his son.

I watched, dumbstruck. The Children were so wrapped up

in trying to figure out how to murder my friend, that they were missing what was going on with the idol. It was glowing. The stone was *glowing*.

When they had broken it free it looked like it was basalt or some other hard stone. There was no way the altar would be glowing this soon, no way the bonfire was hot enough, but it was glowing. Not red or ruddy orange like you'd expect from heated stone, but a deep, festering yellow.

"Now," Black stated, clasping his hands before him.

One of the Children lunged at Wensem, knife in hand, and I watched as Wensem clutched his newborn son in one hand and grabbed the attacking human's head in another and twisted it around in one smooth motion.

A sickening crack silenced the raving crowd. The dead cultist fell headlong into the blaze. His jacket burst into flames.

Black roared with laughter.

"A fight then! Of course. It makes sense. You Bell Caravan boys always have a bit of fight in you. We could waste time trying to cut off your feet or tear out your boy's throat, but why bother? We can always just burn you atop of my Cybill!"

The Children drew closer. I tensed as moments ticked by in my mind.

It was almost time.

"After all!" Peter Black continued. "It's the night of my wife's resurrection!"

TWENTY-FOUR

In the serials, the hero always does something clever. He swings in on a rope and grabs the girl, swinging away and leaving the dreaded pirate captain cursing, or he figures out a way to turn the villains against one another, allowing him time to rescue his friends with little bloodshed. Carter's cross, do I wish this was one of those tales.

I didn't feel clever or quick. I felt trapped. My best friend and his kid were about to be sacrificed to a glowing rock. If I didn't act they'd be dead, and very soon. I breathed deeply, inhaling the heavy air, feeling it enter my lungs, and trying to let it calm me.

The thought of Wensem's body aflame, clutching his son as they burned on Cybill's altar, was too much. Peter Black forced my hand and I had one option.

I rose.

My knee and ribs protested, but I ignored them. Leveling the shotgun at the back of the nearest cultist, I pulled the trigger, gritting my teeth as the rifle bucked in my hand. The sound of the blast boomed. It rolled down the tunnel like a volcanic eruption, echoing off the walls and hammering against my eardrums.

The ranting voice of Peter Black and the noise of celebration from his followers died almost instantly. They turned in unison and saw me standing there murdering one of their members. Their silence intensified the sound of the kresh's body slapping against the floor. I felt its hot blood spatter against the cuffs of my jeans.

A moment hung between us.

We all stared at one another. The weary and wounded caravan master out of his element, armed with a stolen scattergun, spattered with kresh blood, and to my best guess…looking like a sack of shit. Across from me, Peter Black, now hairless thanks to the bonfire, and his red-coated throng of bloodthirsty cultists.

"Stop," I barked in what I hoped was a firm tone.

Mumbles of confusion bubbled from the Children. Eyes widened and mouths dropped open as they gaped at me.

I had expected Black to spin around wildly at the sound of the gunshot. But ever the showman, working his crowd, he turned slowly, methodically. His back hunched in anger and his hands curling into gnarled claws. It was as if he knew what awaited him.

I reloaded, shoving a shell into the shotgun's magazine to replace the one I had fired, and took a few painful steps forward. Advancing like a predator, trying to maintain the momentum. Something would flip, something in these people's heads would turn on, and they'd realize they could destroy me.

The crowd murmured and drew together, huddling near

their master and the bonfire, where the stone idol lay glowing its sickening yellow. My one move had worked, sort of: I had surprised them. Shocked them out of their revelry enough to cause confusion. I watched uncertainty spread through them. Looks of embarrassment chasing questioning glances like the shadows of clouds blown across the open plains.

Black was different. He wasn't unsure or confused: he was pissed. The old satyr glared at me with a dark expression. The placid smile that he had worn in his office had been usurped by a curling snarl. His well-groomed goatee and white hair were gone, exposing a weak chin and a brow that sloped back too early. He bared rows of perfectly white teeth in a frame of fat pink lips.

"Nice to see you again," I blurted, trying to fill the silence. I had spent my last move, my element of surprise was drifting away like bonfire smoke, and now it was Waldo Bell versus fifty crazy people and their weird demigod.

"Guardian," Black spat the word as if it was poison. "I assume from your presence that Child Hübner and Child Talc are dead."

I took a page from Zilla's book and said nothing.

Black huffed out a long, frustrated breath, as if my silence was answer enough.

"Now you kill another of my Children?" He motioned to the body of the kresh at my feet. "Here in this consecrated chamber?"

My stomach sickened, thinking of the body count I was racking up, and trying not to imagine what ritual Black and his creatures performed to consecrate this part of the Humes tunnel. I glanced down at the kresh before looking back up to meet

Black's gaze. I could deal with my guilt later.

I remained silent.

The crowd pressed around the base of the bonfire, forming a half circle facing me, and in the process blocking my view of Wensem and Little Wal. They looked to one another, then over their shoulders to Peter Black, as if waiting for a command. They'd have made terrible caravaneers. I expect anyone in my company to improvise, act without direct orders, adapt. A roader who can't think on their feet is a dead roader. Black's followers stared up at him waiting for his word, reminding me of stupid baby birds waiting for their next meal. Their faces had placid, sheep-like expressions.

It was an unusual standoff. Fifty of them, one of me, by all odds I was dead. A few had rifles, shotguns mostly, similar to my recent acquisition. Must have been a sale. But they were few and far between and knives seemed to be the weapon of choice in this crowd. Almost all of them carried a blade; each different in shape, size and design. A few of the more inventive had tied their knives to poles with thick twine, forming crude spears. They held these makeshift weapons out, as if I was planning on rushing them. I wasn't.

"Let Wensem and his son go," I demanded, taking a step to my left. Fifty sets of eyes followed me.

Peter Black laughed. "From where I stand, you aren't in a position to make demands, Mister Bell."

He was right. I looked at the shotgun in my hand and felt the weight of the Judge in the waist of my pants: two guns. I looked at the throng surrounding Black: more than two guns and a lot of knives. Also a whole lot of crazy.

Crazy is hard to fight.

I tried to do a mental calculation; the Judge had three shots left, the shotgun—I honestly wasn't sure. I had plenty of shells, but I wasn't fast on the reload. I'm no gunfighter. This wasn't a monochrome or a radio serial, and I sure didn't have backup to cover me or barrels to crouch behind.

"True," I admitted. I was not quite sure how to proceed. I went through my options. I *could* start firing. Turn this into a shooting gallery, but Wensem was right behind the mass of Children. I didn't want to risk hitting him or Little Waldo. I could sprint for cover and gamble the armed thugs in the crowd were worse with their weapons than I was; but that seemed like a long shot. Running away might buy me more time, but with my bum knee I wasn't fast, and who knew what they'd do to Wensem?

So I went with the only choice I had left. I pulled the shotgun to my shoulder and aimed it at Black. The crowd seemed to respond to me and hissed in anger. A few moved in front of the barrel, protecting their Father. The sound of more knives and guns being drawn filled the quiet of the tunnel.

We stood there and reality seemed to pause.

There would be only one shot at this. I'd fire my shotgun and the Children would fill me with enough holes to strain water. I breathed deeply, steadying my aim like my old man taught me, slowing my breathing so my shot would strike true.

Well, I thought to myself, *it's time.* My finger tightened on the trigger.

My best friend and business partner interrupted my sacrifice.

Wensem roared from somewhere behind the crowd. With their focus on me and Black, the Children had completely lost track of the big maero. Leaving him to his own devices with two much smaller cultists.

The body of one of Wensem's guards burst through the crowd like a missile, collapsing as it crashed into an overturned cart. The second went running through the gap in the crowd, a panicked look on his face, his arms outstretched as if trying to get as far away from Wensem as possible. He looked over his shoulder, shouting to the others, until a makeshift spear hurtled through the gap and lodged in his back.

The slow burn had become an inferno.

Cultists moved away from the bonfire toward me, then stopped, seeing my leveled shotgun. They looked from me to the enraged maero who had just killed two of their number. Black was losing control. Panic began to spread.

Peter Black had turned his back on me to watch Wensem, but quickly realized his error and spun to face me again. He opened his mouth to shout, but before commands could come, Wensem charged.

Shoulder low, Little Waldo held in the opposite arm, he smashed into the crowd. Protecting his son by any means. Cultists went flying as Wensem either broke or threw anything he could get his free hand on. Little Waldo wailed, sheltered in his father's arm, his face half-buried in Wensem's bicep.

Black's orders came out in a choking squawk. He dove behind his wife's idol.

My moment had finally come, and everything seemed to

flow in slow, precise movements.

I moved toward where Wensem ran. I fired one, two, three shots with the shotgun. Reloaded. Picked my targets. Fired. On to the next. Cultists dropped, some in mid-run, sliding across the smooth tunnel floor. My hands took over, pulled the slide, aiming, firing; while I watched in slow motion as the shells ejected from the chamber and spun end-over-end in a dance.

More gunfire went off. I could feel bullets rush past me, one close enough to cut my cheek. Hot blood ran down my face, but I ignored it; instead I turned to where the near-miss had originated. Pain shot up from my knee, punching me in the crotch and making me gasp for air.

A medium-sized human woman with dark hair and bright gold eyes leveled a fat revolver at me. Those eyes narrowed to slits. Her hand tightened on her weapon. Poor girl.

I shot her in the chest.

A few less brave Children were fleeing down the tunnel; some were banding together on the edges of the circle where the overturned carts had been pushed. Some moved in on Wensem, who beat them back.

I turned to take out a kresh with a wicked dagger, giving myself enough time to look over my shoulder and see Wensem pounce onto two of the thugs at once. He began lifting and slamming the head of one into the ground as he drove a knee into the back of the other. Little Waldo was hanging from the crook of his arm, screaming loudly.

Peter Black poked his head out from behind the stone, his cheeks red, his eyes wide in anger. He yelled something that was lost to the chaos. I fired in his direction, my blast dislodging one of the carved eyeballs and driving Black back down.

To my amazement, the stone bled. Instead of chipped rock, a gaping hole now occupied the spot where the carved eye had been dislodged. It retched jaundiced blood like a sucking wound in flesh.

My brain tried to process what it was seeing. It had to be one of Black's tricks. I didn't have much time to dwell. More Children were rushing toward me. I nearly blew a dimanian in half as he slashed at me with a knife, and brought the butt of the shotgun into the jaw of a maero with beady eyes. The brute stepped back and blinked, shaking off the blow and smiling an insane, toothless smile in my direction. Recognition overwhelmed me: I knew him, he was the maero that had attacked me in the pitch den days earlier. His jacket collar was missing, torn by my hand.

"Hello," he growled, flipping a blade around his hand and bending like he was ready to pounce. "Again."

I leveled the shotgun and pulled the trigger.

Click.

My heart sank. The maero chuckled and lunged. Tossing the gun at his face, I took several hurried steps backwards, trying to put distance between the two of us. The shotgun had slowed him, but he had swung his knife out and barely missed opening up my stomach.

"Father will reward me," he mumbled. I drew the Judge, but had to jump out of the way again, nearly dropping the pistol. The maero slashed again and I backpedaled, my knee promising to make my life miserable if we survived this.

The brute was driving me toward the bonfire, toward Peter Black and the arms of other cultists. He cackled a mad laugh and leapt at me.

Wensem caught him mid-leap and threw him down on the ground with one arm. I blinked, shocked.

"Here," said Wensem, handing me his son.

Little Waldo screamed at me, his face pudgy and fat, his mouth open wide. Blood had spattered his tan baby cheeks, but he was unhurt. A few cultists circled like buzzards and I held out the Judge, daring one of them to try to advance. Wensem spun, now with both hands free, and punched the other maero as he tried to rise. The swing was so fierce that Wensem was caught in its momentum and fell to the ground. There, he began to pummel him.

Maero are hard to kill. Some built-in toughness. Their large size, the thickness of their skin, their blood—it all plays into their resilience. Seeing two of their species fight without restraint was shocking. Wensem punched, bit, and kicked; the other maero struggled, jabbing with his knife, drawing a little blood, cutting an arm, taking a chunk out of Wensem's ear.

I had no idea how long this fight would go on or how much damage they might do to each other. An old road priest once told me a story he'd heard of a maero who had his head cut off in a farming accident. He went on to say the old fella lived for three days without his head while waiting for the doctor. When the doctor finally arrived, his head was sewn back onto his body and the maero healed up as if nothing had happened. Went back to being a farmer and lived for a hundred and nine years. But road priests tend to spin wild yarns.

Wensem stood, lifting the other maero and throwing him headfirst into the bonfire. The maero thug screamed and rolled down out of the pyre. He dragged himself away, clothes and skin smoldering, as he crumpled. The cultists circling us backed away, then fled.

Peter Black's hold over his followers was collapsing.

Wensem turned to me and plucked Little Waldo from my arms. He was very much alive, but looked ragged and worn. I wondered if the road priest's story was actually true. Blood ran from hundreds of small cuts and gashes. He looked like he had taken a shotgun blast to the gut and he was missing a few teeth. He gave me a pained, crooked smile as he held his son close to his chest, breathing heavily.

Shoving the Judge back into my jacket pocket, I picked a shotgun off the ground and began feeding more shells from my pockets into its hungry mouth. I watched for any cultists still keeping the faith, and dared Black to peek up over his cover.

"Thanks for the save," I said, watching a few Children disappear down the tunnel. I looked at my partner and apologized, "Sorry about this. Is Little Waldo okay?"

Wensem patted his son on the back and nodded. His soft voice was odd, juxtaposed with the recent violence. "He's scared and hungry, but he'll be fine. I won't let them touch him."

"Look, get yourself and your son out of here. Head back down the tunnel—there's an elevator there, although I'm not sure if it's working. I heard it was disabled, but there should be some way to the surface, a ladder or something. There's always a failsafe built into those things."

"What are you going to do?" Wensem asked.

I fired my new shotgun twice, sending a few courageous true believers scurrying backwards to the ring of overturned carts. I looked toward the pyre where Peter Black hid.

"I lead that thing to Lovat. Brought these murderers down on its citizens, and on my friends. I need to end this. Forever."

"Wal..." Wensem began, but I wouldn't let him finish. I shook my head.

"No. Go."

"Wal," he said again.

"Go!" I shouted and rushed from his side and toward the bonfire.

Wensem watched me go then rushed from the light of the fire and into the darkness, sending a dauger cultist sprawling as he disappeared. I hoped he'd be okay. Somehow knew he'd be able to hold his own. Maero are hard to kill.

Now it was just me.

Me, and what remained of the most loyal Children and their satyr Father.

Four cultists moved to flank me, standing dangerously close to the fire. They held their weapons at the ready: more shotguns.

Peter Black peeked up over the edge of the stone avatar and, seeing I was alone, stood atop it again, leering down all the while. With his hair missing, he looked more monster than dimanian. Wild horns whipped back from pink flesh, a hooked nose hung off a bent face, small eyes stared out from under a heavy, sloping brow.

"You can't stop it, Bell. She'll awaken. She'll just be angrier. So angry. We didn't follow her commands, we didn't gather all the sacrifices. You've only made things worse! Lovat will suffer! You will suffer! You haven't saved anyone! In fact you have done the opposite. You've killed millions!"

The glow from the idol pulsed now, and the stone seemed to writhe below his hooves. The eyes seemed to move in waves of heat, and the tentacles seemed to press against one another as if shifting. I couldn't look away. Was this stone actually Cybill in some dead and inanimate form? Mummified? Was that even possible? Hagen would have had a field day.

"I will make breath enter you, and you will come to life. I will attach tendons to you and make flesh come upon you and cover you with skin. I will put breath in you, and you will come to life," said Black to the idol. He looked at his followers. "My loyal ones, fetch the Guardian."

Two of the remaining four followed his orders, and I fired two blasts from the shotgun, driving one to the ground and sending the other backwards into the flames. The human screamed and dropped to the ground, rolling out the fire that had burst along his crimson jacket. The sight of their partner on fire broke the resolve of Black's remaining entourage. They fled.

And then there were none.

Black's face dropped.

He leapt down, so now he was between me and the fire.

He was naked and wild-eyed. He bared his teeth like some feral cat.

Dropping the shotgun and pulling the Judge from the waist

of my jeans, I leveled it at Black.

His wild rage choked, seeing the dark end of my handgun pointed at his face. He seemed to regard the weapon with the turn of his head, a motion much like that of his dead gate.

He was a creature I had never seen before, a satyr, possibly a demigod, and I wondered if the gun would have any effect on him. He smiled a sleepy smile and watched me lazily for a heartbeat.

Then he burst away: rushing from the fire, the stone, and into the belly of the ancient tunneling machine.

I surveyed the scene around me: A few bodies lay scattered around the open space. Most of the Children had fled, but a few hid behind overturned carts, unsure whether to remain or flee. Survivors were dragging fallen comrades away from the center of the ring with looks of panic as they spied the bonfire.

Odd.

I had been so wrapped up in Black that I hadn't noticed what had begun atop the bonfire. When I looked up, I felt my heart stop.

You couldn't call the object in the fire a stone. Nor could you call it an idol. Stones and idols are still, dead things. The altar was *writhing* in the flames. The festering yellow that had glowed from deep within the stone had brightened to a sulfur-tinged green, and it moved…the thing *moved*. I blinked and rubbed my eyes, unsure of what I was seeing and wondering if I was going insane. It wasn't heat waves causing optical illusions—the thing actually moved.

Thoughts slowed like sap in winter as I struggled to compre-

hend what I was seeing. Not stone. Not stone at all. Mummifi-
cation. Flesh hardened to rock. Frozen in a stasis more protective
than the best armor. I had heard the tales. Seen tiny idols in curio
shops, but never did I expect such a thing to actually be true. It
was madness.

Warmed by the flames, fueled by the flesh of the murdered,
Cybill was stretching, struggling to awaken, and as she did, she
seemed to be growing. The beak that was her mouth clicked together with loud bangs, and her hourglass irises rolled around
on her eyeballs lodged in their sockets. I shuddered as tentacles
pressed and stretched, watched as they loosened from their stony
sleep. Spiders who had lodged in the creature's cracks tumbled
into the flames with a hiss. Loose arms slapped about in the
coals that warmed the creature and sparks burst from the slaps,
sending glowing ash soaring into the air.

Cybill.

The Mother.

A First.

Fleeing was an option, but to what end? Black was still here.
Cybill was awakening. She would escape and she would murder
millions. This was what Black had meant. Cybill was angry. She
would take her rage out on Lovat. I should have been in a mad
panic, but rationality seemed to save me. I stared. Awestruck?
Horrorstruck? Something. Amazed, repulsed, and dumbfounded at what I was seeing.

I was discovering giants were real.

I stumbled backwards, and any thought to the dangers at
hand were lost as I took in Cybill's immense form. It was just…

wrong. Forget about the young races of Earth. Ignore the howls of the Purity Movement's pro-human agenda. It wasn't the kresh, the dimanian, or the cephels that didn't belong: *this* creature didn't belong. It didn't fit. It wasn't right. It was predator, ruler, and slave master. It was an abomination.

My mind pulled away from what I was seeing, unwilling to witness any more. Thad's face appeared, his eyes narrowing as he studied a pair of spectacles. Fran came next, hidden behind her mask, but still elegant and beautiful as she played her flute. August appeared, my former friend, my possible betrayer, his laughter filling the room as he devoured one of Mrs. Sardini's signature dishes. Even Doctor Inox, brutally murdered for our brief association. So many dead, so many murders, a city terrorized, and for what? This thing? This bizarre monstrosity that didn't belong?

I shook my head, trying to clear it, stepping backward as Cybill flopped about. She lifted her heavy mass upward, then collapsed into the red hot coals beneath her. Pain shot up from my knee, snapping me back into reality. My ribs complained of their treatment, and I realized it hurt to breathe. I was exhausted. My limbs felt like they were tied to millstones. My mad rush into Black's flock had taken more from me than I realized, and adrenaline struggled to hold back the waves of pain.

Cybill roared an ear-splitting shriek that shook the tunnel, an awful combination of warping metal and screaming voices. I clamped my hands over my ears in an attempt to close out the sound. Rocks rained down from above. She flopped about, roaring all the while, and sent more sparks exploding upward.

My hands had little effect. The noise was tremendous. I couldn't withdraw from it and it pulled me from my pain.

This was Black's scheme? This was his wife? His reason for killing so many innocent people? This...thing? My stomach churned in disgust.

Cybill roared a second time and I watched as cultists were enraptured by the sound. Madness overwhelmed them. Wide, stupid grins split their faces as they witnessed the birth of their profane goddess.

Fools.

More dust rained down from above us. I imagined the weight of the Sunk pressing downwards, crushing Cybill and drowning her followers. It was a lovely thought.

The tunneler loomed above the scene. Ancient and rusted, but still lodged in the tunnel's structure, its girders fighting to keep the sea at bay. Its beams barely holding. If it came down, if its support failed, it could collapse the entire tunnel and bring it all down on top of Cybill. Bury her under bedrock. It was rusted and broken and its engine had to be seized up and dead. It wouldn't start, but I imagined it'd be simple enough to destroy the rotted supports.

It was madness, but what choice did I have?

The creature was too big for my shotgun. I had no explosives. I was out of options. I could tell the wave of adrenaline my body was riding would soon subside. I was delirious from exhaustion and pain, but something pressed me forward.

I left the bonfire, left Cybill, left her prostrate followers, and followed Black into the stomach of the ancient machine.

TWENTY-FIVE

B ehind me Cybill roared as she stirred. The sound of her thrashing grew more and more intense, regardless of how far away I moved from her. Below my feet, the floor of the ancient tunneler vibrated, kicking up dust. I hobbled along painfully, making my way deeper inside the machine. As I went, I knocked out girders and pylons, swinging my shotgun like a club, intent on bringing the tunneler's structure down. It wasn't going very fast. I needed a different plan...this would take forever.

Names and dates were carved, painted, and scrawled onto any exposed surface, hundreds of them in hundreds of languages, like the discarded flags of ancient explorers atop a mountain. My mind wondered who they were. Adventurers? Homeless? Kidnapped victims such as myself? Did the owners of these names know what was going on in this tunnel? Or were these the names of Cybill's worshipers?

A lattice of girders and supports formed a tangle behind me as I looked over my shoulder. In some ways I was relieved. I didn't want to look at the monster behind me. Having her twisted, horrific form blocked was a small comfort.

Another roar shook the tunneler, the structure around me absorbing some of the sound as I moved deeper and deeper inside.

Running down the center of the machine was a train of carts. Hardened stone sat in their bins, felled centuries earlier from a broken conveyor another two floors up. Catwalks ran around me like cobwebs, running the length of the tunneler, disappearing behind walls, and reemerging like the digestive system of an ancient leviathan.

It was growing darker. I picked my way carefully and wished I had a lamp or a flashlight. In the increasing gloom it was difficult to get a sense of the ancient machine's scale. Occasionally a low-hanging beam would appear from the murk like an umbra from the shadows and attempt to crack open my skull. My pace slowed. I didn't need a whack to the head, and the thought of cutting myself on one of these rusty beams made me shudder. A cut could mean lockjaw, and I had seen one of my uncles die from contracting the disease. I didn't want to go that way.

Somewhere in the distance water dribbled. Light from the bonfire would occasionally flicker through a recess, revealing pathways blocked by rubble older than my great-grandfather. In a few places the floor had collapsed, creating traps that disappeared into shadow and threatened to swallow even the most wary explorer.

My progress changed from a hobble to a crawl. I used the shotgun as a cane, holding it out before me and feeling for obstructions in the dark. I was careful to test each step before I put weight on my foot. It was easy to imagine the floor collapsing, and I saw myself ending up somewhere deep below the earth in the chambers of the Sleeper.

Black was somewhere nearby. I could hear the sound of hooves on metal ahead of me and something else, something very different from the metallic echoes. A deep thrum. It was slow. Less regular than a breath, but constant and vibrating through the rust like the heartbeat of some great whale.

Cybill? No. She was massive and growing larger still, but to thrum like that? When I had last seen her she was the size of a small building and throwing a fit like a two-year-old. She was enormous, but not big enough to make that noise. At least not yet. This was the heartbeat of a giant.

My mind became occupied trying to place the noise. I forgot my diligence at picking my way through the blackness.

The floor creaked and then gave way.

I slipped.

My arms shot forward like javelins as I scrambled for a handhold. As I fell broken metal snags tore at my forearms, my hands, my chest. Something hard scraped skin off my forehead. For a second I was in free fall, then my fingers tightened around a beam.

A hold!

My shotgun fell away, I heard it clatter against something below and then nothing, as if it fell forever.

Heart hammering, I wrenched myself upward, and felt my ribs pop and my shot bicep complain as I hauled myself from hanging over the abyss and back onto a small square space of rusted floor.

I breathed deeply.

My hands shook. I was grateful for the breath. I leaned against a wall and listened to my own heart beat against my sternum.

The tunneler shook and I tensed. Cybill roared, but the sound was difficult to pinpoint. The fall had disoriented me. I wasn't sure which direction was forward or which led back to the bonfire.

I wanted to give up.

I was exhausted. I was in pain. I felt defeated.

As if on cue, Wensem and Little Waldo seemed to emerge from the gloom, smiling at me. Behind them stood Samantha, her dark eyes flashing, and next to her was a beat-up looking Hagen, broken horn and all.

I blinked. I shook my head trying to clear it.

Were they real or was I hallucinating? As if in answer to my question Thaddeus stepped out; the expression on his frog-like face seeming to urge me forward. I rubbed my eyes in time to see August smiling at me from behind his mask, and somewhere over his shoulder were Fran and Doctor Inox and a shadowed Lilly Westmarch.

I watched them and they watched me.

Stand up, Wal. They seemed to say.

I shifted. I hurt so much. I was disoriented. I was tired.

Stand up. Stand up, Wal.

Wensem and Little Wal needed time to escape. Samantha

and Hagen might already be out, but what about the rest of Lovat? What about the innocent folk in the Sunk and upward through the city's levels? They'd be doomed if Cybill escaped.

Stand up.

Leaning against a wall wouldn't solve anything. I had to end this.

Cybill was rising, her mind emerging from her long sleep. Right now her actions were awkward, slowed from generations of slumber and an incomplete ritual. As the fire warmed her, she'd become more aware. She'd want to escape, and she'd destroy anything in her path. What had Hagen called her? The Awakener?

The thought of Cybill pulling herself through Lovat's levels and killing its citizens moved me into action. I needed to collapse this tunneler, crush Cybill before she could escape.

But how?

I was without my shotgun—my makeshift club. If I was in better health I might be able to push some of the most rotted beams over, but I couldn't muster the leverage or strength in my present condition. I had to find another way to collapse the tunneler and with it—hopefully—the Humes tunnel.

The shotgun shells in my pockets bulged, feeling worthless and cumbersome without a rifle. I pulled them out and dropped them on the floor with echoey plunks. I felt for the Judge and breathed a sigh of relief when the warm metal greeted me. I was grateful it had remained in my waistband.

Catching my breath, I tried to get my bearings. I could hear Black move somewhere to the right and above me. Hooves on metal. *Plink plink plink.* Again, I felt a thrum from whatever resided in this relic. A power conduit, perhaps? Some ancient generator? I stepped out gingerly, expecting the floor to give way a second time. It didn't.

Wandering around in the darkness, trying to follow the sound of Black's hooves, I eventually found a ladder. I couldn't tell how stable it was, but my catwalk had ended and I wasn't left with another choice. Peter Black—Pan—was above me and I needed to find him before he found me.

I climbed, testing each rung as I went. Groping in the darkness and each time putting my trust in the rusted steel bar, hoping it would hold my weight.

I reached what I assumed was the next floor of the tunneler. It took me a few moments before I released my death grip on the ladder and felt out with a foot for purchase. Images of the floor collapsing kept my hands clung tightly to the ladder. It took even longer before I entrusted all my weight to the floor.

All was shadow. Light from the outside was all gone now. I couldn't see a thing. I could hear Cybill roar occasionally and feel a shake as one of her tentacle things slammed against the tunnel, but there was no visible light this deep inside the machine.

My progress across the second floor was even slower. I was that much higher above the broken floors below me, and that much more wary. I moved with the speed of a tortoise who expected each footstep to be his last.

A fresh surge of adrenaline—my drug of choice now—burned through me like pitch. My heart hammered loudly and I worried it would give me away. Most of the pain in my knee, my chest, and even my arm was numbed, distant feelings on the edge of my senses.

I can't say how long it took me to reach the room. Five minutes? Ten? An hour? Time is odd in complete darkness. When I first noticed the scant traces of light I thought I was hallucinating again. I half expected the forms of my friends to reemerge from the blackness.

Delving into the tunneler had allowed my eyes to grow accustomed to the pure darkness, and something was dancing across my irises. As I moved cautiously down the catwalk, more lights seemed to emanate before me from tiny portals, distant stars shining from a doorway I could barely make out.

The room was small, with a bank of glowing objects that looked like mushrooms or eyeballs poking out from a black mass. The lights that burned from behind their plastic casings were so minute that I normally wouldn't have noticed them. They thrummed in chorus alongside the giant's heartbeat, glowing brightest at the apex and then receding to almost blackness as it faded.

I carefully ran my hands over them, feeling the hardness of their shells and wondering what bizarre creation the ancient Lovatines had built. A few had play, allowing me to jiggle and maybe even press them like a button; others were shattered, barely hanging onto life as the dampness had eaten away at their shells.

I stared at them with utter fascination. Finally reaching out, I touched the largest one labeled with some sort of runes that looked like a simplified version of Strutten. I was sure Samantha or Hagen would have been able to easily translate them. The object resisted any interaction at first, so I tried harder, pressing down on the button with my good arm.

The heartbeat that had been so subtle boomed loudly. Then boomed again. The whole tunneler shook, and I could hear a few other sounds: a high-pitched whine, followed by another, and then a rattle like bones being dragged over stone.

Machines long silent coughed into life. A bank of lights from somewhere behind me were flicking on one at a time. Their glow was harsh, cold, and white—nothing like the warm sodium lights of Lovat. They flickered and buzzed, bathing the interior of the tunneler in their frigid glow.

The brightness forced my eyes shut as it ran toward me. Row after row of lights popping to life, growing brighter and brighter. I slumped in a corner trying to squeeze it out but it clawed its way in, forcing my eyes to readjust.

It took a few moments before I was able to reopen my eyes. Even as I did, my vision was clouded and blurry. A form stood in the doorway I had passed through. I thought it was one of my hallucinations, but as my vision cleared, I could see it was Peter Black.

I tried to recoil, but my back was to the wall of the little cabin.

Black stood like some crazed demon. His hands curled like claws. His naked flesh looked paler and more alien in this new light. He rose above me on twisted, naked goat legs, like a grotesque statue carved by a madman.

"Why. Don't. You. Leave. Me. Alone," growled Black, each word its own short sentence.

I squinted up at him, feeling the machine's heartbeat below me booming to life, rising with more intensity and shaking the tunneler.

Somewhere I could hear the screech of metal tearing itself apart with unyielding power.

Black raised a hoof with the intention to strike me, but I was quicker, rolling away as it smashed into the space where I had sat.

He was a blur of pink, twisted in the wrong ways.

To my adjusting eyes he looked more like some blurry cartoon character, not the evil mastermind that reanimated the mummified corpse of a First. He barreled into the room, blocking my exit as I pushed myself into a standing position to face him.

"You killed my friends," I stammered. My vision was sharpening up.

The room we stood in appeared to be a small control room. A wall of knobs and buttons occupied one whole side. They were broken up by banks of small screens displaying odd patterns in blacks and greens. The only entrance was to the left of a large cracked window that occupied the wall opposite the buttons, giving the tunneler's operator a view on the comings and goings of his great machine.

"I did what I needed to do. This world is wrong. The inhabitants are wrong. They are twisted mockeries of creation. Abhorrent, mewling simpletons who consume all they touch. We need a fresh Aligning. The world needs to be corrected," Black said, as he failed to kick me again.

Dodging the second strike, I shook my head in disagreement.

"You murdered innocent people. You wanted to murder an innocent child. The world isn't wrong, Black. You're wrong. You and...and..." I struggled for the right word, "...the things like you, things like you and that monster out there."

"That 'monster' is my goddess! My queen! My beloved!" Black screamed.

Now it was my turn to lunge, and Black wasn't fast enough. I slammed him against the wall, feeling his head smack backwards. I reached up and grabbed one of his swooping horns, pulled him forward, and used his momentum to carry him headfirst into the opposite wall. He grunted, slumped to the floor, then rolled over onto his pale backside and started up at me. A trickle of blood dribbled from the corner of one eye.

I regarded the panel of buttons. Something I had done had awakened this machine. If it was still somehow working, perhaps I could try to get it to dig again. It would never truly work. The structure was too rotten, and I was sure it was too far gone to perform its intended function. But perhaps the very act of trying would cause the machine to tear itself apart, and maybe bring the tunnel down on top of it.

It was a gamble, but my options were limited.

I started smacking buttons, advancing across the small room to where Peter Black lay.

He growled up at me, "Two thousand years ago, I'd be eating your heart while being sucked off by virgins in a glade."

"Yeah?" I said, grabbing Black by a horn and jerking violently, lifting him to his feet and sending him sprawling behind me into a rusty bulkhead. He didn't fall over, but stumbled and shook his head, slightly dazed, then turned on me.

"Yeah," he said, mimicking my tone. "You mortals are such fools. You face a demigod and yet treat him like a sad OLD MAN!"

He kicked out at me, catching me in the chest. I heard a rib pop. I was flung backwards, struck an empty wall and smacked my head against hard metal. I could feel a warmth trickle down the back of my head and ooze onto my neck as I collapsed. My chest felt like it had been struck by an ox at full run. Something had to be broken. Pain lanced through my core. I struggled to breathe.

Black advanced across the small room, his hooves banging like hammers against the floor. My mind reeled, body focused only on breathing.

Breathe.

Just Breathe.

It hurt.

BREATHE, dammit!

"I hate you humans. Always have. You're always meddling. Always interfering." Hands clasped my throat like a vice grip. Black grabbed my neck and dragged me across the floor. "Always sticking your noses where they don't belong."

He slammed me face-first into the wall. My eyes welled with tears and I think my nose broke, but so much of my body hurt that it was impossible to tell. My mouth tasted coppery and I knew it was blood. I was rolled onto my back. Black stood over me, his ridiculous penis swaying like a pendulum between two equally ridiculous-looking legs.

My eyes rolled to the paneled wall. Knobs and buttons protruded and looked like forlorn faces. Somewhere in the distance Cybill thrashed.

I hoped my friends were safe, and that my earlier visions of them weren't some ghosts returning to me. Wensem, Little Waldo, Hagen, and Samantha. Beautiful Samantha.

I gazed up at Black's sneering face.

Samantha.

Black spat. Hot, wet spittle striking my forehead.

Sam. Her eyes. That smile.

My head lulled and I was staring at the panel again. Buttons. The largest in the panel with massive labels. One the color of a bright green apple, a large circle with some weird symbol next to it of angles and lines. Ancient letters. Beside it another button, another object, festooned with another set of hieroglyphics. This labeled in red with symbols I recognized as warnings all around it.

I felt Black strike me, but it hardly hurt. My head lulled to the other side, staring out into the tunnel behind me, now lit with the bright white light. Blood seemed to arc away from my face and spattered across the floor. The slap was weak. I had hardly felt it. My ribs, knee, arm, head, nose, legs, stomach, and even my hair hurt more. My cheek was strong; it could take a few slaps.

Black struck me again. It was almost comical. My view changed as my head lulled again to the other side. The panel. I studied it some more. Hoping to glean more information.

Stand up.

Black slapped me a third time, and now I was laughing.

"What's so funny?" Black snarled. In my delirium—feeding off madness and staring up into the eyes of a crazy demigod—I decided to make him guess. I suppose it was funnier at the time. More slaps followed. My view shifted from door, to panel, to door, then back to panel.

"What's so funny?" Black demanded with a scream. I could feel his hot breath against my face. I blinked at him, and choked out my response in a blood-filled sigh.

TWENTY-SIX

Y ou...are...."

It came out like a whisper, but I saw my blood spatter upwards against Peter Black's pink cheek.

His eyes widened as the blast hit him in the stomach and threw him backwards. Confusion on his face.

He hit the wall opposite me, struggled to stand, and stared at the smoking Judge. Black made a feeble attempt to cover a wound in his stomach the size of a dinner plate.

"You are," I stated again—stronger—with a bit more self-assurance. I wiped blood off my face with the arm holding the gun, and wondered if Black would try anything. I was grateful that he didn't.

He stared at me; hate, confusion, fear and pain all playing across his face.

"Two thousand years," I said, repeating his words from earlier.

He stammered and struggled to speak, but couldn't find his voice. I saw genuine fear on his face. Pools of blood darkened his pale flesh, and his breathing was rapid.

"Eat my heart in a...." I thought, "What was it? A glade? Virgins and the like?"

I leveled the Judge at him a second time.

"Look, B-bell...." Black stammered. "Look...."

With my free fist, I slammed the big green button on the panel, and somewhere in the heart of the tunneler, the machine roared to life. The floor quaked around us.

Black's mouth dropped open. He understood what I was trying to do, and he was afraid it might work.

I was going to collapse the Humes tunnel.

"You killed my friends," I said, and I pointed the gun at his face. The room was small, but large enough that he couldn't lunge at me and knock the weapon from my hand. Dust was filling the air around us, setting in like a morning fog. A conveyor outside the window tried to move, but it was too far seized by rust and instead began tearing itself to pieces.

Black looked to the self-destruction, then back to me.

"I d-did what I...n-needed to," he stammered as I pulled the hammer back on the Judge. The click filled me with confidence, and Black began pissing himself. "She's my WIFE!"

I shook my head.

No.

The great machine swayed and I heard the sound of splitting rocks somewhere around me. Black looked up at the ceiling, and whimpered.

"Children? Innocents?" I shouted over the sounds of the machines and the cracking stone.

"Mister Bell...Waldo...Wal...."

"It doesn't work like that. Not in this world!"

"Wal, please...j-just listen," Black yelled. The room around us shifted slightly and he stumbled against the wall, nearly slipping on his own blood.

"No more listening. It's over, Black."

"I can explain," he shouted holding one hand out in a pleading gesture. It was pitiful. A naked old satyr, covered in his own blood from the waist down, pleading for his life while the world around him crumbled.

Dying machines groaned around us, drowning out Cybill's angry bellowing. Somewhere I heard—or felt—something rumble as it tried to continue its quest started generations earlier. Below the conveyor, I saw a mechanical arm move an arched piece of tunnel and try to stamp it into place. The cement form shattered as it collided with the exposed rock. Ignoring its failure, the machine continued lifting another piece of tunnel lining, slamming it upward. The second piece shattered like the first. The arm didn't stop.

A girder collapsed somewhere in the distance, along with a whole catwalk. The tunneler twisted intensely, and the window shattered, sending waves of glass cascading outward. I felt the ground around the machine begin to shake. The integrity of the tunnel giving way.

So much dust.

I hoped my friends were all right.

Black—bloody and mortally wounded—rushed me, head down, like a billy goat charging a rival. He was slow. Too much blood loss. Too much arrogance. I shifted, throwing him into the wall at my back. He groaned, but didn't go down. Spinning slowly, he stared at me with hate-filled eyes.

I didn't wait for another attack. I fired the Judge a second time, and Black's kneecap shattered. He screamed in pain. He scrambled out of the way as I aimed the gun at him a third time. The Judge's cylinder clicked into place.

We were only feet apart from one another, his back to the broken window.

Outside, the tunneler continued its work, destroying itself as it chugged on, slamming ancient stone against far more ancient stone and shattering it in the process.

Water was streaming in from somewhere, and I saw the dust and rocks collapsing as the dying machine threw itself into its work. Structural beams that ran the length of the tunneler's tube form twisted and broke. Parts that supported the Humes tunnel for thousands of years collapsed under the weight of stone. Somewhere in the distance, I heard screams.

Black twitched like he was going to rush me again, and the Judge barked in protest. My finger pulled the trigger before my brain could even issue the command. The slug erupted from its chamber.

Peter Black's eyes widened.

His face froze in a mix of shock and anger.

The slug caught him full in the chest and lifted him up and out the window, throwing him into the workings of the tunneler.

The world moved in slow motion as he fell. His body—dead or alive, I could not tell—was caught in the arm as it pushed upward to lay another piece of the unfinished tunnel into place. It slammed against the rocks, and Peter Black—Pan, Puck, The Black Goat with a Thousand Young—disappeared in a spray of mist that was part liquid, part solid, and utterly dead.

TWENTY-SEVEN

For a moment I just stood there.

Peter Black was gone. Pan was gone.

Dead.

It was hard to comprehend, but it seemed like it should be the end. Music rises. Fade to black. Yet, I was left just standing there in the control room.

I was broken. It hurt to breathe. My knee was shouting at me. My arm hurt. My nose bled, and I could feel the stinging cuts along my arms and face.

My stomach growled and it made me laugh.

I stood there, tucking the Judge into a jacket pocket.

Around me the world broke apart. Rock rained down as the tunnel collapsed. The tunneler in which I stood thrashed about, breaking itself against the ageless stone it had once bullied into submission.

I smiled, oddly proud.

My idea worked, in a way: the tunneler was too old to work

properly. Its gears, flywheels, and hydraulics were seized. Permanently frozen by age, rust, and rot. The energy being fed to them was very real and operated with or without the machine's consent. It built pressure, it forced the machine onward in a herky-jerky mimicry of its original design.

Lines burst and the structure of the whole machine twisted in place as its cutting teeth tried to work against the ancient stone. I heard pops and saw streams of sparks as the brilliant white lights exploded and power panels burst. A hiss of steam, followed by a thrumming boom as a boiler or a hydraulic line ruptured. The sound of metal grinding against stone was so loud, the rest of the world was drowned out.

I saw Cybill.

Much of the tunneler had already collapsed, and her great twisted form writhed a hundred or so yards away. The bonfire that warmed her to life was embers now, partially drowned in the rising water. Her nightmarish form thrashed about as her massive, foggy mind realized what was happening.

A few of her great eyes turned their focus on me. The weird hourglass irises shrank in the light. Her hate was obvious. So similar to that of her fallen husband.

Cybill's great maw, ringed by the boney beak, opened into a roar, but I was deaf to it. It was pointless, and she knew it. A tantrum. An angry fit.

She lurched toward the tunneler, toward me, as if she could stop the inevitable. It made me smile, which I hoped only angered her more.

Tentacle arms as big around as an ox pulled the tunneler's

backside apart, bringing more parts of the tunnel down. Rocks fell like rain with each swipe. She pulled her bulk into the back of the machine, howling as mangled girders punctured her yellow flesh. She tried desperately to stop the machine, so intent on finishing its job that it was destroying the space it once created.

Cybill was too slow, too seized by her years of slumber to get to me, to stop the tunneler. Bigger rocks above broke free and fell. First one tentacle was pinned, then another. She writhed and tried to pull free as more rocks crumbled down. With one last scream she shouted at me, her mouth a wide and silent hole.

My control room shuddered and slumped forward, and it was all I could do to not fall out. When I regained my footing, I looked out to see Cybill staring at me. All her eyes were focused on me as I crouched by the broken window in the small control center at the heart of her undoing.

The world seemed to pause for a heartbeat of a moment, a half breath.

"I got you, you bitch."

The stone that crushed her was massive. Four, maybe five times her size. Forced down from the weight of the Sunk above it. Her scream was silenced with a pounding finality. Behind the stone, water rushed in, filling the space. Drowning the Humes tunnel.

I was lost.

I knew it.

I accepted it.

Leaning against the wall of buttons, I hoped my end was swift.

A man ain't nothing without his name. My old man would be pleased. My name would be restored. I smiled. I thought of my friends.

Hagen's nervous drumming of the spurs along his knuckles played in my memories. It was odd how fate had thrown us together, and how willing he had been to see it through with me.

I jumped as part of the tunnel slammed into the top of the small control room. I saw a dent in the ceiling where the rock had landed. It wouldn't be much longer now.

More water was rushing in—torrents of it—swallowing up the lower half of the tunneler. Its color was turning from a rushing white to a churning red as it mixed with the rust and blood.

Wensem would escape with Little Waldo. I knew it. There was a reason he and I were partners. I felt sad. I'd miss walking the roads of the territories with him, guiding whatever caravan needed help. Bell Caravans would be more than fine in his hands. He'd take care of the company. Build it into the caravan empire of which we often spoke. He'd look after my folks. He'd make sure they were okay.

As more rock rained down, my last thoughts were of Samantha leading her brother to safety. Her instant trust in me. The bravery she showed following us into this tunnel. How she saved us both from Zilla's straight razor. It was a debt I'd never be able to repay. I closed my eyes and thought of her smile, her dark eyes, the curve of her chest and her hips. The spurs near her temples, and the small ones jutting from her chin. The way she would tilt her head as she read some tome of forgotten knowledge, and the occasional glance she would cast in my direction. Carter's cross, she was beautiful. It was a shame I'd never be able to take her to dinner. I knew a few places she might enjoy.

My stomach growled again. I really wanted—

A wall of cold water struck me in the chest, pinned me to the wall of buttons, and then sucked me out of the small control room as it flooded the Humes tunnel. Heavy stone slammed against my back and my skull. I struggled against the current, but everything moved so fast I never had a chance to take a breath, I never was able to finish my thought.

My lungs ached and I gave in, my body unwilling to struggle. The world became liquid blackness.

I let it take me.

TWENTY-EIGHT

I awoke to a choking cough, and it annoyed me.

Firstly, I was having a damn good dream, and it involved Samantha. I'll keep the details to myself, thanks very much. So there's that.

Secondly, it felt *really* good to get sleep. I had been in pain since the day I escaped Lovat Central and was shot, and this sleep had become a wonderful place of escape where my head ignored the signals the rest of my body was sending.

So waking to someone continually coughing was annoying.

It was my chest that hurt first. My lungs.

I was further bothered when I discovered that I was the one doing the choking cough, and I was doing it a lot. I could feel water come up out of my lungs, and with each hack, I spat it out. My chest burned. I hacked and choked. My insides felt raw and bloody by the time it began to subside.

Opening my eyes, I saw the form of someone pull away from me. Everything was blurred, like looking up from underwater.

I blinked and tried to tell my hands to wipe the water from my eyes, but my hands decided they weren't moving.

I was cold. I was soaked. I shivered and inhaled sharply.

It hurt. The cool air of one of Lovat's lower levels filled my chest. Above me, a yellowed sodium lamp buzzed in the ceiling, its curved bowl filled with a handful of dead bugs that dulled the light and cast my surroundings in the constant glow of twilight.

Samantha's beautiful face leaned in, soft, the features not quite sharp.

I smiled.

Another hallucination. I've heard of worse.

She was still as beautiful as I remembered. Those eyes, those dark eyes, flashing. The small horns protruding below her temples. A smudge of dirt across her forehead. Her lips turned into a smile, and I felt a warm hand touch my face. It made everything instantly better.

The hallucination spoke.

"He's breathing," she said, her eyes focused on me, though she was speaking to someone else. She wiped my face dry with the sleeve of her shirt. Careful not to touch my nose. "He's alive."

I wanted to move, I wanted to sit up, but my body was taking its sweet time reacting to my commands.

"Thank God," said a masculine voice. The alpha male in me felt a little jealous. This was my hallucination; I shouldn't have to share it with someone else.

Where was I? My brain didn't process the question quickly. Last thing I remembered was Peter Black. His face. Hatred and shock as he fell from a window, gunshot wound to the chest, stomach, and knee. I tried to focus on remembering what had happened after, but it was all muddled. It was like waking up after a bender. Only along with the headache, everything else in my body hurt. I remember Black falling, falling, and after that... nothing. Blankness.

Here.

Was I dead? Was the afterlife real?

"Wal? Can you hear me?"

It was my Samantha hallucination again.

I gave what I thought was a nod and then tried to speak, but my mouth rebelled and all I could do was flap my lips and cough up more water. Always the charmer.

"Wal? Can you hear me?" Samantha repeated.

Guess it wasn't much of a nod.

I breathed deeply and tried to speak again. I was able to force out a mumbled moan that I hoped sounded like a yes and was delighted when Samantha smiled.

"Thank God you're alive." Her smile widened. "Look, you rest here, there's a medical cart on its way. They're going to take you to Saint Phillip's on Level Six. Do you understand? Saint Phil."

Ordering my hand to touch hers was a small victory and I gave it what I hoped was a gentle squeeze, feeling the small spurs along her knuckles. Guess I was a little off with the whole hallucination thing.

I moved to sit up.

"Wal, don't move, wait for the doctors."

"Wha—" I began, finding it difficult to speak. I coughed up

more water.

"Wha—" I tried again, before eventually finding my voice. "What...what ha-happened?"

The male voice came again. "We were hoping you'd be able to fill us in. Last we saw, you were heading down the tunnel, gun in hand and hell-bent on finding Black."

I turned my head and saw Hagen standing with his hands in his pocket. The broken stub of his single horn looked like the knot of a tree springing from his forehead. His unruly nest of hair was caked with dirt and dried blood. His eyes were ringed by dark circles, and one remained swollen shut matching his puffy lips. He looked like hell. He gave me a reassuring smile despite his wounds.

"Is...is Wensem okay?" I asked. I could remember my business partner's last look at me before disappeared down the dark tunnel. His jaw set, the kid who now bore my unfortunate name screaming in the crook of his arms.

His words came playing back through my memories, "Maero are hard to kill."

Carter's cross, I hoped that was true.

"Haven't seen him," admitted Hagen, then as if to reassure me, "If he was down there, I'm sure he got out. He is tough."

Flashing red and blue lights danced on his skin. I panicked.

Bouchard.

Lovat Central.

This wasn't over—they'd still be after me. I couldn't let Bouchard catch me like this. I couldn't face the cells of Lovat Central for a second time. It was lost. My memory of events were foggy. Black was gone—drowned, right? Somewhere beneath me? Wensem hadn't surfaced. With him went my alibi. I'd be back to where I was when this started. Hiding among addicts in pitch dens and doing my damnedest to avoid the police.

I moved to sit up.

"Lovat Central," I stated as Samantha placed a gentle hand on the center of my chest and shook her head. Her eyes were kind, so kind. I wanted to just lose myself in them.

"Calm down, Wal. Lovat Central knows what happened; when we got to the top of the elevator shaft, we found the first officer we could and explained everything. They're arresting any of the Children who survived. There is going to be a full investigation. Hagen and I have agreed to come forward as witnesses."

"You're safe, we'll make sure you're safe," Hagen said with a smile.

I laid back and closed my eyes.

Safe.

Was it true? Was this nightmare all over? Was that it?

I struggled to remember.

Everything was such a blur.

When I opened my eyes again, I was inside the sterile interior of a brightly lit hospital. At once I could tell it was both expensive and highly elevated. Sunlight—real sunlight—flooded in through windows to my left. A pot of flowers sat near, drinking in the sun. The walls were painted a fresh pale yellow. The borders near the ceiling were decorated with painted marigolds of fine oranges and rich yellows. The linens that lined the bed in which I lay in were nicer than anything I had ever used before, soft and warm.

Looking down the length of my body, I could see my right leg elevated and braced in a contraption that reminded me of the bones of the tunneler. As I rolled my head around, I could see bandages across my chest and wrapping around my upper arm where a Lovat Central bullet had torn through.

Two transparent tubes ran from my arm up to a pair of glass bottles hanging upside down in wire cages and mounted to poles. One was clear, and the other looked a lot like blood. Something itchy sat astride my face, holding my broken nose in place.

On my left sat Samantha Dubois. An old leather book in her hand, legs crossed. When she saw I was awake, she looked up at me and smiled.

"Welcome back."

"What happened?" I said, my voice a painful rasp. "Last thing I remember was lying on my back somewhere in the depths of the city."

"You almost died. When the Sunk seemed to, well...collapse, everything was a bit crazy. Cephels and anur were scrambling to get out of the water. Shortly after that, bodies started rising. Yours among them. A Lovat Central officer pulled you out of the water, but you were blue and you weren't breathing."

"So...." I began.

Hagen stepped from behind his sister. A few bandages covered cuts across his face and the majority of his features were swollen. The flesh around the stump of his broken horn looked red and tender, but he had his color back.

"Sam knows how to resuscitate someone if they aren't breathing."

I'd be lying if the thought of Samantha's mouth on mine didn't stir something inside me. I grinned. "Sorry I missed that."

It was probably the most honest I had been in a long time.

"Hey, she is my little sister," said Hagen with an annoyed smile.

Samantha interjected, "Before you get too excited, Waldo Bell, you should know it involves more than just breathing into your mouth. I had to press on your chest." She paused and watched me for a moment. "With the broken ribs."

I winced.

"Yeah," Samantha continued, "I'd imagine it's probably a good thing you missed it."

"Then I owe you twice," I said with a smile. "Once for the tunnel and once for bringing me back."

"You helped Hagen. You stopped Black and the Children. I don't think you owe me anything."

Footsteps in the hall interrupted our conversation. Detective Carl Bouchard came around the doorframe.

My heart skipped a beat. I instinctively tried to scurry backwards, but stopped myself as I saw Wensem and Kitasha—Little Waldo in her arms—trailing behind him.

"Wensem! Kit!" I rasped. "Little Wal!" And finally, with less gusto, "Detective...Bouchard."

"Probably not the person you want to see right now," said the detective.

I didn't say anything.

"Look, I spent a good six hours talking with your business partner here, not to mention the Dubois siblings. I got the details on the Children. Wensem filled me in on the circumstances and most, if not all, of what he said was corroborated by the cultists we pulled from the Sunk. Look...." He sighed, inhaling a deep breath and scratching behind one of his sweeping horns. I could tell this bothered him. "I was wrong. I saw it wrong and I called it wrong. On behalf of Lovat Central you have our utmost apologies...."

He didn't meet my eyes. Despite what he was saying, I was sure Bouchard couldn't get past what his cop's sense told him. He probably still thought of me as a killer.

In a lot of ways, Bouchard was right. I thought of the cultists I had killed in the tunnel, the looks on their faces. The light disappearing from their eyes. I was a killer, but I didn't have any other choice. It had been them or the city.

"...for everything," Bouchard continued, following my eyes. "Look, I'd say no hard feelings, but if the situation was reversed I'd have hard feelings, so I know that's bullshit. I'd say let bygones be bygones, but I almost threw you to the wolves based on circumstantial evidence. We probably won't ever be friends, Bell, and I understand. If you want to go after my badge I'd understand that as well, but please realize how sorry I am.

"I screwed up. It's hard to say, but I did. I screwed up, and I nearly threw an innocent man in prison because of my mistake."

We stared at one another for a long while but never met each other's eyes. I could tell the silence that hung between us was unnerving my friends.

When I held out my hand, it was like the dam broke. A palpable feeling of relief seemed to wash through my fancy hospital digs. Bouchard stepped forward and took my hand in a bone-crushing grip with a serious expression.

"I still think you're a bastard," I said with a forced smile.

"I do have a reputation to keep up," said Bouchard. "Look, Lovat Central is picking up the tab on your hospital stay; whatever happened down there—we've heard some wild tales from the Children—all is forgiven. We have a whole task force set up to figure out how much damage they have done. Our best guys.

"Get well, and next time you're in my city, keep your nose clean. I don't want to see you in my interrogation room again."

I nodded and turned my head to look out the window, seeing the sun low over the water in the distance. The lines of towers and the roads and streets that hung between them broke up my view of the sky. Thad would have loved this, Fran had probably seen this more times than she could count, August would have dreamed of it.

I would miss them, all of them.

Bouchard retreated from my room, shaking hands with Wensem, Kitasha, Hagen, and Samantha before disappearing with a nod.

Little Waldo was forced into my one good arm. His oddly proportioned maero features gave him an adorable, comical look, and he reached out with a pudgy seven-fingered hand and went to grab the bandage on my nose. Kitasha caught him before he could do any serious damage, which caused his features to screw up into a pre-wail. Wensem swooped him into his arms before Little Waldo could scream.

"He seems to be in fine spirits," I rasped.

"Thanks to you," said Kitasha, looking at Little Waldo with a motherly smile.

I waved a hand dismissively. "Wensem did all the hard work. I just made the noise."

"That's not what he tells me," said Kitasha, turning to me. "He said you were a proper hero."

"He said that?"

"Well, not in as many words," Wensem interrupted, giving me a crooked smile.

Kitasha bent down and gave me a kiss on the cheek. "We're going to get some dinner, you rest up."

"Can we get you anything?" asked Wensem.

"Vermouth?" I asked, which caused my business partner to chuckle and shake his head. "Rest well, my friend. We'll have plenty of work when you're healed up."

"Mind if I join you?" asked Hagen.

"Of course not."

He followed Wensem, Kitasha, and Little Waldo out my door, leaving me alone once again with Samantha.

I looked over at her and felt a lump grow in my throat. Bouchard's visit had hit me harder than I could have imagined. Relief seemed to fill every crevice inside me and it was all I could do to keep myself from shaking. The tension that had lodged itself in my muscles was washed away. I tried to think of the future, not to dwell on what had happened or on the people I had killed. Dead, by my hands. Fools, maybe, but they had been living and breathing people.

Samantha's warm hand slipped inside mine and I gave it a squeeze.

"You're going to be okay," she reassured me, and for whatever reason I knew she was right. I looked over at her, blinking rapidly.

Time passed.

I could dwell on the morality of my actions later.

I breathed.

I relaxed.

"I'm famished," I finally said, after waiting for the wave of emotion to pass. "I know a great pierogi place in Frink Park. Let me buy you breakfast. We got started off in all the wrong ways: violent cults, serial killers. Let's do this right. Breakfast. You and me."

I grinned.

Samantha responded with a smile of her own, a smile I could get lost in. "Wal, it's eight-thirty."

"So?" I said.

"At night," Samantha stated with a laugh. "eight-thirty at night."

I wasn't dissuaded.

"Dinner then?" I asked with a laugh, feeling better than I had in...well, forever.

ACKNOWLEDGEMENTS

Writing is a team effort and there are a few people in my own caravan company that need special recognition.

First and foremost my wife Kari-Lise. Thanks for dealing with me as I began to spin the tale of ol' Waldo Bell and badgered you with questions and demanded you read chapters in various states of completion. I love you so much. I couldn't ask for a better supporter and partner in this crazy journey.

My family also deserve huge thanks in constantly supporting, cheering and pushing me forward. Even at its best writing can be exhausting and without their support and love I don't know where I would be.

Special thanks to my editors Ben Vanik, Josh Montreuil, Lola Landekic, and Victoria Shockley for helping me write words that don't make me sound like an uneducated simpleton. I'll get better, I promise.

A huge thanks to Jon Contino (and his daughter Fiona). Without your offer of assistance the cover of *The Stars Were Right* would have been seriously lacking in style and polish. I still grin every time I see it.

Special thanks in particular to my best pal Josh Montreuil who has constantly been a sounding board for all my crazy ideas and who first thought up a weird post-Aligning world with me.

Also thanks to Ana Lopez-O'Sullivan and Paul O'Sullivan, whom I badgered with medical questions at all hours of the night. Without you guys, Wal would have been a more whole man. I thank you. Wal probably doesn't.

And of course, I need to thank my extensive crew of beta-roaders who read, re-read, challenged, and gave me loads and loads and loads of notes: Alison Fisher, Andrew Wilson, DawnWaswick, Jedediah Voltz, Kelcey Rushing, Kevin Mangan, Lauren Sapala, Sky Bintliff, Steve Leroux, and Sarah Stackhouse. Your input, encouragement, and advice helped me get here, so thanks for giving your time and effort.

Finally, the good people of B3S. *Magna voce ridere æterna.* You all know who you are. Your support means the world to me. Thanks.

K. M. ALEXANDER is a Pacific Northwest native and novelist living and working in Seattle, Washington with his wife and two dogs. *The Stars Were Right* is his first novel. You can follow his exploits at: blog.kmalexander.com.

Waldo Bell and company return in:

Old Broken Road

Available Now